Sniper Jackson

Sniper Jackson

Frederick Sleath

Foreword by Martin Pegler

FRONTLINE BOOKS

Sniper Jackson

First published in 1919 by Herbert Jenkins Ltd, London

This edition published in 2014 by Frontline Books,
an imprint of Pen & Sword Books Ltd,
47 Church Street, Barnsley, S. Yorkshire, S70 2AS
www.frontline-books.com

ISBN: 978-1-84832-745-0

CIP data records for this title are available from the British Library

For more information on our books, please visit
www.frontline-books.com, email info@frontline-books.com
or write to us at the above address.

Printed and bound by CPI Group (UK) Ltd, Croydon, CR0 4YY

Typeset in 11.75/14.1 point Caslon Pro by JCS Publishing Services Ltd,
www.jcs-publishing.co.uk

Contents

Foreword

Frederick James Sleath

Born in Boro'ness, West Lothian, Scotland on 28 September 1889, Frederick was the third of six siblings. The world that he entered was to prove to be the golden autumn of a British colonial summer that had lasted for almost 100 years. Since defeating Napoleon in 1815, Britain had enjoyed a virtually unchallenged position as the world's primary global power, both economically and militarily. It had become the largest empire in history, greater even than that of ancient Rome, at one point controlling some 458 million people across 13 million square miles of the earth's surface. Unknowingly, Sleath and his generation were to aid in the dismantling of this great Empire, the catalyst of which was the Great War.

He proved a bright student, obtaining a place at Edinburgh University in 1907, where he read for a pure science degree, before taking a masters, which he received, somewhat ironically, the month before war was declared, in July 1914. As had so many of his contemporaries, Frederick joined the Officer Training Corps (OTC) at Edinburgh University, and enlisted in the regular army as a private soldier on 30 November 1914, at the age of twenty-five. No photographs of Frederick have been found, but from his enlistment papers, his physical description appears typical of the period. He was of average height, 5ft 7½in with a modest 32½in chest span, making him about the comparative size of a modern-day fourteen-year-old boy. Whether by accident or design, he was attached to the 16th Battalion Royal Scots which consisted mostly of players and supporters of the Heart of Midlothian Football Club. The regiment, based in Edinburgh, held the distinction of being the oldest and thus most senior line regiment in the army, having been raised in 1633. His cadet experience clearly stood him in good stead, and he was promoted to corporal in January 1915, having applied for a commission on the 9th of that month and he was gazetted second lieutenant on the 12 March, after which he was initially attached to the 14th Battalion.

Military service

Frederick went to France in July 1915 and was seconded to the 2nd Royal Scots. By his own account, he was serving in the Ypres sector by the end of the year, but at what point he became the battalion sniping officer is conjecture. At this period, such an appointment did not imply that Sleath possessed any special abilities, as any subaltern was likely to be put in charge of specialist units such as snipers, bombers or trench mortars, simply because such jobs were considered suitable for men with a lack of combat experience. This left the more senior and experienced officers free to keep effective control of the day-to-day running of a battalion. At this period, with little in the way of proper training or effective sniping rifles, British soldiers were doing their best to combat the dominant German snipers along the front-lines and regiments occupying trenches would have had to provide men to form sniper sections, often against the wishes of their commanding officers. Many senior officers were reluctant to detail good men for what was widely regarded as yet another unnecessary task. Quite frequently, therefore, sniper sections were made up of 'difficult' men that the CO was happy to sideline and this is hinted at in Sleath's opening chapters.

However, as an OTC cadet he would certainly have learned to shoot and in his book mentions that he gained the approval of his snipers by his accurate shooting. It appears that Sleath was in charge of the sniping section for some time, probably several months and he left it, not through any personal desire, but as the result of a freak accident. On the night of 7 March 1916, he was aiding stretcher bearers to recover three men sunk to their necks in deep mud near an area known as The Bluff. One stretcher bearer slipped and the trench-board being used at a makeshift stretcher swung round and struck Frederick hard over the heart. He developed bronchitis and during routine tests it was discovered his heart had been damaged and he was evacuated to England. In November he was passed fit by a medical board for desk duty only and he worked at the War Office for the duration of the war. After much correspondence with the War Office, in 1919 he was eventually awarded a small war pension and the silver wound badge.

The Books

Although it reads as a novel, *Sniper Jackson* can be justifiably viewed as 'faction', weaving true events around a mythical character. This was a commonplace method of writing at a time when serving or ex-soldiers did not want individuals or events in their books to be identified, and many used pseudonyms to conceal their identities. Some more familiar examples were A.M. Burrage (Private X), Max Plowman (Mk VIII), John Hay Beith (Ian Hay) and Siegfried Sassoon (George Sherston).

Sleath's work bears all the hallmarks of personal experience, and the twenty-nine chapters are each self-contained short tales, which include those small details of trench minutiae and insights into the close-knit camaraderie commonly found in specialist units that only those who have experienced it could know. Unusually for such a work, Sleath includes many personal details of the men in his section, particularly in Chapters IV and V. Few officers' memoirs give much information about the civilian lives of the men under command, but the close and dangerous nature of sniping threw the men into very close contact with their officer, whom they had to trust implicitly. Failure to achieve this bond could have fatal consequences, however, for it took only a casual suggestion that an unpopular officer have a quick look at the German trenches where a sniper was known to lurk for the end result to be a foregone conclusion. It was thus a matter of great importance to all concerned that Sleath gain this acceptance, and his satisfaction at the close of Chapter V in having done so is palpable. *Sniper Jackson* covers most of the regular tasks that befell snipers, which were more than simply attempting to shoot unwary Germans. Hours were spent in silent observing, examining aerial photographs for tiny clues and then patrolling No Man's Land to see first-hand what the enemy were doing. Their understanding of camouflage and expertise in moving silently and unobserved made snipers ideal for the task, but the cost was high. Few accurate statistics are available of casualty levels in sniper sections, but the Canadian Brigade estimated that almost 80 per cent of their snipers were killed or wounded during their tours of duty and for a neophyte sniper on the Western Front in 1916 the life expectancy was under two months. Sleath's book covers the earlier part of the war, when British snipers were still under-trained, ill-equipped and less numerous than their German adversaries and life was particularly trying. It also documents many of the more commonplace events of life in the line. Parted from their own families, the love the men had for the French children is touchingly and sadly portrayed in Chapter VII, and the near obsession that the British had with spies, in Chapter XV. Rest, leave and the sometimes uncomfortable relationships with French soldiers and civilians are all touched upon. Because no locations were mentioned, and the names of those involved have been changed, it is impossible to place exactly where these events occurred, but much of the section's work was to the east of Ypres, along the Menin Road and around the area of The Bluff and the description of the ground conditions there is extremely vivid and accurate.

One must, after almost a century, perhaps make allowances for a certain amount of Victorian sentiment in some chapters, but it would be a mistake to dismiss this literature as imagination or fabrication, bearing little relationship to reality. The truth is that such books actually contain a wealth of information and *Sniper Jackson* is a very rare piece of eyewitness history about a little-known and rarely discussed element of trench warfare. Perhaps the most important element of the book is how Sleath portrays the relationships that the men had with each other, and the dependence that they felt towards one another. This was not unusual in the Great War of course, but it is seldom so openly represented.

After the book was published in 1919, Sleath continued to write, producing another five novels of the mystery thriller genre, *The Seventh Vial* (1920), *A Breaker of Ships* (1922), *The Red Vulture* (1923), *The Gold of the Sunset* (1927) and *Green Swallows* (1929). Several gained good reviews and it appeared that Sleath had a promising future ahead of him as an author, but no further books appeared after 1929. It is known that he married after the war, but his profession and personal life remains, for now, a mystery. He died in Durham in 1966, aged 76.

Martin Pegler

CHAPTER I

Ronald Jackson, Subaltern

IS BATTALION, THE 2ND Eastshires, was in the trenches due east of Ypres when he reported himself at the rest camp. The interchanging battalion occupied all the billets, and the quartermaster was the only officer of his own battalion remaining there. This wily old soldier did not want the bother of finding accommodation for the new arrival; so, after giving him a meal, he packed him off to the trenches. Here a more thoughtful adjutant posted him to a company holding the most comfortable position in the sector, a group of reserve dug-outs, near the northwestern fringe of Sanctuary Wood. In one of these, Second Lieutenant Ronald Jackson of Buenos Ayres, ex-medical student of Edinburgh University, eventually settled himself down for the night.

He was awakened next morning by the sound of a violent explosion. A shell had burst just behind his quarters. He was out of that dug-out before the upheaved particles of earth had ceased falling. It was only a frail structure, hardly proof against shrapnel, and he had sense enough to realise that his best chance of safety lay out in the open, where there was no likelihood of his being buried beneath a mass of timber baulks and sandbags. Another shell was coming. Its dull groaning sound turned him all a-tremble. He lay down on the ground and waited for death. It is a curious fact that the dominant feeling within him was one of annoyance at having got himself into such a position by enlisting, when so many men of his acquaintance were safe at home.

Just before the shell arrived, a man rushed out of one of the dug-outs. He turned first one way, then another, completely panic-stricken. Finally he seemed to run right into the explosion. He was lifted up into the air; his body crashed against the roof of the dug-out, and rebounded thence to the ground. 'This is war,' thought Ronald, and without a moment's hesitation he rose and walked to where the soldier was lying. The man was still alive, so he dragged him into a narrow ditch which drained the communication trench a few yards away. It was what he thought was expected of an officer.

The men of the company were running out of the dug-outs in twos and threes, scattering towards the reserve trenches. He saw the captain running with them. In a dim sort of a way he began to wonder if he ought not to be running also. Then he heard another shell coming, and felt almost too frightened to fling himself down in the ditch.

Several of his platoon poured out of a dug-out near by. He stood up and shepherded them into the ditch, and had only just got down himself when the shell burst. A mass of earth avalanched over the top, covering the man behind him up to the waist. The shell had barely missed the ditch itself. The man tried to struggle clear, clawing vainly at the top of the low parapet. Another shell was droning its way through the heavens.

'Lie down, you idiot!' said Ronald sharply.

'But I'm buried, sir,' said the man, ceasing his clawing, and looking plaintively at his officer.

A ludicrous mixture of fear, wonder, and annoyance showed in his face. Little more than his head and shoulders were visible, and these were plastered with surface mud and loose soil. Supporting himself on his inturned palms, with elbows jammed firmly against the trench walls, he looked like a prehistoric reptile emerging from its slimy lair. So grotesque a picture did he present that Ronald choked with laughter.

'You have better cover as you are,' he said, when he had regained sufficient control of himself.

Then the shell arrived. It split a tall oak into fragments. A large splinter landed right athwart the ditch where the men were lying. A shower of powdery resinous wood poured down on the subaltern's head and neck. The sweet smell of the raw wood reminded him of the countryside of the homeland, with all its beauty and peace. The contrast went to his heart like a knife. A feeling of dull fury transfused his being. The thought of having to lie helpless in a ditch while the Germans coolly dropped their shells around, made him long madly to get his hands at some foeman's throat and tear at it. He bit savagely at the powdery fragments and ground them between his teeth.

A noise of scrambling behind made him look round sharply. The man who had complained about being buried was trying to bury himself still further. He was digging frantically at the trench walls and pouring the earth over his head and shoulders. The ludicrous aspect of the incident again struck Ronald, and again he laughed.

The soldier lying head to head with him looked up in amazement. He was the platoon sergeant. His face was ghastly white, but his lips were firm set and his gaze was clear. He seemed to think the officer had gone crazy.

'You're not hit, sir, are you?' he enquired.

'Good Lord, no. Are you all right?'

'Yes, sir,' said the man, reassured as to the mental state of his officer. 'So far,' he added mournfully, crouching down in the trench bottom while the next shell burst.

'They've got Silent Sue on us,' he mumbled, when the splinters from the explosion had ceased falling.

'Who's Silent Sue?' asked Ronald.

The sergeant raised his head and looked questioningly at Ronald. 'I forgot, sir,' he said, his face suddenly clearing. 'You've only just come out. I somehow thought you'd been with us quite a while, and ought to know Silent Sue. They say she's a big naval gun. You never hear the sound of the discharge; just the shell coming groaning towards you. It always makes me sick when I hear her. Oh, God! here's another,' he groaned, and dug his nose into the muddy bottom.

At regular intervals for about ten minutes shell after shell burst among the dug-outs. The air was full of flying fragments, and the silence of the wood echoed with the sound of falling débris and rending timber. Somehow or other Ronald could not associate anything very terrifying with one gun solemnly firing shot after shot at definite intervals of time. He had expected to see the whole ground being churned up by massed shell-fire, and he kept thinking that this was only a preliminary bombardment, that the real thing was still to come.

After a while he noticed that the time since the last shell had fallen was lengthening appreciably. A stillness had settled down everywhere. 'Now,' he thought. 'Here it starts in earnest.' He lay silent and tense at the bottom of the ditch, straining his ears to catch the first sound which would herald the commencement of the hellish chorus. But no sound came, and the stillness continued.

'Where are you off to, sergeant?' he enquired, as he noticed the man beginning to get out of the ditch.

'The show's over for to-day, sir,' replied the sergeant.

It was Ronald's turn to look questioningly at the sergeant. 'Surely not,' he said. 'That can't be all.'

Sergeant and officer stared at each other in wonder.

'I don't know about it being "all", sir,' said the sergeant at length, 'but it's quite enough for me. There's scarce a blessed dug-out left untouched, and I bet a few of our fellows have been done in.' He moved off on a tour of inspection, and Ronald silently followed him.

Fully three-fourths of the dug-outs had been destroyed. The position was strewn with broken rafters and dislodged and disembowelled sandbags. Great pits gaped in the earth where dug-out roofs had been entirely blown in, and here and there a smudge of blood told of the death of men. Seven men had been killed, five in the dug-outs and two in the reserve trenches. Over a score had been wounded.

The men of the company came trooping back from the reserve trenches, eager as schoolboys to see the effects of the shelling. The recent terror which had descended among them from out of the skies was forgotten. All engaged in a hunt for souvenirs. Some worked singly, some in gangs, peering and poking inquisitively among the ruins. One group even skylarked about an unexploded shell, until a sergeant discovered them and set them to bury and wire off the monster. But there was no hilarity among the working parties which had been immediately organised to search the dug-outs where missing men had been sheltering. One by one the poor broken bodies were found and reverently carried away to await burial. Then the whole company was split up into fatigue parties, and the work of repair set agoing.

As Ronald passed from group to group he noticed that many of the men paused in their work to stare at him rather curiously. Each time a vague dread stole into his heart that somehow or other he had shown the white feather during the shelling. His case was on a par with that of the schoolboy who, receiving only two stripes instead of an expected dozen, treats the punishment as nothing, and gains a reputation for hardihood among his companions. And the cause of the men's curiosity was the astonishing coolness under fire which the officer, a new-comer, had displayed. But he did not know this, and their staring made him extremely miserable and self-conscious. He felt lonely and insignificant, horribly inexperienced compared with the greatest duffer in his platoon. It seemed the height of impudence on his part to give an order: his men knew so much more than he did. As soon as the work was finished he stole away to the seclusion of his dug-out.

He was roused by the entrance of the company commander.

'How do you feel, Jackson?' enquired the captain. 'I noticed that you stayed on in the middle of it all. Next time get the men away. No sense in remaining while the Germans plump shells at you. I want you to take your platoon up to Sap C to-night. Complete the filling in, and join up the gap in the wire there. Corporal Smith here will take you up just now, and show you the place. I'll explain to you anything you don't understand.'

'Right, sir,' said Ronald in as matter-of-fact a tone as the captain's own. He had not the slightest idea of what was expected of him. But Corporal Smith was an entity within the field of his consciousness. He saluted smartly, and went off with his guide.

'Cool youngster, that,' said the captain to himself.

'Told off already,' his subaltern was murmuring.

About a hundred yards from the dug-outs the ground began to slope up towards the firing-line. It was thickly wooded with tall trees, many of them oak in the full pride of autumn foliage. The slope seemed to have protected them somewhat from the havoc of the shells, for hardly any damage was apparent. Here and there, however, a riven trunk bore witness to the passage of some screaming missile; and in places the white raw wood scars gleaming through the leafy screen, the green leaves on the ground intermingled with the freshly broken twigs, showed where the shrapnel had been busy hastening the hand of time. Half imbedded in the trunk of one giant oak was an unexploded 'whizz-bang' shell.

'You take the turning here, sir,' said the corporal, drawing Ronald's attention to this landmark. 'If you go straight on, or to the left, you'll get lost.'

As it was, Ronald was quite lost already. He had tried to keep his bearings, but the innumerable twistings and turnings of the trenches made his head reel with the effort. The wood was a maze of trench and cross trench. He had to content himself with blindly following the corporal.

At last the firing-line was reached. The corporal came to a halt and produced a periscope. Handing it to Ronald he told him to look over. Ronald looked over. All that he saw was an oblong patch of wet clay, interspersed here and there with bits of sacking. It was the first time that he had used a periscope, and he did not realise that he was scanning the top of the parapet. But he simulated a wise understanding of all his mentor was saying, striving to pick up landmarks in the wet clayey mass which danced before his eyes. A chance jerk of the periscope brought No Man's Land into his field of vision. Very gravely he told the corporal to begin his tale over again.

To his left front was a wooded knoll. The trees which covered its slope were the furthermost outpost of the wood, and the open ground swept past its base and away to the right in a wide gulf. The knoll itself was in German possession. The British firing-line skirted its lower slope and ran along in the open ground at the edge of the wood. The shattered tree-stumps in front of the trench, round which a few straggling wire strands were curled, showed that the line once had run just within the wood border. About two hundred yards away was a dishevelled mass of loose soil and blue-grey sandbags, seeming to come right down from the top of the knoll. The corporal told him that this was the German firing-line. Halfway in between was a line of upturned earth – Sap C, he was given to understand. He could make out a stretch or two of trip wire two or three yards in front of the sap. But there was still an extensive gap without a vestige of wire showing. This was to be the scene of his night's labours. He wondered vaguely, almost rebelliously, how anyone could be expected to work out in the open so near the German lines without being discovered and shot.

'A party of the South Irish were working on this last night, sir,' said the corporal. 'But the Germans turned a machine-gun on them, so they did not get it finished.'

Ronald felt that such an occurrence was not to be wondered at. He came down from the firing-line feeling like a man condemned to die. He thought of all the men he knew who had been killed on just such a job, and felt horribly afraid. Again he experienced that weird sense of annoyance at having got himself into such a disagreeable situation. Only a few months ago he had been a careless, ease-loving medical student. How was it that he had allowed himself to be mixed up in such a bloody business? He did not want to be killed. He did not want to kill. Had it been in his power at the moment he would cheerfully have signed peace and gone home.

At times he found himself wondering whether it was not all a bad dream from which he would presently awake. Yet he moved about his duties throughout the rest of the day with apparent unconcern, simply because months before his arrival in France, he had steeled himself to taste of Death itself, if need be; and now that the cup was presented to his lips he had no intention of flinching.

He spent what time was left to him in bringing his diary up to date and writing a few letters. These he tied up into a parcel, along with his money and his watch, and handed them over rather shamefacedly to the keeping of a brother officer. The latter was a youthful Sandhurst boy, John Rankine by name, but nicknamed 'Cissie' because of his girlish appearance. Being new to the trenches also, he received the charge with due solemnity.

'If anything happens, Ronald old man, I'll write at once to your mother,' he said.

'Thanks, Cissie,' Ronald replied, comforted by his friend's remark.

CHAPTER II

A Night Adventure

BOUT AN HOUR AFTER darkness Ronald set out for the firing-line at the head of his platoon. The trenches were crammed with soldiers, fatigue parties and companies of New Army battalions up for instruction as well as the ordinary garrison; and it was no light task for his men, burdened as they were with all the implements and material for their night's labours, to make progress through the crush. But at length the point opposite Sap C was reached, and he led the way over the parapet into No Man's Land.

Just for a moment he had paused, like a bather shrinking from the cold of the first plunge. Then he had taken the parapet in a wild scramble, slithering down into the ditch on the other side, and remaining crouched upon his hands and knees waiting for the death-dealing bullet to strike.

His heart was pounding away against his ribs. He fell to counting the beats, thinking that each would be the last. But nothing happened. The wind whispered among the long grasses of No Man's Land. The broken foliage of the trees rustled in sympathy. A loose strand of wire, twanging to the gentle touch of the breeze, lent a more strident note to the chorus of the wild. He began to feel better. Like the shrinking bather after the first plunge has been taken, he found his new surroundings not so unpleasant as he had anticipated. He saw his men swarm past him, each one standing straight upright, making no attempt to seek cover. With an assumption of indifference Ronald crawled out of the ditch and joined them.

A covering party had already been told off by the sergeant. It was their duty to lie out some distance in front of the working party so that they might hold up any attempt of the Germans to rush their comrades. The men detailed for this work casually sauntered to within fifty yards of the enemy trench and lay down. Should any attack take place, these fellows would have little chance of escape. Yet their attitude showed no trace of concern. Ronald began to feel the effect of their coolness, and his spirits mounted higher and higher. Not the slightest quiver sounded in his voice as he gave the order to start the filling in of the sap.

But the sense of bewilderment of it all never left his soul for an instant. Rather did it grow. Here was he standing in No Man's Land within a few yards of an enemy trench, surrounded by a toiling working party. On either side of him other working parties were labouring noisily right away down the line. For some hundreds of yards away he could hear men patting sandbags into shape. Yet never a hostile rifle spoke to interrupt the proceedings.

Before coming out to France he had often wondered how wire entanglements could be erected in front of a trench with the enemy so close at hand. Now he was seeing it done, and it looked very simple. There was no moon, but the night was clear. The outline of objects thirty yards away could be seen quite distinctly. And every now and then a star-shell rose and illuminated his surroundings with a light almost as bright as day. There was a mystery in it all that he could not fathom. His heart had ceased throbbing unduly. He was outwardly cool. But he felt every nerve strung to the utmost pitch; he walked about like a creature of the wild, expecting danger from every point, and ready to counter it immediately.

Within an hour the first alarm had come. Ronald was standing a yard or two from the edge of the wood which clothed the little knoll, when he heard it. He sank silently to the ground, and drew his revolver. His men, he noticed, had heard the alarm and taken cover before him. Longer experience of the firing-line had rendered their senses more acute than his own. Nothing could be seen but the rough tumbled shadows of No Man's Land. A slight clicking sound here and there told him that some men were testing the bolt-action of their rifles.

High up on the side of the knoll a crashing had sounded among the trees. Louder and louder it grew. Someone was crushing his way through the undergrowth with all the careless confidence of known strength. The sound was coming directly towards him, and from the enemy trenches. At length Ronald could see a tall figure moving through the sparser marginal growth. Out into the open it strode, and paused within a few feet of his crouching form.

Slowly he raised his revolver and took aim. His finger pressed against the trigger. He was about to kill his first enemy. How weak his arm felt! How strong the trigger spring seemed to be! He had never quite realised its strength before. Was it going to fail him now? Would his enemy get in the first shot at him? He felt the spring slowly begin to yield. Another moment and the hammer would fall.

'That you, Jackson?' said the voice of his captain.

Still holding his revolver, Ronald rose drunkenly to his feet and glared at the intruder. It was his captain sure enough. God! He had nearly killed him. He slipped his revolver out of sight, praying that the captain had not observed it.

'Couldn't get through the crush in the trenches,' went on the latter easily. 'Got out the other side of the knoll and took a short cut. Seem to have alarmed your crowd. Tell them to carry on.'

Ronald gave the direction and accompanied the captain as he inspected the progress of the party.

'Getting on quite nicely, Jackson,' he said, when the inspection had been completed. 'Keep them going as long as you can. You'll possibly have a few interruptions when the Germans waken up to what's going on, but do as much as you can. Remember we've got a reputation to keep up. Good night.'

Ronald watched him disappear into the firing-line. 'I saw him running from the shells this morning,' he said to himself, 'and I wondered at it. But this shows me what he really is. By Jove! I'll keep them going.' And he moved off to spur his men to greater efforts.

The last spadefuls of earth were being stamped down in the sap, some of the men were already drawing out the concertina trip wire to form the first entanglement, when a faint creaking sound was heard coming again from the knoll. It came from the direction of the Bird Cage, a strongly-built German bombing post screened over with wire-netting to deflect any bomb landing on top. A trap-door in the screen allowed a bomber to hurl his bombs at the British trenches, and the noise of this being raised had caused the alarm.

In the wilderness the human senses are keyed up to an extraordinary fineness, and the slightest sound carries a meaning and a warning very seldom neglected by experienced trenchmen. At the first creak the men silently dived for cover, and waited expectantly for what might happen.

Something hurtled out from among the trees near the bombing post, something that sputtered and sparked viciously, and left a long parabola of sparks behind it to mark its course.

It was a bomb from the Bird Cage. It struck a tree, pitched to the ground, and came rolling down the slope, still sputtering and sparking. A friendly log stopped its course, and the bomb burst harmlessly ere half the slope of the knoll had been traversed. The blood-red flash of the explosion showed up the ghastliness of the shattered wood, and the terror of war again entered Ronald's soul. The flick of the air wave in his face made him fancy that a splinter had hit him. He very nearly panicked. Only by sheer will power was he prevented from rushing madly for shelter.

A second bomb was caught and deflected by the trees. A third shared a like fate. Others followed – how many he could not count. The dazzling flashes, the sharp stunning barks of the explosions, completely bewildered him. He lay almost unconscious, incapable of movement, defensive or offensive. Fortunately the range was too great, and none of the bombs reached the party. The splinters whistled vainly into the shadows, and left the crouching men unscathed.

At last he realised that no more bombs were falling. Looking up, he tried to peer into the blackness. For a time his narrowed pupils failed to fasten on anything palpable among the shadows; but gradually they expanded and he was able to take in the situation. The working party on his left had retired to the trenches. Being nearer to the Bird Cage, they had suffered several casualties. His own men were sitting up, waiting for instructions, their attitude plainly hinting that they thought work for the night should be suspended.

'Carry on,' he ordered, and the men carried on.

Roll after roll of the trip wire was expanded and securely pegged down, until the bank was complete. The covering party were recalled within its shelter, and a start was made with the inner layer of the barbed entanglements. Posts had already been driven into the ground, the work of the unfortunate fatigue of the previous night, and the men quickly and skilfully festooned the wire about them. A supply of strongly-made knife-rests had been prepared by the trench garrison during the daytime, and the loose wire layer was backed by row upon row of these formidable obstacles. The work went on smoothly. In another hour the men would be back in the trenches. But the most fearsome adventure of the night was yet to come.

So far the trench directly in front of the party had been unoccupied. There were many similar trenches at this time on the German Front, every available German soldier being away in the East adding to the Italian and Russian calamities. Now one of the covering party came in with the word that the trench was filling with Germans. A sharp-whispered order from Ronald sent the men to cover.

They were only just in time. One moment the enemy trench was but an indistinct blur, a line of shadow a little blacker than darkness. The next moment it was illuminated from end to end by the stabbing flashes of many rifles, belching out rapid fire. The bullets droned through the air with that peculiar note which the bullet makes in the earlier part of its course. Like a swarm of angry hornets they sounded; hornets eager for their prey, but blind and flying too high.

Underneath the leaden storm crouched forty desperate men, clawing their mother earth in an agony of suspense, their ears ringing with the thunderous cracking of the rifles, their nostrils pricking with the acrid smell of burnt cordite. They tasted of the bitterness of death many times over in those few crackling, flaming moments.

Ronald lay towards the rear of the party. Like his men he fancied that the end of his life had come. Yet in all the tumult of his feelings he could diagnose some subtle undercurrent of self-satisfaction, the satisfaction of a prophet who, having prophesied the end of the world, lives to see his prophecy come true, although he himself is involved in the general ruin of its culmination. His imagination had built up for him a certain picture of the firing-line. Hitherto his short experience had yielded nothing bearing any resemblance to it. Not only had he been disappointed, but the discrepancy existing between his preconceived ideas and his experience had bewildered him. He had felt strange, helpless, ill at ease. Now his picture was filling in. He was faced with something familiar, with a situation which he had met and mastered in fancy many times before.

Only one thing his imagination had not prepared him for – the awful physical terror which had gripped him at the first German volley. Every nerve-centre of his body tingled in apprehension of being struck, until his whole being was raw and full of torment. Every rifle report, every bullet crack, impinged on his nervously tautened fibres, making them twang and thrill with agony. But the greater moral fear that he would break down, that he would show himself afraid before all the veterans lying around him, gradually asserted itself as an antidote, and he was able to keep himself under control.

He raised his head and tried to sum up the situation. The rifles were still flashing, the bullets still droning and cracking overhead. Near by he noticed the prone forms of one or two of his men. One man was crawling towards him. Ronald began drawing himself forward until he was face to face with the moving figure. Almost with a shock he realised that the man was crying. He recognised him as a young recruit who had come out at the same time as himself.

'What's the matter?' he asked.

'Oh, sir,' wailed the boy. 'This is awful work. Dae ye no think we should gae hame?'

'No, I don't,' said Ronald, catching hold of the boy's shoulder and gently slewing him round in the opposite direction. 'No one leaves this party without my permission. You understand! This is nothing at all. It will be over in a minute or two. Then we get on with the work.'

The boy ceased his crying. 'Oh, dinna be feared, sir,' he replied coolly. 'I'm no gaun in, if you're stayin' oot. I didna ken whaur ye were. That's all.'

The presence of the officer had steadied him. He slung his body round, and began to crawl back again. It was Ronald's first lesson as to how much an officer really counts when the scene of action is the open, and German bullets are seeking for British lives. The realisation of his responsibility banished the last vestige of his fears.

Somewhere on his right he heard a sound of scuffling and snarling. Crawling towards the spot, he came on a small whizz-bang shell-hole, hardly big enough to give cover to a good-sized man. But in it were two men; two men who fought and snarled and struggled, each actually endeavouring to turn the other out.

Ronald swung his leg over the top of the hole, and kicked both of them soundly. The scuffling and snarling ceased. The men recovered their senses and surveyed each other in astonishment. He heard them begin to talk, and paused to listen.

'Is that you, Wullie?'

'Ay, it's me, Jimmie. What way were ye tryin' tae guzzle me?'

'What way were ye tryin' tae guzzle me?'

'I didna ken who ye were,' said the first speaker.

'Nae mair did I,' said the second. 'I was that feared that I thocht ye were a German when ye tumbled in on me.'

A momentary silence followed, as each man settled himself down to the best advantage. Then the conversation began again.

'Was it ye that kickit me?' said Jimmie. 'Naw,' said Wullie. 'Somebody kickit me tae. I wunner whae it was.'

'Ma conscience! I'd like tae ken. I'd gie him a kick,' said Jimmie wrathfully. 'Look ower and see, Wullie.'

'Look ower yersel' if ye want tae,' replied Wullie discreetly.

'Go on! Look over, Wullie,' Jimmie urged. 'The kick cam frae your side.'

'Naw it didna,' Wullie replied. 'It cam frae your side.'

'You're a leear.'

'I'm no.'

'Ye are.'

'Ye're anither.'

Things were becoming strained again in that shell-hole, and Ronald could not help chuckling softly at the thought of these two simple Tommies busily working up a personal quarrel in their own quaint way, despite their mutual peril and the fearsome battle tumult going on around them. The men seemed to hear his chuckle as they were getting into grips again. They released each other and stopped their snarling.

'Whae was that laughing, Wullie?' said Jimmie after a pause.

'Gode, Jimmie, I think it was the officer.'

Another pause followed, apparently used by Jimmie to digest his friend's information.

'Keek ower and see, Wullie,' he said at length.

Ronald burst out laughing again.

'Ay! it's him,' said Wullie. 'I believe it was him that kickit us.'

Wullie and Jimmie relapsed into an abashed silence, and Ronald crawled quickly away.

Someone spoke his name, and he called out softly in reply. A sergeant moved up alongside of him. He brought an order for Ronald to bring in his men, adding the information that the other working parties had already been called in. But owing to the noise of the firing and the sergeant's nervousness, Ronald only caught part of the message, and what he did hear he misunderstood entirely. He thought the sergeant was offering him a bit of gratuitous advice as to the desirability of retiring to the trenches.

Under normal circumstances he would have treated the sergeant's suggestion politely. But just at the time that the latter intervened a bullet struck the earth a few inches away in front of Ronald's nose. A spurt of soil sprayed into his face, making it smart most vilely, and under the influence of the pain the sergeant's intervention appeared nothing short of a gross interference by a subordinate with his functions as an officer. He told off the astonished man in such a way that he hurriedly withdrew to the firing-line, and Ronald gave his attention to what was happening around him.

Some distance to the right a British machine-gun had begun to stutter. The machine-gun officer had only been waiting for No Man's Land to be cleared of working parties before starting to reply to the German fire. His bullets now thrashed through the air above Ronald's party, and played steadily along the enemy parapet. The German rapid fire ceased with the first traverse. The line of the flashes merged into darkness, like a chalk line on a blackboard under the sweep of the master's duster. For about another minute the machine-gun kept on firing. When it ceased, a silence settled down over the trench area and a blackness. Out in No Man's Land forty silent men slowly awoke to the fact that the peril had passed away, and no harm had befallen them.

Ronald staggered dizzily to his feet. Now that the danger was over he felt as weak as a child. It was with some difficulty that he roused the men and got them started again. Their recent experience had shaken them badly. They wanted to get back to the trenches. But he got them back to work and led the way himself in the more dangerous parts nearer the enemy trenches, so that for very shame they had to follow. No Egyptian taskmaster could have worked them more shrewdly, and they sometimes cursed him under their breath even while doing his bidding, wondering greatly at this boy-officer who had so suddenly taken on the manner and speech of a veteran.

The work progressed slowly. The nerves of everyone were jangled. At the slightest sound the men would throw themselves on the ground. No other working parties were out. The only sound came from their own trenches, where a perfect babel of conversation was going on. In reality it was nothing out of the ordinary. But to the labouring fear-racked men the noise seemed to grow louder and louder until each one believed that it was only a question of time before the Germans would hear it also and open fire again. Many an angry fist was shaken in the direction of the firing-line, and many an imprecation uttered at the thoughtlessness which exposed less fortunate comrades to greater peril.

Ronald also became infected with the general annoyance. His wrath boiled over eventually and he made off towards the part of the trench whence the greatest disturbance was coming. There seemed to be a regular parliamentary debate going on. An unusually strident voice was making most of the din. He leaned over the parapet above the debaters, and reviled them with all the wealth of language at his command, even threatening to use his revolver if the disturbance caused him to return.

The debate stopped instantly with his appearance. He heard a gasp of astonishment and saw three white faces staring up at him out of the trench darkness. As he made his way back to his party, he heard the strident voice commanding silence, and noted in a vague sort of way that the hubbub immediately ceased. He was too much immersed in his work to wonder at the time why a command from the possessor of the strident voice should prove so efficacious. But when the wiring was finished the impression began to emerge from its subconscious state, and it troubled him.

As he passed down the firing-line on his way to the reserve position, he saw a head pop out of a dug-out whose owner seemed to be watching him intently. Other curious faces appeared beside the first, and as he rounded a traverse which would hide them from view he thought he heard a broad Doric voice exclaiming, 'Ah wudna like to be in his shoes.'

CHAPTER III

The Colonel's Revenge

RONALD WOKE UP NEXT morning to find Cissie Rankine leaning against the dug-out wall regarding him with much the same look as might be bestowed on a man about to be hanged. 'Morning, Cissie!' he said cheerily. He got up from his bed and began pulling on his boots. Cissie fidgeted about impatiently.

'Whatever is the matter?' asked Ronald, at last noticing his friend's unusual manner. 'Has anyone been killed?'

'No, Ronald!' replied Cissie seriously. 'But you have made an awful bloomer.'

'Me! Whatever have I done?'

'You cheeked the colonel last night. Yes, you did! And threatened to shoot him too.'

'Wha-at? You're raving.'

At first it occurred to Ronald that possibly he might have got up and committed the crime under the influence of the rum he had taken on turning in the night before. Then the memory of his uneasiness at the close of his last night's labours came back to him.

'For Heaven's sake! Cissie, explain yourself,' he yelled frantically.

'You did! You did!' said Cissie excitedly. 'The colonel sent Sergeant Somerville out to tell you to come in last night. You disobeyed the order and tried to brain the sergeant. Then, when the colonel was discussing the new traverse in Oxford Street, you came in and swore at him. Said you would shoot him if he didn't shut up. Oh crikey! I would not like to be you. The colonel is simply awful.'

'Was that the C.O.?' asked Ronald weakly, as remembrance of the incident came back to him. 'Oh, Professor Glaister! What have I done?'

He sank back on the bed in dismay, oblivious to everything but the awfulness of his situation. Colonel Stewart, the Eastshires' commanding officer, was a brilliant disciple of the 'Hellfire' school, a stern martinet at whose slightest nod the regiment straightened itself up to a man. Even the older men, who knew him for a very gallant gentleman indeed, stood in awe of him on the parade ground. To the new-comers, especially the subalterns, he was a veritable terror, and Ronald turned sick at the thought of what he would do to him.

'You'll be sure to be put under arrest,' said Big Bill Davidson, the senior subaltern of the company, who had drifted in soon after Cissie to hear what had actually happened. 'Then you'll be court-martialled and possibly sentenced to be shot in the Tower, or something like that.'

Bill's legal knowledge was delightfully deficient on this point, nor did he seriously think that such penalties would be inflicted. But, being a born practical joker, he considered this too good an opportunity to be missed of ragging a greenhorn. In an unholy glee he exerted himself to add to Ronald's fears. But the latter hardly heard him. After breakfast, however, he cheered up sufficiently to reply quite effectively to Big Bill's chaffing. Yet throughout the day, on the arrival of every messenger from headquarters, he looked up apprehensively, expecting each one to bring a summons for him to go before the colonel.

But no such summons came. Late in the evening the Eastshires marched out of the trenches to the rest camp. Ronald was more than thankful for the gathering darkness which hid him from the colonel's notice. Whenever the latter passed up and down the line he took care to slip behind the tall form of his platoon sergeant. It was a case of using every subterfuge to stave off the time of reckoning, even if only for an hour or two.

In his dreams that night he careered madly from trench to trench along the whole battle front, while close behind him followed the colonel, shrieking out awful maledictions, and threatening him with fearful punishments. For hours he dodged his relentless pursuer; slipping down side-saps, hiding in shell craters, only to find the colonel still bearing down upon him. With a horrible sinking sensation he realised that he was unable to elude capture any longer. An iron handgrip closed on his shoulder. He shook it off wildly but the grip returned and grew stronger. With a yell for mercy he awoke to find Big Bill Davidson shaking him by the shoulder.

'Yes, Jacky,' said Big Bill, eyeing him critically, 'I am not surprised at your nerve giving way.'

'Great Scott! What an ass you are!' growled Ronald.

'Oh! Very sorry I bothered about you,' said Bill huffily. 'I thought I would rouse you early to give you a chance of getting down the lines out of the colonel's way. He stays next door. No use running into trouble before you need to, you know.'

Ronald's own forebodings made him fall into the trap at once. Big Bill listened to his apologetic thanks without a hint of the joy that filled him at the success of this new venture in leg-pulling. It was hours before breakfast, but Bill routed out some bully beef and biscuits, the stalest and hardest that he could find, and solemnly watched his victim gulp down the unappetising meal. His pent-up emotions gave vent in a huge guffaw – which he carefully smothered in the folds of his sleeping-bag – as Ronald with a further word of thanks hurried away down the lines.

A soft drizzle was falling. The ground was slippery underfoot with an inch of creamy surface slime. Everything was wet and depressing. The tents hung dankly in spite of their straining guy ropes, and for what seemed an eternity Ronald dodged about the miserable camp trying to find something to do to explain his early appearance. He turned out his platoon and subjected them to the most minute inspection, until the men cordially hated him for his officiousness and thought gloomily of their future under so meticulous an officer. But at length he had to allow the wretched fellows to go, and then he forced his company on the sergeant-major and watched the latter self-consciously eat his breakfast. By this time the camp was thoroughly awake, and when he again ventured out among the lines he had to pass among a crowd of men busy preparing themselves for the morning inspection.

The news that the officer who had sworn at the colonel was present in the lines travelled from group to group, and Ronald soon became conscious that he was the centre of an unobtrusive, yet very thorough examination. The men had fully appreciated the humour of the episode, and had Ronald only known it, the scrutiny was exceedingly friendly and sympathetic. But being very sensitive at best, the little ripples of laughter breaking out behind him wherever he wandered proved too much for his composure. He was making his way towards the officers' quarters when something happened which sent him hurriedly back to the shelter of the lines.

From somewhere among the officers' huts a voice rose in anger, a familiar strident voice, pouring out a stream of biting abuse with neither pause nor falter. The whole camp heard it. Everyone put on an appearance of businesslike bustle. Officers came dodging stealthily out of the huts towards the lines, and all kept casting an apprehensive eye in the direction of the disturbance.

'Oh, Heavens, Ronny!' gasped Cissie Rankine, who had come down like a frightened hare with the dogs at its heels. 'The colonel is in an awful rage. He's caught someone asleep in his hut. Crikey! He'll be coming down here now.'

The voice had suddenly stopped roaring, and Cissie hurried off to turn out his platoon. Every other subaltern was doing the same thing, anxiously going through every point of equipment to prevent anything being left undone which might catch the colonel's eye, and bring his wrath down on the head of the unfortunate platoon commander. In the midst of all the nervous bustle Big Bill Davidson strolled casually down to the company tents. There were tears in his eyes, but tears of mischievous joy, and his face was contorted with the effort to keep his merriment within bounds.

'The funniest thing in the world has happened,' he chuckled, in response to the excited queries thrown at him. 'Oh! Carry on, sergeant! – You know how keen the colonel is that we should be out early, especially the morning after relief,' he continued, addressing his brother subalterns. 'Well, he was coming down the lines when he saw someone asleep in D Company hut. I was just behind him, and I saw everything. The C.O. just went into that hut like a pug-terrier into a raccoon pit. Lordy! He did swear! He must have learned something from you, Jacky. The best of it was that the fellow asleep paid no attention to him, and the colonel got madder and madder. Then the sleeping-bag suddenly opened, and out of the mouth shot the head of the R.C. padre, looking as shocked as a girl asked to go off a week-end for the first time in her life. Oh, the dear little fat priest, you should have seen him! And the colonel's face as he shut up his jaws and tried to apologise! He nearly burst. You'll be for it with a vengeance, Jacky. O Lord! Here he comes,' he added, making off towards his platoon as the colonel's figure appeared from out among the huts.

The whole camp saw him coming and the bustle increased tenfold. Everyone glanced nervously over the various parts of their habiliments, and neglected buttons were hastily put in their places while the owners thanked their stars that they had discovered their remissness in time. Ronald got away to the far end of the camp, determined to keep away from the colonel as long as possible. But the C.O.'s attention was too quickly engaged for him to retain any special vendetta in mind, and Ronald could not help smiling gleefully when he noticed that Big Bill Davidson was marked out for the greatest share of the colonel's dammed-up invective. Bill had dressed himself rather carelessly, and his boot-laces, his puttees, his buttons, his neck, in fact every part of him, came in for a merciless criticism which made even Big Bill wince, master cynic though he was himself.

When the inspection was nearly over, Ronald took cover in a company store tent which had already been visited. He heard the tumult of the colonel's progress gradually recede. As it died away he began to congratulate himself on his escape, and after waiting a minute or two to make sure that the colonel had really gone, he walked boldly out of his hiding-place.

'Mr. Jackson!' thundered the colonel's voice. He was standing only a few yards away talking to the adjutant and Captain MacMichael, C Company's commander. 'Where the deuce have you been? Come here, sir!'

'Now I'm for it,' thought Ronald.

The whole camp was taking up position to witness this culminating explosion of the colonel's wrath. But he stuck his chin forward and prepared to take his beating manfully. He felt like an errant schoolboy going up to the Head's private room for special punishment. Ronald had often been sent for by the Head in the old days, and the remembrance gave him courage.

'Good morning, sir,' he said, saluting with an extra degree of smartness.

'Good morning, Jackson,' said the colonel cheerily, extending his hand.

Ronald took it gingerly at first. Then in his astonishment he gripped it as hard as he could.

'Damn!' rapped out the colonel, withdrawing his hand with a jerk. The adjutant hid a grin under his hand and winked at Captain MacMichael.

'I believe I have met you before, Jackson,' said the colonel questioningly.

'Yes, sir! I am very sorry for what occurred then. I acted under a complete misapprehension,' said Ronald quickly.

'You did a very fine bit of work, Mr. Jackson, in getting that wiring done under such circumstances, and the regiment has been complimented by the brigadier. I was very pleased to hear also that you were the first officer down the lines this morning. Keep that up, Mr. Jackson. Always see to your men first. By the way, MacMichael tells me you were a medical student before the war. Edinburgh? Good! Did you go in for athletics?'

'I got my rugger blue,' said Ronald modestly.

'You did! I saw one of your tussles with 'Sonians. Egad! It was worse than the Retreat. I am going to make you sniper-officer, Mr. Jackson. MacKelvie has just been invalided down the line. See the adjutant about taking over the books and papers. He will tell you anything you want to know. And, by the by, Jackson,' he added slily, as he turned towards the officers' quarters, 'when you are finished with the adjutant, if you feel inclined, you might drop in and give me a few lessons in vocabulary. I seem to need a little fresh instruction. Good morning, good morning, Jackson.' All the way up to his hut everyone could hear him chuckling.

Ronald was immediately surrounded by a crowd of curious subalterns, all eager to know what had transpired.

'That means promotion for you,' said Jimmy MacLauchlan, one of the company subs, when Ronald had given them the news.

'Jove! he shook hands with you,' murmured Cissie Rankine. 'More than he did with me.'

'I tell you what it means, Jacky,' said Big Bill mysteriously. 'This is the way the colonel is taking to get his own back on you. You simply can't live with the snipers, and the old boy knows it. It's a deep-laid cunning plot, my boy, to get you under the sod. Mark my words! You see if I am not right.'

Ronald was so amazed at the unexpected reception he had received from the colonel that he was just a little tempted to consider Big Bill's suggestion. Like all new-comers to the trench area, he regarded the sniper's existence as the most precarious of all the army services, and he certainly did not like the prospect of taking over such a command. But experience had taught him not to take everything that Davidson said at its face value. To avoid any leg-pulling he broke away from the group and made towards the adjutant's quarters.

'Hail to the Sniper who in triumph retireth,' chanted Big Bill mockingly.

The adjutant handed over to Ronald a mass of books and maps, told him to study them thoroughly, and to come back again if he wanted anything explained. Ronald carted off his belongings to C Company hut and sat down on his bed to carry out the adjutant's instructions. One book was the log of the sniping section, and the more he read of it the more distasteful did the prospect of his new command become.

'You don't look very cheerful about your step, Jackson,' said Captain MacMichael, entering the hut.

'I am not, skipper, I don't mind admitting. It seems to me that I have got the job under false pretences. The colonel thinks I was very plucky the other evening, when I was in the greatest stew of my life. And from what I hear of the snipers, they will be simply furious at an inexperienced fellow like myself taking over the command.'

'I've no doubt that they will. Our snipers think themselves the salt of the earth. But you are an officer, so you ought to know what to do if they show any sign of their displeasure. Jump on them good and hard. Before you are with them a month they will be swearing by you, and you by them.'

The captain told Ronald a good many things about his section, and gave him many useful hints about individual snipers, and how best to deal with them. The sergeant, he said, was too keen on his job not to do all in his power to help him. But he advised Ronald to get on terms at once with his corporal, Old Dan Haggarty, as wily an old tough as Mephistopheles himself. The two brothers Saunders, Argyleshire men, were fine reliable fellows and would help him a lot. But another dangerous man was Brown, an ex-Oxford undergraduate with a kink somewhere in his nature, who, before joining the snipers, possessed a conduct sheet which was a regimental record for petty crime.

These five were by far the most skilful of the snipers, and the rest of the section were completely under their influence. They were a wonderful quintette – the speaker's enthusiasm often boiled over when talking of them – Sergeant Ferguson and Old Dan Haggarty especially, being known all over the line, their reputation dating from the early months of the war. The captain also spoke of another man, Matthew Oldheim, a Dutch-American, who was fast attaining the standard of the others. But as yet he was little more than a recruit, and 'The Five', as the captain called them, were the men most to be reckoned with.

An incident concerning these five snipers, which had happened a few months previously, gave Ronald a good idea of their character. The Government had just sent out consulting snipers to form schools behind the lines to train up sniping sections for every battalion. The idea was that each battalion should send so many men to receive instruction, and then they were to go back to their battalion to form the nucleus of a definitely recognised sniping section. A senior officer from the Staff was commanding the Eastshires at the time, while Colonel Stewart was off on sick leave, and to the amazement of everyone he decided to send Ferguson and the other four to undergo the training.

Ferguson and his gang had been furious, but they had to go. They were still more furious when they found that the instructing staff was composed of musketry people from the schools at home, fellows who had never seen a trench at all. It had ended in the five of them giving their instructor the finest showing-up a man could get, a showing-up which had quickly developed into a first-class row, as the instructor naturally objected to being exposed to ridicule by subordinates.

Fortunately the consulting sniper, a big-game shot from Africa, had heard of the Eastshire snipers, and he took their side. He sent them back to their regiment by the next train, along with a letter explaining his action and asking for men to be sent him who really required instruction. When the colonel heard what had happened, the gilded staff officer had received the biggest telling-off of his life.

'You read up the log-book thoroughly, and get a good preliminary grip of the work, and you'll soon be all right,' the captain concluded. 'I know I'm sorry to lose you. Your fellows are great poachers, by the way, so remember the company mess when you get any of the spoils.'

Ronald settled down to a systematic study of his papers. As he read more deeply he could not help becoming interested in the subject. He was undoubtedly getting a very fine section, and he gave a little whistle of astonishment as he came on a list of the various snipers' successes. The numbers simply appalled him. Sergeant Ferguson's name was first, and then followed the other men mentioned by Captain MacMichael; a big gap existed between the last of their scores and the next in order.

This tally filled the last few pages of the sniping log-book. But the book contained other things besides. It was really a history of the doings of the section from a very early period. Thus, under date 3d April, 1915, the first two entries read: 'Enemy working party observed at 10.30 A.M. extending communication trench at M.B.5.6, Sheet 21. Information sent to Artillery. Party shelled and dispersed. Four left on the ground.' And also, 'At noon L.-Corp. Adam Saunders shot the Jaeger in the post to the right of the Wall at Hooge.'

The book had been begun by the second sniping officer of the section, an officer from the Special Reserve, who had joined the regiment early in the war. In peace time he had been a Divinity student, and in the cloisters of a stately Scottish university he had dreamt his dreams and wrestled in an academic way with the problems of the be-all and the end-all of human existence. The call of duty brought him face to face with the realities of life and death. As one result of his university training he had filled the early pages of the log-book with beautifully written notes and observations; and when death claimed him, his successor fell heir to a manuscript textbook in which was treated, in scholarly fashion, every aspect of the sniper's art. Even the grisly nature of the details with which he dealt could not hide the culture of the man.

Three other officers had carried on the record. The differing handwritings traversed the allotted number of pages. Did Fate laugh as he watched his victims scrawl the period of their days? At the end of each was an entry in another hand, always the same hand and the same form – 'Lieutenant X was killed to-day. Signed, Andrew Ferguson, Sgt.' Perhaps it was imagination only, but to Ronald each signature appeared to grow bolder and more aggressive than its predecessor. They seemed to say – 'Officer may come and officer may go, but I, Andrew Ferguson, sniper sergeant, will go on for ever.' Ronald determined to come to an understanding with that sergeant as quickly as possible. After a careful study of all that the log-book contained, he set off for the section's quarters.

'Sergeant Ferguson,' he shouted outside the tent which he knew belonged to the sergeant.

A head popped out from beneath the tent-flap. Ronald got a glimpse of a tousled mop of hair surmounting a dirty unshaven face, before the head was withdrawn. The owner had only retired to put on his cap, and a second later the tent-flaps opened out and disclosed him to view.

'Yes, sir!' he said, smartly saluting.

In spite of the sergeant's untidy appearance he certainly was a remarkable figure. Not that his height or build was anything out of the ordinary. It was his eyes that immediately attracted attention. They were the eyes of a killer of men. Set deep beneath rugged eyebrows, the hair on which formed an unbroken jet-black arch almost from cheekbone to cheekbone, their pale dull blue colour made his glance peculiarly impersonal and passionless; and whether in times of crisis or in the peace of the rest camp this expression did not alter. His mouth was that of a gambler, tight pressed at the corners with the skin of the lips all pursed up and crinkled from tension. When confronted with any problem he had a curious trick of bringing his lip down tight against the upper teeth and running the tip of his tongue along its edge. When the problem was settled satisfactorily, his jaws would come together with a snap. He gave no indication of great physical power, yet he could slide himself forward on the ground for hours at a time by the strength of his wrists alone. Not a movement of his body seemed to be wasted; not even a flicker of his eyelids. Every motion was purposeful, quick, and incisive. He was dangerous.

'I'm taking over from Mr. MacKelvie, sergeant,' said Ronald.

'Yes, sir,' was all the sergeant said.

He remained standing at attention, his eyes never leaving his officer's person. Coldly and impassively they summed up his every point. Ronald felt that they were searching into his very mind.

'Turn out the section, sergeant,' he ordered.

The sergeant gave the necessary order. Instantly the tent-flaps were switched aside, and the occupants streamed out and smartly took up their position in line along the duck-boarding running in front of the tents. Ronald's heart thrilled as he watched them. Physically and intellectually they were the pick of the regiment; and they were his charge.

One quick, penetrating glance each man cast at him as he left his tent; then they ignored his presence. They stood stiffly at attention, staring steadily to their front. But as he passed down inspecting them, he realised that their glance 'to the front' was not the unseeing stare of the ordinary soldier at inspection time. The eyes were focussed directly on him. They did not follow him. Only for the time he took in passing was he in their field of vision. He felt as if he were passing before a row of mechanical figures, into whose eyes flashed a spark of intelligence as soon as he confronted them.

It was the depth of the eyes which attracted his attention. Later he learned that this curious property was the result of the long intensive gazing which their calling imposed. But the subtle hint of disapproval which each glance conveyed he detected at once; and that not merely because he had been led to expect it. They knew they were men above their fellows, and obviously resented the fact that an untried boy should be sent to command them. Once, even, when he had paused to examine a telescopic sight, the owner had snatched it from him in his anxiety lest Ronald's inexperienced touch might displace its delicate setting.

'Dismiss the section, sergeant,' he said grimly. He remembered Captain MacMichael's advice, and had all his plans ready for showing the section that he was their officer, and would be regarded as such.

'How is it, sergeant, that the clothing of the men is in such a disreputable state?' he enquired, when the snipers had fallen out and retired to their tents.

'That's easily explained, sir,' said the sergeant, rather taken aback. 'We have to go to our companies for anything we require, and I think you know, sir, that company quartermaster sergeants don't, or can't, give men attached to different units the same attention as they give to those parading with the company.'

'All right, sergeant. To prevent your giving that excuse again, appoint one of the lance-corporals, say Adam Saunders, to act as quartermaster to the section. I'll see it past the colonel. Draw up an indent of everything required, and send it to me for signing. I shall expect everything to be made good by to-morrow afternoon – clothing, equipment, iron rations, gas helmets, everything. Just one thing more. The section seems to have taken advantage of Mr. MacKelvie's departure. Several of the men have not shaved this morning. One or two have not even washed. You yourself, sergeant, might set a better example to them. Parade the section again, and let them know what I have said to you,' he added, as he turned towards the officers' quarters.

The indent arrived in due time. The inspection next day was completely satisfactory. All the week Ronald watched his section at work, and learned his business. The sergeant was friendly and respectful, and very helpful. But the attitude of the other snipers was doubtful. He knew they were watching him closely, and he was glad when the rest period was over, and the return to the trenches gave some prospect of opportunities for him to justify his charge.

CHAPTER IV

Old Dan

THE SNIPER (RONALD) WAS sent on in advance to take over the trenches from the battalion which the Eastshires were relieving, as Colonel Stewart believed in teaching his officers to undertake responsible duties from the beginning of their careers. He was ordered to take one man of his section along with him. The Sniper chose Corporal Haggarty, in the hope that he might get to know his second senior N.C.O. a little better. The two were seated opposite each other in the limber which the quartermaster had provided to carry them and their stores to within easy walking distance of the firing-line, and throughout the early part of the journey the Sniper studied his subordinate with interest.

The corporal was an old man with curly grey hair and glassy eyes perennially inflamed. There was a mocking light in them. Everybody called him Old Dan. Dressed in sober black, he would have suited to perfection the part of a moneylender's confidential clerk. His lips were blue and flaccid with age. The underlip drooped a little. But the corners of the mouth were compressed tightly, and the same gambler's look showed on his face which the Sniper had noticed in the case of the sergeant. He was under middle height, yet brutally strong, with great bulky shoulders, a legacy of his trade as a Glasgow coal contractor. A curious contradiction of his general appearance were his hands, which were small and well-shaped, almost as white and delicate as a woman's. It was the corporal's venerable appearance that astonished the Sniper most, and he wondered why such an ancient should be allowed in the firing-line.

'How old are you, corporal?' he asked suddenly.

The corporal hesitated a little before replying. When he spoke the Sniper was irresistibly reminded of the Broomielaw on a Glasgow holiday when the Gallowgate is streaming 'doon the watter'.

'Ah'm thirty-nine, sir,' he said briefly.

'I'm not the recruiting officer, corporal.'

The old man stirred uneasily. 'Oh weel, near aboot saxty,' he amended.

'How in all the world did you manage to get out here?' queried the Sniper in surprise.

'Ah did them fine, sir,' said the old man gleefully. 'It was this way. Me and ma faither and ma twa sons ran a coal business thegither. Ma sons were reservists. So was masel' afore them. They got a notice tae report, an' by mistake fower notices cam' instead o' twa. So Ah pit ane o' the twa addressed tae Dan'l Haggarty in ma pocket, and packit aff wi' ma sons. Ah wasna examined the first day, but the next day they were for sendin' me hame though Ah'd been served wi' a uniform. But Ah wasna gaun back! Ah would never have heard the end o' it frae the wife. Ma sons were gaun off with a draft that day, so Ah just pinched a chap's rifle and equipment, and hid behind a dyke on the road tae the station. When the draft came by, Ah just steppit intae the ranks, and oot Ah came. They were needin' men ower bad in France at the time tae send me back, an' Ah've payed ma way ever since.'

'Yes, you've paid your way, corporal,' said the Sniper, thinking of Old Dan's record in the log-book.

Old Dan chuckled softly to himself at this remark. His eyes flickered over the Sniper's face, dropping instantly as soon as they encountered his officer's gaze, but constantly returning. He pulled out a dirty 'cutty', and commenced filling it with army shag.

'You come from Glasgow, I see,' remarked the Sniper.

Old Dan stopped filling his pipe and blinked across at his officer.

'Oh! ye've noticed that, have ye? Perhaps ye came frae doon that way yersel', sir?'

'No! I come from a good bit further on.'

'Mebbe frae Hamilton, then, sir?' quizzed the old man.

'I come from Buenos Ayres,' said the Sniper, seeing that he would have to satisfy him.

'Never heard tell o' it,' remarked Old Dan complacently. 'There's waur places than Glesca, though,' he added, striking a match and applying it to his pipe, drawing and puffing vigorously the while.

'Are your sons with the regiment now?'

Old Dan had lit his pipe. He was in the act of fixing the perforated tin containing cap to the top of the bowl when the Sniper asked the question. His puffing stopped immediately. The hand holding the pipe fell limply to his side. The pipe rattled between his teeth, spraying out a shower of smouldering fragments all over his knees. He quickly recovered himself, carefully sweeping the burning shag from his trouser-leg before replying.

'They're baith deid,' he said at length. 'Doon by the Petit Bois. Ah saw them killed.'

The Sniper felt guilty of an awful *faux pas*. He would have changed the conversation, but Old Dan went on speaking. His eyes had lost their blinking look. They were keen and steady. His lips were no longer flaccid, but tight drawn and purposeful. The Sniper realised with a start that he was looking into the face of an old man suddenly grown young.

'Ye've been wonderin', sir, since ever ye set your een on me, hoo it was that an auld man like me was oot here, far less in the snipers.'

He glanced steadily at the Sniper, almost as if he were daring his officer to contradict him.

'Ah saw baith ma sons killed last May; doon by the Petit Bois, and they werena killed fair. They werena killed fair,' he repeated fiercely. 'The colonel offered tae send me hame or doon the line, after that. But Ah joined in with Andra Ferguson instead. Ah couldna gae hame and have ma sons' bairns askin' me hoo their daddies were killed, an' me no able tae tell them hoo many Germans Ah killed for killin' them. Ah'll kill a wheen mair afore Ah'm done, tae.'

He turned away from his officer and spoke no more during the journey. The Sniper would have liked to hear how the younger Haggarties had been killed; but as the old man showed no signs of telling him, he refrained from asking. He lit his pipe and thought over what the corporal had said. Occasionally he would look questioningly in the corporal's direction. Old Dan was staring unseeingly over the country to the left of the road. Sometimes he would chuckle softly to himself.

At the furthest limits of daytime traffic the limber came to a stop, and the Sniper and Old Dan alighted to continue their way by communication trench. On the right was the Wytschaete buttress, with a shattered house or two showing gauntly against the sky. On the left the ruined towers of Ypres reared themselves amidst the poplars – black and sombre and broken these towers, yet with such an appeal to the eye and soul of man that the Sniper would fain have interrupted the journey to linger over the scene. But time was pressing and the corporal was impatient, so he had reluctantly to push onward.

The communication trench ended in the main street of a little village. A large screen of green cloth erected at the further end protected the street from the notice of the German observers, and it was possible to walk freely between the rows of shattered houses without attracting hostile shell-fire. The holes in the screen showed that the village was well within the range of even a rifle-shot, and at night the fixed rifles of the enemy made the locality very unhealthy. Quite close to the screen were the remains of an old street barricade – upturned carts, barrels filled with earth, and other lumber. The Sniper afterwards learned that the Belgian troops had fought a pitched battle there against the German advance guards.

About four hundred yards beyond the village a narrow grove of tall trees stretched between the road and a ruined mill about a quarter of a mile to the right. Here was located the headquarters of the battalion from which he was to take over. A small stream ran through the midst of the trees, and throughout the unrecordable years of its course it had succeeded in hollowing out for itself a deep bed out of all proportion to its size. The headquarters dug-outs had been built into the bank nearest the trenches. It had been impossible to dig very deeply, as the stream rose at intervals and sometimes flooded the shelters, placed though they were as high as was consistent with safety; and they jutted out of the bank the whole length of the plantation like a row of large beehives, or the propped-up dwellings of ancient lake dwellers. The Sniper reported himself at the colonel's dug-out, while Old Dan wandered off to exchange views with his brother snipers.

The taking-over business was soon completed. It was hardly more than a formality, for the battalions had relieved each other so often all over the sector that every detail, both of the trenches and the trench stores, was already known to them. It was just a case of 'drinks' and general talk. Many a pleasant afternoon can be spent in some old dug-out in France or Belgium, even in the hottest part of the line. The brigadier dropped in for tea after an inspection of the firing-line, and added to, rather than lessened, the conviviality of the gathering. For a brigadier-general is a most human individual in the trenches. Even the humble subaltern looks on him as a fellow adventurer in the same great undertaking as himself. A soldier steps off the parade ground when he enters the first communication trench. Thereafter he is but a member of that great mutual help society, the Brotherhood of the Line.

Late in the afternoon the brigadier took his departure. The Sniper went outside and lounged lazily on the sloping bank to watch the general's progress down the road. It was the early evening of a lovely autumn day. The rays of the sinking sun shone on the ruined village, showing up clearly every detail of objects three hundred yards away and more; and through the trees the Sniper caught the flicker of the brigadier's scarlet shoulder-tabs and the gleam of his polished buttons, as he rapidly passed down the road towards the village. Not a rifle-shot was being fired. The stillness of content was everywhere.

Suddenly he heard a sound which sent a curious premonitory thrill through his being, a low groaning sound rapidly increasing in volume. Only a week ago he had heard it as he lay in that trench near the north of Sanctuary Wood while the company dug-outs were being crumped in. Silent Sue was speaking again. Again he was clinging tightly to the earth, waiting for the burst of her shell.

The shell struck the ground just a few yards beyond the bank, directly in line with the spot where the Sniper was lying. The débris from the explosion poured over the top of the bank like a miniature landslide, nearly burying him. A second, then a third shell followed. Three guns were at work, and all of Silent Sue's kind. One shell burst in the gum-boot store and wrecked the place. Dozens of big thigh-boots, joined in pairs by the supporting straps, whirled like chainshot into the air. Some became entangled in the trees, and for days after the branches were festooned with gum-boots slung by their fastenings. The third exploded in the dug-out next door. This contained trenching tools, and, with a clattering and a clanging, picks and shovels slithered all over the place.

Instantly the dug-outs woke to life and disgorged their occupants. The colonel roared out the order to scatter. Silently and quickly the men filed over the footbridge crossing the stream, and bolted for the village. They were Kitchener Army men of less than two months' experience, yet they evinced hardly a sign of panic. Their departure was hurried, but without confusion.

Two men were crossing the stream by a duck-board a little further down from where the Sniper lay. A shell arrived just at the moment. It stamped one into the stream. His blood dyed the water dark purple. The burst hurled the other man into the air and impaled him on the spikes of a portion of iron railing which ran along the top of the bank above the dug-outs. A large splash of blood drenched the Sniper's hand.

Slowly the Sniper rose to his feet, gazing in a fascinated way at the blood as it slowly trickled along his outstretched fingers and dripped to the ground. He felt sick, almost fainting. The whistle of a pick-shaft by his head steadied him a little. He saw it strike and fell the battalion sergeant-major as he came out of a dug-out. His nerve came back to him completely at the sight. He was starting forward to the man's aid, when a hand closed on his shoulder.

'Ah came back tae see if ye wanted any help, sir, when Ah saw ye standin' there a bit dazed like,' said Old Dan's voice in his ear. 'We'd better be runnin' for it now.'

'We'll take this man with us,' said the Sniper. 'Come and give me a hand.'

Old Dan pushed his officer aside and lifted the wounded N.C.O. on his shoulder as easily as though the man had been a child.

'Run for it, sir, run for it,' he exclaimed.

Ronald waited till Old Dan came up with him. He stepped out of the way for the old fellow to pass, and in this order they raced through the barrage of lighter shells which the Germans had locked across their path. Once a shell burst inside a ruined barn bordering the road just as they were passing. Only a timely push and a jump by the Sniper saved the three of them from being buried under the toppling wall. The effort sent them sprawling, and the watchers in the village thought for a moment that they had been hit. But, quickly regaining their feet, they raced clear of the danger zone into the village, where the sergeant-major was quickly carried away to the dressing station.

There is only one way of showing appreciation in the trench area – 'Have a drink?' Rum, whisky, oxo, or tea. You please yourself. The Sniper gratefully accepted the colonel's invitation to 'come in and have a spot'. 'In' was a cellar which had formed the headquarters of the reserve company stationed in the village. The colonel had annexed it as his own headquarters, and in one corner a rather disconsolate company commander was discussing with a number of no less disconsolate-looking company subs the possibilities of other cellars in the village.

Over the drink the colonel said some very nice things to the Sniper about himself and his regiment, much to that officer's embarrassment, so that he was greatly relieved when some battalion business diverted the senior man's attention. He left the cellar in time to see Old Dan finishing off the few remaining drops of a capacious mugful of rum which the battalion sniper sergeant had procured for him.

'They've given up the auld headquarters, sir,' he said, grinning cheerfully at his officer. 'It micht be as well tae tak a look roun' the place for a billet for the section, afore the rest o' the battalion arrives and grabs up everything.'

'I leave that to you, corporal,' said the Sniper.

Old Dan saluted, and hastened off on his search. The Sniper walked down the village street towards the old headquarters. The shelling had now ceased, and a party of soldiers were at work among the débris. They moved about carefully, almost nervously, for there is always something awesome about a familiar place which the guns have just laid in ruins. The rude interruption of its long-standing immunity shakes the trenchman's belief in the reality of any such thing as safety. When the nerves are raw, the mental processes resulting in the conception of 'What is', are too readily influenced by suggestions from 'What might have been' or 'What might be'. Their duty was to recover the bodies of the two men who had been killed, a gruesome mission requiring the employment of waterproof sheeting as a means of carrying the remains; a bursting shell is a devilish agent of destruction when applied to the human form. As soon as the poor mangled corpses had been laid amid the ruins of the sniper's old dug-out, the party hastily returned to the village.

It was nearly dark when the Sniper returned. He let Old Dan make his report on the available billet accommodation without making any comment, and sat down on the broken wall of a ruined house to await the arrival of his battalion. The corporal similarly settled himself a few yards away, wondering greatly what his officer's intentions were.

As soon as the battalion arrived, the Sniper took charge of his men and led them down the street and out of the village in the direction of the old headquarters. The sergeant marched silently beside him. Old Dan was in the rear. When the path leading off the road along the line of the dug-outs was reached, the officer stepped aside to allow the section to pass on.

'The headquarters are now in the village, sergeant,' he said. 'Take the men to the old bombers' dug-out. I think it is a better one than your old place. I am going to stay in the colonel's dug-out.'

'Very good, sir,' said the sergeant, leading the way into the side path.

The column silently filed off the road and was gradually swallowed up in the darkness of the tree-covered gully. As the Sniper watched them disappear, he thought he heard Old Dan laugh softly.

He went back to the village and reported himself to Colonel Stewart. The colonel had accepted without question his predecessor's report that the headquarters had been completely destroyed. He had already given directions for the building of a new headquarters in the village itself, and the Sniper did not see fit to tell him that his former dug-out had entirely escaped damage. He merely reported that he had been able to find habitable quarters for himself and his men, and the congestion was so great in the village that the colonel gladly gave his consent without asking any questions. As he returned from the village the Sniper could not help laughing at the comparison between his own splendid accommodation and the cramped squalid cellar which the colonel was sharing with the adjutant and the second-in-command.

His servant had nearly completed the preparations for dinner when he reached his quarters. After taking off his equipment he went outside and climbed to the top of the bank to await the man's summons. Above him was the deep blue moonless sky. Behind were the dark outlines of the village where the transport carts were rattling. In front was the 'line', ablaze with its night's splendour of star-shells. Tomorrow he would be on duty there in command of his men. Would success or failure be his lot? The thought did not depress him unduly. He no longer felt himself an untried man. The crowded events of the last few days had made him a veteran, in experience if not in time. He ceased thinking of what the morrow would bring, and let his mind wander where it would. His senses drank in the night's mystery. His consciousness was full of a supreme content. The trees whispered dreamily above him. The stream gurgled a soft response from its invisible depth. An occasional bullet whined overhead. But of individual sounds he was scarcely conscious. His soul was listening to the chorus of the wild while his physical being slept.

The low murmur of voices gradually came to his ears; his sleepy mind slowly tracked them to their source. They came from right beneath him. He was standing on the roof of the snipers' dug-out. Once the problem which had forced itself on his consciousness had been settled, his mind would have slipped back again to its waking oblivion. But ere the forgetfulness was complete, a ruder interruption brought him out of his restful trance. Someone had come racing into the dug-out beneath him.

'Sairgint, Sairgint,' the man called out excitedly. 'There's twa deid men lyin' in our auld dug-out, and the place is crum-pit tae blazes.'

'You've been a long time in discovering it,' he heard the sergeant reply coolly.

'But dae ye think the officer kens?' said the original speaker.

'Ay, does he. He kens a' richt. He was here when it happened,' – it was Old Dan who spoke.

Several of the snipers began to leave their dug-out to make investigations. Not wishing to be discovered, the Sniper stole silently away towards his dug-out. Above the clamour of their voices sounded Old Dan's chuckle – 'Hoo! Hoo! Hoo!'

From the ruined tower of the village church a desolate owl hooted a reply – 'Oo! Oo! Oo!'

CHAPTER V

The Snipers Accept their Officer

B EFORE DAWN THE SNIPER was roused by Sergeant Ferguson, and together they made their way to the firing-line. About two hundred yards to the left, in line with the dug-outs, was the beginning of a well-dug communication trench. But the road leading by the dug-outs was the shorter route, and the sergeant led the way along it, despite the stray bullets which were always whistling across. About a mile up the road was another ruined village. The firing-line skirted its further side; and the Sniper stepped down from the cobbles of the village street to the duck-boards of the front-line trench. He found the morning watch of the section already on duty, the men all standing by their loopholes, eager to avail themselves of any opportunities which the first flush of the morning might disclose to them. The sergeant conducted him from post to post, explaining its construction and purpose, and adding much useful information on sniping generally.

Trench warfare has killed much of the romance of sniping. As the firing-lines crept closer to each other, the sniper was forced to leave his self-chosen hiding-places in No Man's Land and take refuge in the trenches themselves. Only after an advance is there any general recrudescence of the old stalking practices. Where the nature of the ground permits it, sniping posts are found outside the shelter of the trenches, and the making of camouflage contrivances has been developed to a fine art. But broadly speaking, in normal trench warfare, sniping is done through loopholed steel shields fixed into the parapet of the trench. Two snipers are generally attached to each post, the one to act as observer, or to relieve the other when the strain of constant gazing through the narrow loophole becomes excessive.

The British sniping shields are small and readily lend themselves to concealment. Some of the plates which Sergeant Ferguson set up were used for weeks without being detected and shot at. The early German shields, on the other hand, were huge, cumbrous steel plates, defying any attempt to hide them. They used to stand up brazenly on the German parapet, sometimes right against the sky-line, so that the loophole was plainly visible whenever the protecting panel was swung open. This little carelessness cost many a German sniper his life, for it is not above the skill even of an average sniper to put a bullet through a German loophole once the light background clearly defines it. Some of these shields had as many as three loopholes. Later on, however, the Germans employed much smaller plates, far more difficult to detect and put out of action.

When it was light enough to see, the sergeant pointed out the sectors which each loophole commanded, explaining how every part of the German line was thus brought under constant observation. He was obviously bent on helping his officer as much as possible. The man was too much immersed in his vocation to be affable. He never seemed to speak an unnecessary word. But the Sniper perceived that he had won the sergeant's whole-hearted support. The other snipers also received their officer in a far different fashion from that of their first meeting. They did not volunteer any information, but they were decidedly responsive to any questions. Old Dan had evidently made them acquainted with the Sniper's conduct when the headquarters were bombarded; they had begun to realise the possibilities about their young officer.

Old Dan himself was there, as N.C.O. in charge of the morning watch. He came out of a sniping post dug deep into the parapet, like a primeval caveman emerging from his underground dwelling, and gave a cheery 'good morning' to the Sniper's greeting.

'There'll no be muckle doing this mornin', Maister Jackson,' he said. 'We've got Saxons opposite us, and they're a quate set o' buddies. Ah'm thinkin' they'll stick tae their trenches like a sheltie in a gable-end hole when it kens the laddies are after it, an' no give us a shot at all.'

The Sniper was particularly taken with the personalities of the two brothers Saunders, 'Adam' and 'Geordie'. They were fine big burly Highlanders, speaking the soft speech of northern Argyle, and looking out on the world with the clear, steadfast gaze of men whose lives have been spent in the open. Both gamekeepers before the war, their skill with the rifle was such that within a month of their enlistment they had been sent out to France as recruits for the volunteer sniping section which Colonel Stewart had set himself to form long before the authorities made the sniping sections general throughout the army. To them sniping was merely a continuation of their previous vocation, and the Sniper soon gathered from their conversation that they regarded their German adversaries much as they would a game pest threatening the welfare of their preserves. Even in their attitude to him he could detect traces of the respectful, almost paternal, treatment which the Highland gamekeeper bestows on a younger member of a shooting party.

Another man who attracted the Sniper's attention was Matthew Oldheim; in the first place because Oldheim was one of the ugliest men he had ever seen, and in the second because he was an American. He had lumpy red features and the kind of ears seen in pictures of elves and gnomes. The only regularity about his nose was an abnormally flattened bridge. It was just as if a designer had pressed it down with the flat of a modelling knife. His mouth was hardly describable, taking different shapes according to his mood; sometimes like the pursed-up entrance of a tightly strung leather sovereign bag, sometimes like the half-extended jaws of a dead cod-fish. His chin was just an appendage of his lower jaw, as if someone had struck him a blow there and the resulting lump had solidified. He had deep-set blue eyes, with a curious dreamy quality about them, giving his face a charm and gentleness of expression which made one forget its astonishing ugliness. Slimly built but as tough as steel, he had proved himself a most dangerous fellow in a rough and tumble. Those who tried to 'pull his leg' very quickly found this out for themselves without seeing him in action. If his accent was not typically American, it certainly could not be described as British. Indeed, he confessed to being of Dutch extraction through many American descents.

Before the war he had been stationed in London as representative of a large American concern, but somehow or other he had drifted into the recruiting station, showing the usual preference for a Scottish regiment. The explanation he gave for his enlistment was that he got tired of the British papers and wanted to see what was doing for himself. His skill with the rifle had very quickly brought him into the sniping section, where he was one of the most promising of the younger members. As Old Dan put it, 'Matthy is no bad,' and this, coming from such a source, was praise indeed, for Dan was as dour and cantankerous a Scot as ever came from North the Tweed, exceeding hard to please, and parsimonious to a fault with his commendations.

The early morning is the sniper's harvest-time, and the other member of the Five, John Brown, was also on duty with the first watch. He was a good-looking fellow, with the type of features that always suggests aristocratic descent. But the downward twist of his mouth at each corner spoke of some chronic warp in his nature, and did much to explain Captain MacMichael's story of the disreputable conduct sheet. He occupied a double sniping post with George Saunders, but he let the latter do all the talking, his keen restless eye never ceasing to peer out of the open loophole. Though naught but a 'Good morning!' passed between them, the Sniper was favourably impressed with the man. He looked dangerous, capable of much greater things than his more steady-going, if more skilful companion.

Old Dan proved to be right in his prophecy regarding the unproductiveness of the morning. The enemy clung to their trenches and gave the watching snipers not the slightest trace of a target. The morning stand-to passed off quietly with not a shot fired on either side, and about eight o'clock the Sniper walked down the long communication trench to his dug-out in search of breakfast. There was still nothing to report when he returned. For want of something better to do the section were engaged in dislodging shields by shooting away their foundations, a monotonous job at best, but extremely useful in destroying the nerve of the enemy.

The Sniper grew weary of watching the efforts of his men. The Germans were making no effort to retaliate, and the one-sidedness of the business bored him. He was not yet accustomed to the cramped conditions of the sniping posts, and the narrowness of the view which each loophole gave of the enemy trenches irritated him. He longed for a more unrestricted outlook, a comprehensive view of the German line, instead of having to piece laboriously together the various disjointed segments which the loopholes gave him.

The most critical time in a soldier's experience is his first month in the trenches. The first day or two are full of novelty, but thereafter his interest begins to flag. He wants to see more, and the danger incurred in gratifying his desire appears less and less menacing as the days go by. The daily monotony of the trenches becomes almost unbearable. He degenerates into such a state of boredom, that the wish for a change at any price proves well-nigh irresistible. This is the danger stage for a new-comer. If he manages to keep his curiosity within bounds, experience will gradually come to him. If he fails, the penalty too often is the sniper's bullet.

Such was the Sniper's state of mind on the very first day of his command in the trenches. Nor was he long in finding a means to gratify his curiosity, which yet appeared to offer him a fair measure of safety while doing so. Just where the firing-line crossed the village street, the battered gable wall of an old house was still standing. The street itself was visible from the German trenches, but the further end of the wall rose up from a much lower foundation, well below the top of the British parapet and wholly screened from German observation. He made up his mind to crawl out from the firing-line and get behind the broken wall from its lower end, to see if some chink in its shattered brickwork would not give him a better view of the German trenches than the more lowly situated loopholes.

He succeeded in reaching the wall in safety, and to his great delight he found a convenient spy-hole from which he could overlook a wide sector of the German line. There for over an hour he stood drinking in the unfamiliar scene. In front of him was No Man's Land, meadowland once, but with little trace of its tender green now visible. It was all a tangle of craters and crater débris. About two-thirds of the way across, the rusty masses of the German entanglements showed indistinctly against the brown earth, and beyond that again was the parapet of the fire-trench, a solid breast-work erection seven or eight feet high, here and there composed of solid layers of sandbagging, for the most part just an untidy heap of earth from which isolated blue, and red, and white sandbags peeped indiscriminately.

The trench ran along the crest of a ridge, and to the left and front little could be seen of the ground which lay behind it. On the extreme left, however, the ruins of old Hollebeke Château showed wanly from a clump of branchless trees. On the right the ridge dipped down to a kind of saddle, disclosing the road beneath Wytschaete Hill, and the gaunt steep of the hill itself, with the melancholy ruins of Wytschaete village on its brow. A desolate scene, but with a fascination all its own, the fascination which an explorer would feel when setting foot on a crater-field of the moon.

It was a typical Indian-summer day. The plate smashing had ceased for the moment, and no rifle-shot disturbed the stillness. The soft northern breeze brought to his ears the distant croak of the solitary yellow-beaked wild-fowl inhabiting the old monastery pool near the village in the hollow below. A spirit of well-being was stirring over that blasted countryside. The experienced sniper would have known the feeling, and his guard would only have become the more wary. He would have known that death was but casting a spell for fresh victims. But the Sniper could not yet read such signs. His vigilance relaxed. He forgot his presence outside the continuous shelter of the trenches. Quite casually he strolled from behind the ruined wall on to the open village street.

Mercifully realisation came to him instantaneously. For one brief awful instant he saw the German line stretched out before him barely two hundred yards away, every detail of it appearing in his field of vision as comprehensively and exactly as the objects on a photographic plate. Only that instant; then he had flung himself headlong on to the cobbles of the village street. A bullet cracked past him. It burst a brick in the further wall of the ruined house. He heard the fragments trickle down on the débris below;

and then a deadly stillness. The low breath he drew sounded in his ears like the roar of a hurricane. He knew that he was quite visible to the German sniper. His only chance was to lie still as if the bullet had killed him. If he moved the German would certainly complete his work. He realised all this as he lay there. He set himself purposely to simulate the appearance of death. He was quite conscious of everything, even the chill of the paving-stones on which he rested, even to the ticking of the watch on his wrist. What a long interval there seemed between each tick!

A voice broke the stillness like a thunderclap. Someone was speaking to him, into his ear. Old Dan's voice. . . . He wondered why the old fellow was making such an unnecessary noise. The Germans would hear him. As he comprehended what was being said, however, his hearing became normal again. Old Dan was scarcely speaking above a whisper.

'For God's sake, sir, keep quate,' he whispered, 'or they'll have ye pluggit. Ah'm richt ahint the auld wall. Ah'm gaun tae reach ower an' pu' ye in. Gie yersel' a wee bit spring when Ah grip ye.'

A hand closed like a vice on the slack of his tunic. The Sniper felt himself switched through the air in behind the old wall. The grip on his tunic relaxed; he scrambled weakly into a sitting position and stared giddily at his rescuer. Old Dan was sitting opposite him as white and shaken as himself. The Sniper quickly unscrewed the cup from his flask and filled it full of raw spirit. The flask he handed to the corporal. Each man drained off his portion to the last drop.

'I'm much obliged to you, corporal,' said the Sniper simply. 'It was a dashed plucky thing to do.'

'Never a word aboot that, sir,' Old Dan replied. 'Ah'm obliged for that nip o' speerit.'

After resting a little, the Sniper led the way back by the route by which he had entered the house. The trench opposite the old wall was crowded with men, and they raised a low jubilant cheer when they saw that he was unharmed. All the morning watch of snipers were there. They helped him in over the low parados, bustling about like a group of excited schoolboys. Old Dan received an ovation when he toppled into the trench. They shouldered off all the other soldiers who did not belong to the section. It was as if they were determined to keep their own to themselves.

'You'll never have a nearer escape, sir,' said the sergeant, eyeing his officer critically. The quickness with which the Sniper had recovered his presence of mind had impressed him. 'We all get a close call when we begin. It's a lesson we never forget.'

'It wass ta spirit of ta auld summer tat cast a spell over you, sir,' said Adam Saunders. 'I haf known of a man tat stepped over ta cliff at Craigellachie chust because it wass ta last good tay of ta year. We sall not haf any more good weather whateffer.'

Sergeant Ferguson at length ordered the watch back to their posts, and the Sniper hurried off to the battalion headquarters. The narrowness of his escape had made him thoughtful. One cannot look closely on the face of death without being appalled at what one sees there. But in a vague sort of a way he felt satisfied and almost happy. His men had been so genuinely concerned about him. Their interest had been almost proprietary, so different from the semi-hostile attitude with which they had first regarded him.

The rest of the day passed uneventfully, a blank so far as sniping was concerned. Soon after darkness the Sniper made his way to the section dug-out, carrying a bottle of whisky with him. At his entrance the snipers scrambled hastily to their feet, but he motioned them to be seated.

'I have come to tell you, men,' he said, 'that Colonel Stewart has recommended Corporal Haggarty for the D.C.M. I want you to drink his health.'

He handed the bottle to the sergeant, who deftly uncorked it 'Bush' fashion – inverting the bottle and tapping smartly on the upturned end until the cork was gradually forced out. Each sniper produced his mug and poured out a tot of the spirit as the bottle was handed round. Then Old Dan's health was solemnly drunk.

The corporal stood by as bashful as a child receiving its first school prize. He chewed nervously at the back of his right hand, even after the ceremony was finished. Then a thought seemed to strike him, and he gave a low gleeful chuckle.

'Ah wonder what the Gallowgate folk will say. Gode! Ah'll chairge them an extra penny a bag for their coals efter this.'

He would make no further reply to the toast in spite of his comrades' exhortations, and the Sniper turned to go. But the younger Saunders' voice stopped him.

'Sergeant,' he said, 'will Mr. Jackson no tak a sup o' ta hare soup tat Adam is making?'

The sergeant courteously extended the invitation. Everyone looked so anxious that he should accept it that the Sniper did not demur. A seat was made for him near the big glowing brazier in the centre of the dug-out, where the dixie was stewing. One of the younger men ran off to his dug-out for his canteen and a spoon. When he returned Adam served out to the

Sniper a generous helping of the savoury stew. The other snipers passed up their canteens in turn, and the big Highlander gravely dished out their portion. No one can beat a gamekeeper in the making of hare soup, and the Sniper lingered long over every sip.

One by one pipes were lit; the conversation became general. The presence of their officer did not seem to embarrass the men. Rather did they seem to regard him as one of themselves. Yet there was evidence of a deference paid to rank and experience. The snipers nearest the officer were the veterans of the section. The youngest members sat farther away. The Sniper silently studied the features of the men around him, and pride of his command stirred in his heart. The unwonted gravity which he saw there betokened men accustomed daily to walk in the Valley of the Shadow, who yet were confident and unafraid. But for the lack of any trace of boredom in their looks the gathering might well have been compared to Hudson's manikin crew of the Catskills.

The flickering light from the few tallow dips fretted the walls with strange tremulous designs in shadow-work from the straps and pouches of the equipment hanging there, and whenever a sniper moved across the floor, great shadows swooped up out of the nowhere, and silently disappeared whence they came. The smoke from a score of busy pipes mounted upwards to feed the billowing cloud which clung to the raftered roof. So dense was the cloud that it hid the head of a sniper standing by the doorway, making him appear like some headless figure, a stranger entering from another world. There was a serenity about everything in that old dug-out which reacted pleasantly on the Sniper's nerves, still throbbing from the experiences of the day. It was with a sigh of regret that he at length rose to go.

'Good night, men,' he said.

'Good night, sir,' every voice replied.

It had been his initiatory feast. Something told him that these men had admitted him into their circle, that he was now a full member of the Brotherhood.

CHAPTER VI

The Lurking Death

NEXT MORNING DAWNED COLD and forbidding. A drizzling rain had been falling all night, and a light mist was rising from the evil swamps of No Man's Land, hiding the German trenches from view; though, here and there, isolated sandbags on the top of the parapet appeared above the low-lying vapours, like the half-submerged, foam-girt rocks of a Highland torrent. The Sniper was kneeling on the fire-step close beside a sniping post, observing the German line through a high-power prismatic periscope.

The periscope had been procured by Colonel Stewart as part of the private equipment of the sniping section, and was one of the best of its kind. Yet so deceptive were the mist forms dancing round every hummock and irregularity of the ground that the Sniper's eyes ached with the strain of using it. He had to lean his wrists against the trench wall to keep the periscope steady, and the rain-water, squeezed out by the pressure from the sodden sandbags, trickled down inside the sleeves of his trench-coat, soaking his arms to the elbow. His knees were in no better plight, and he longed for the day to break properly, for the time when he would be hastening down the communication trench to the warm breakfast awaiting him in his dug-out.

Slowly the mist cleared. The German line became more and more distinct. A group of ruins stood behind the enemy trenches directly opposite the point from which he was observing. He was examining them curiously, trying to picture what kind of buildings they had been before their destruction, when out from behind a broken-down wall strolled a German soldier, obviously a straggler from a night working party who had missed his way.

It was the first German soldier that the Sniper had ever seen, and he nearly dropped the periscope in his excitement. The German walked boldly out on to the roadway; his clothing was drenched and muddy. The fellow looked so bedraggled and wretched that he hesitated to indicate him to any of his men. But the man on duty in the post had seen the target. His rifle cracked and the German dropped out of sight.

'Hoo! Hoo! Hoo!' Old Dan's chuckle sounded out of the post.

The Sniper drew aside the sacking which shielded the back of the post and looked in. Old Dan was sitting beneath his loophole writing something down in a little note-book. The sniper surmised that it was a private list of victims which the corporal was compiling. In spite of the knowledge that he owed his life to this man, he could scarcely repress a shudder. It all seemed so brutal.

Old Dan looked up and saw his officer, and seemed to divine immediately what was passing in the latter's mind.

'Come ben, sir,' he said simply. 'Ah ken just hoo ye feel. Ah used tae feel the same masel'. Ah couldna bring masel' tae take tae snipin', till after Ah saw ma sons killt; though Ferguson pestered me sair. Ah'll tell ye the story. It'll dae ye guid.'

The old fellow put away his book and glanced down sadly at his rifle for a little.

'It was doon by the Petit Bois,' he began, 'Mairch, 1915. We had advanced. But the French was held up on our richt. So was the rigiment on oor left. So we had tae gae back. Ah saw ma sons comin' back thegither. Baith were wounded, helping each ither alang. A sniper got on tae them. He killt ane first, and then the ither as he bent ower tae see what ailed his brither. Ah crept oot that night and brought them in. Ferguson helpit me. Ah laid them in the same grave, doon by the wee kirk a mile ahint oor lines.'

The corporal ceased speaking, there was silence for a minute or two. His fingers played aimlessly with the bolt of his rifle. He stared steadily ahead of him out along the trench, an old man bowed down by his sorrow. There was none of the vengefulness which the Sniper had noticed when the corporal first had mentioned the death of his sons. In its place was the softness, the humanity of the man who has suffered. When he spoke again his voice was so low that the Sniper heard him with difficulty.

'Ah didna want tae start the game,' he said; 'nane o' us did. But the Germans would play it. Oh, the braw laddies Ah've seen them kill! An' what's mair, they dinna play it fair. They're worse noo. They hardly fire a shot without first nickin' off the heid o' their bullet. When it strikes a man's heid, there's no much o' that heid left. Ye'll see for yersel', sir, afore ye're lang here. Ah suppose there are dacent men in the German Airmy. But efter what Ah've seen, it's vera difficult tae believe.'

He bent down, clicked another cartridge into the breech of his rifle, then rose and commenced to peer steadily out of his loophole. The Sniper silently withdrew from the post. What could he say? He had heard many tales of the German soldier's dirty tactics. He had hitherto viewed them all with the vague scepticism of the inexperienced man. But it was impossible to disbelieve Old Dan. The thought of the old man crawling out at night and searching among the bodies of the slain for the murdered sons caused a lump to rise in his throat.

About an hour afterwards he saw another German sniped. The fellow had looked impudently over the parapet and remained staring there for some time. By his actions he seemed to be beckoning other of his comrades to come and look over also. John Brown spotted him just as the Sniper passed his post. As his rifle would not bear properly from the loophole, Brown coolly climbed up on the fire-step and fired over the parapet itself. The Sniper saw the German's head go back with a jerk as the bullet struck him. The sight turned him sick. He had to leave the firing-line and go down to his dug-out to rest for a while. He was not yet accustomed to the killing of men.

In the evening came the antidote, as Old Dan had foretold. Just after the evening stand-to, he was standing on the fire-step with the sergeant and another sniper, gazing over No Man's Land. The light was bad, and the dark background of a ruined building was behind them. Only with difficulty could they make out the outline of the German parapet. It seemed impossible for them to be seen by the Germans. But it is at such moments of relaxed watchfulness that Death avenges herself on those who have so often made her their handmaid. A bullet sang between officer and sergeant. Their companion slid down into the bottom of the trench with a hole in his head into which a man could have put his fist. His brains were on the parados; yet he lived for three hours.

'Tampered bullet,' said the sergeant curtly.

They buried him next morning behind one of the ruined houses at the farther end of the village. It was the first break in the section since the Sniper had taken command, and as he stood by the padre and watched the body being lowered into the grave, he felt as if he were mourning the death of a near and dear relation. But he had learned his lesson. The casualty had revealed to him the unscrupulous brutality of the men who were his foes.

The spell of bad weather continued until the close of the tour in the trenches. Day after day it rained steadily. The conditions of existence became wretched. There is a rude comfort in trench life when the weather is fine. It is a very different thing when the weather breaks down, for wet or fair the fire-step has to be manned. Passing down the trench at night, the Sniper would see the silent figures of the sentry and his reliefs. The sentry standing up in a corner of the traverse, in his swathings of dank sacking like some desolate woman of the street. His two reliefs crouched up on the fire-step, their only covering a waterproof sheet. The trench wall wet and slimy, the water in the trench bottom washing over the duck-boards. Often he wondered how men were able to endure such conditions.

The rain searched out every weakness of parapet and parados, and soon whole lengths of trench wall began to sag inwards. It is always thus with the first rains of the winter. The whole battalion had to labour hard to save a general collapse of the position. The extra work involved, combined with the miserable weather conditions, heavily taxed the endurance of the men, although everything was done to alleviate their hardships. There was no rum issue, but dry socks were served out to them each evening, and at midnight big kettles of hot soup were placed at intervals along the trenches for the men to go and help themselves at will. But in spite of all the extra comforts, life during these soaking days was but an existence even for the strongest.

The main route of supplies for the trenches at night was the road which led past the old headquarters' dug-outs. It was barricaded at two points where the reserve and the support lines crossed over, and thus was fairly safe from an attempt of the Germans to rake it with fixed rifle fire. Night after night, as soon as darkness gave cover from watchful German artillery observers, the ration parties would leave the trenches and walk in regulation order down the road to the regimental 'dump', or stores depot, in the ruined village below. Later, in such order as their burdens permitted, they would return laden with food and stores for their comrades in the trenches.

Digging parties went up and down between the trenches and the billets of the reserve company, and larger working parties from the brigade reserve fed the constant stream of men which filled the little roadway. The protecting barricades reached up and caught the more dangerous low-flying bullets, and the men laughed at those which whined and hissed harmlessly overhead.

But there is no such thing as constant immunity from danger in the trench area, and ere long the Germans found a means of breaking into the comparative security which the ration parties had hitherto enjoyed. Away on the right where the ground rose up to Wytschaete, they placed a machine-gun, carefully fixed with swinging traverse to enfilade the road; and at intervals the measured purposeful note characteristic of the German machine-gun in action would be heard hammering its way through the night hubbub of the trenches. Sparks would fly from the metalled roadway as the cone of fire swept across it, and ration parties prayed that the gun might not speak until their work was accomplished.

It was just at the break-up of the weather that the Germans got their machine-gun to bear properly, and one of the snipers was destined to fall a victim to its fire.

Snipers are not usually called upon to do 'fatigues'. The strain of their daily duties is considered a sufficient reason for relieving them from this extra work. But every man was needed in the firing-line for the repair of the collapsing trenches. Men could hardly be spared for the ordinary ration parties; yet more men were required on account of the extra work in bringing up the huge soup kettles. Colonel Stewart was compelled to call on the snipers to undertake this duty.

On the fourth night of their stay in the trenches, Old Dan set out with half the section to carry up the kettles. Early in the evening the German gunners had been particularly persistent in their attentions to the roads, and though a silence had fallen when the party set out, every one of them knew that it was only a lull in the storm. The most dangerous part of the journey was the stretch which lay between the two barricades, and when they came to this part of the road, each pair of men, carrying a kettle between them, hurried across as quickly as possible. But one man lagged behind, one of the younger snipers, a fine strong lad from Perth, who had manfully volunteered to carry a kettle alone, in order to save a comrade a double journey. Ere he could reach the shelter of the barricade, the wicked hammering of the machine-gun rang out. Its bullets snapped and whistled across the road, and the soul of the sniper went out into the night.

Just below the last barricade grew a deep bed of wattle stems, and in a little clearing stood all that the German shells had left of a Belgian peasant's humble dwelling. Amid the débris of broken brick and mud and blackened timber, one untouched gable-end reared itself appealingly to the skies, and cast its shadow from the midday sun protectingly over a little patch of green, which shrank close to its side away from the encroaching wattle stems. In the centre of the sward they buried him. They placed the little black cross at the head of the grave, where the rays of the sun could just light up the lettering which gave his name. Instead of a wreath they pinned down his cap on the top of the mound with the brass nose-cap of a German shell.

Among the letters which the Sniper censored next day was one to the dead man's mother telling her of her son's death. There was a touch of human sympathy in the letter which made his eyes grow strangely tender. The writer was Sergeant Ferguson. Thereafter the Sniper forgot all about the sergeant's impassive ways, and the dull expressionless look of his eyes; for the letter told him that these were but a cloak beneath which throbbed the great big heart of a man.

That week the section sent thirty-two Germans to attend to the needs of their slaughtered comrades in the Valhalla of snipers.

CHAPTER VII

Goo–Goo

THE SPELL OF BAD weather caused the abandonment of the rest camp which the battalion occupied between the bi-monthly trench tours. It lay on the lower slope of a hill, and the heavy rains washed down the higher surface soil until the camp was a slimy morass, a foot or two deep where the paths had been, and inches deep over the tent floors. The rain eased off sufficiently for the quartermaster and the men remaining with him to get the floods under control; but the camp was scarcely habitable, and the quartermaster determined to take advantage of the visit of a high engineering personage to get the locality condemned.

All the rest camps in the neighbourhood were being inspected at the time, and though every one of the battalions concerned wished to move to positions which they had long been coveting, none of them succeeded in impressing the inspecting officer with the necessity for the change. He suggested certain improvements in the already existing conditions, and with that they had to content themselves.

The quartermaster had noted down an ideal position; and he had not served thirty years with his regiment without learning how best to acquire anything he had set his heart on. He cheerfully informed the inspecting officer that the battalion was completely satisfied with its quarters – an attitude which impressed the officer very favourably when he remembered the long lists of complaints of the other battalions – and after detailing the various improvements which he had effected in drainage and equipment, he guilelessly led the way on a tour of inspection.

A man who knew the camp could cross from one end of it to the other without sinking in the mud more than an inch or so above his boots at most. But there were old bog-holes and drains where the depth was much greater.

These were given a very wide berth by the initiated. The quartermaster seemed to have temporarily forgotten such pitfalls, for he led that engineer general through the deepest and slimiest of them all. He had donned a pair of big thigh waders. His charge wore a pair of small-sized knee-boots – the kind with the grey waterproof leggings – and a very natty pair of light fawn breeches. Before a score of yards had been traversed, boots and breeches had disappeared into the mud and the general had come to a stop waist deep, cursing Heaven and Hell and the god of the weather, the god of war, and the comfortable little gods whose duty it is to choose rest-camp localities and billeting areas.

The quartermaster was the tallest man in a regiment of tall men, but even his long legs hardly kept his middle clear of the treacherous slime when he bore down to the rescue. But he dragged the general clear with a minimum of discomfort to himself, and hurried him off to the store hut, where a fine warm fire was burning, and other comforts in the way of hot whisky and dry boots and breeches stood marvellously ready to hand.

'You see, sir,' he explained, 'being at the foot of a hill, we are constantly troubled with fresh springs bursting out and causing bog-holes like the one you fell into. We only discover that they are there when the men get bogged in them.'

The general departed full of thanks for the attention he had received, and wondering how some regiments were able to put up with so much and yet complain so little about it. The quartermaster had judiciously hinted at the desirability of the site he had in mind. The general at once gave orders that a new rest camp should be prepared there. So impressed was he, moreover, with the discomfort of the present situation, that he cleared out various depot units from billets which they occupied in a neighbouring town, and placed them at the disposal of the battalion until the new camp was ready.

'Is it the case that we are going back to Poprinbusch, sir?' asked the sergeant of the Sniper when the news came to the battalion. 'I hope you will get us the billet behind the Anglais Estaminet. We've always occupied it before when we've been billeted there.'

The Sniper at once saw the adjutant, and it was to the Café Anglais that he led his section when the battalion marched out for its weekly rest. The café stood near the station in a side street in the poorer quarter of the town. The billet for his men consisted of a shed behind the estaminet proper. The noise of his section drawing up in the street outside the house roused the inmates. The door opened, disclosing a woman with a child at her side.

'We have come to occupy the billets here, Madame,' the Sniper explained in his best French.

'Certainly, Monsieur,' replied the woman in very good English. 'Will you take your men through dat gateway dere?'

He turned to give the necessary order when a cry from the child interrupted him.

'Grandpère! Grandpère!' she called, running out into the street. 'You come back to Goo-Goo.'

Someone detached himself from the rear of the section. The little girl was swept up into his arms, and the Sniper heard Old Dan's voice speaking the babyish prattle with which grown-ups greet a favourite child.

'Is dat you, Monsieur Ferguson?' called the woman. 'Oh the good chance! Come in to de estaminet. At once! Why do you stand in de street so long?'

'We are known here, sir,' said the sergeant to the Sniper. 'Goo-Goo – the little girl there – is a great friend of us all, especially Old Dan. It will be quite all right to leave us here, sir.'

'Fall out,' called the Sniper immediately.

The sergeant hastened off to greet Madame. Several of the men followed him into the estaminet. But others gathered round Old Dan and Goo-Goo.

'Hey, Daniel!' expostulated Adam Saunders. 'Just you be not so greedy with ta bairn.'

'Get oot o' the way, ye muckle big Hielantman,' called a man whom the Sniper recognized as Walter Finney, one of the roughest fellows in his section. 'The bairn kens me better nor you. Ah have the next chance.'

'Oncle Jean! Oncle Jean!' cried the child.

To the Sniper's great surprise John Brown's voice called back in reply. The man moved up to Old Dan and took the child into his arms, and he and the corporal disappeared into the estaminet. The men seemed so much at home about the place that the Sniper hurried off to his own quarters without worrying further about their comfort.

The section had first come to the billet a long time ago when the 2nd Eastshires were moved up to the Salient after the first Battle of Ypres. It had not always been an estaminet. Before the war Monsieur who owned the place had been a thrifty citizen, whose weekly wage more than sufficed for the needs of his little family. But the Battle of the Aisne had left him a cripple, and now he could only sit by the fire and sometimes reach out with his crutch to rock the cradle when his baby daughter proved fretful. The arrival of the British in the town gave Madame her opportunity. She opened the place as an estaminet, and the prices paid by a generous soldiery soon solved the problem of ways and means for the little household.

It was then that Old Dan gave Goo-Goo her name. She was in her cradle when the snipers entered the billet, and Old Dan went down on his knees beside the cot to talk and play with her. She stretched up her chubby little arms, and murmured 'Goo-goo-goo!' 'Goo-goo-goo,' Old Dan chuckled in reply. And Goo-Goo she was to the section and to all other men who frequented the estaminet.

The snipers had since occupied the billets on several occasions, and even when they went to a new rest camp with a change in their battalion sector, they were never so far away but what a short walk would bring them back to the estaminet during rest periods. And Madame welcomed their visits, not merely on her own account, or for the sake of the life which flushed Monsieur's pale cheeks when he saw them, but because of Goo-Goo, who cried when they were away too long.

Old Dan was easily first in Goo-Goo's favour. She called him Grandpère in the pretty Anglo-French patois which she had learned through their association. John Brown came next, and then possibly the sergeant, whom she sometimes called Papa, because he always sat talking to Monsieur and the little maid had come to associate the two with each other. As to the other snipers she showed little distinction in her treatment of them. But she was keenly conscious of their different individualities; and when any were missing she noticed their absence at once and mourned them bitterly, refusing to understand why the angels should have taken any of her big playfellows away from her.

She seemed to regard them on a level with her doll Bi-Bi, which Old Dan had brought to her from Glasgow, and a sly bull pup called Fi-Fi, found by him in the ruins of Ypres; and she would play with Bi-Bi or romp with Fi-Fi and the snipers indiscriminately. But every game had the same ending. 'Goo-Goo tired, Grandpère,' she would say, and Old Dan would gather her up in his arms and nurse her till she slept. Then the only attention the other men would get from him was an angry look when their conversation became too noisy.

The Sniper soon found himself marked down for her attention. He belonged to the section, and the section belonged to her, therefore – was Goo-Goo's line of reasoning. It was rather embarrassing for him at first, especially when Goo-Goo would come out of a morning while he was parading his men and demand to be kissed. But he went through the ordeal nobly, and soon he bade fair to rival Old Dan in her favour. Often when he was seated in the barn in the midst of the section doing compass work and map-reading, Goo-Goo and Bi-Bi and Fi-Fi would descend like a whirlwind among them, and demand to be amused. He would get her interested in the swinging compass needle or the colour scheme of the map, so that she became as attentive a student as any one of them.

When Madame came, and in horrified tones called her sharply away, he would never permit her to go. He always treated her as a big brother would a tiny sister, and the men appreciated his kindliness. She was an object of mutual care and interest to them all, and the community of feeling thus engendered between officer and men reacted on all their dealings with one another, so that the section became more and more a brotherhood, wherein the sanctions of discipline were overlaid by the ties of mutual trust and friendship.

From the beginning of his career with the section, the Sniper had realised that he could not run such a unit like an ordinary platoon. Sniping was an art in which excellence of attainment was bound to carry with it a degree of authority over those less skilled, independent of the military rank which the successful sniper might hold. He had five of the finest snipers in the British Army under his command, and he recognised that the best way of managing his section was to work through them and accord to them all the deference which their skill merited.

The standard of conduct which the good sense of the snipers enforced among themselves relieved him of any fear with regard to discipline, and he completed the good understanding which had grown up between him and his men by unobtrusively showing that in matters concerning the efficiency and well-being of the section, he was willing to be guided by the general opinion of the snipers themselves as expressed through the Five. The need for filling the places of the two men who had been killed during the last tour in the trenches gave him the first opportunity of putting this policy into effect and he commissioned Sergeant Ferguson to select likely candidates, thus making sure that he would get two men who, while being fairly good marksmen, would at the same time be possessed of personal qualities likely to make them harmonise with the other members of the section.

'I've put two men through their preliminary tests for the vacancies, sir,' said the sergeant after one morning parade. 'Mackie of A Company, and Smith of D. Both are fairly satisfactory. Perhaps you would test them this afternoon, sir?'

'Right, sergeant,' said the Sniper. 'Parade the section at two o'clock sharp, and we'll go to the range. I'd like to see how the whole section shoots also.'

The range lay in a valley about two miles from the rest camp. The butts consisted of a natural bank with a trench at its base to shelter the markers.

Two hundred yards was the distance of the furthest firing-point. The target was a three-inch circle on the top of an oblong nine inches by three, the whole painted black on a white canvas screen two feet square. A hit on the circle counted five points; on the part of the oblong immediately below the circle, three points; on the rest of the oblong, one point. The idea underlying the scoring was the relative seriousness of a wound in the head, neck, or shoulders, for such the target was supposed to represent.

Each of the snipers fired five rounds at two hundred yards. Eight of them made the maximum score of twenty-five points. The lowest score was twenty-one.

'Will you try five rounds, sir?' said the sergeant to the Sniper.

The Sniper had not hitherto fired before his section. Not one of them knew whether he was even a marksman, and the sergeant's tone was uncertain, clearly showing that he did not want to convict his officer of any lack of skill before his men, but just as clearly expressing the hint that an officer in charge of snipers should himself be able to shoot.

The Sniper had been an extra marksman in his cadet-corps days. With the greatest of ease he put up a score of twenty-three, four heads and a neck. The sergeant's relief was obvious. The looks of the other snipers also showed their appreciation of their officer's skill. He was no unworthy commander after all.

Mackie and Smith were then put through their test. The former managed a score of twenty, but the best Smith could do was only eleven points. The boy was painfully nervous, and the result of a second attempt was even poorer. The sergeant looked anxiously at his officer.

'Perhaps the rifle is flinging wide, sir,' he said.

'Possibly, sergeant. Here, Saunders, try five rounds with Smith's rifle,' said the Sniper, turning to the elder of the two gamekeepers.

Very deliberately Lance-Corporal Adam fired the rounds. His score was the same as Smith's. The very shots were identical – three necks and two shoulders.

'You are right, sergeant,' said the Sniper. 'It's the rifle's fault; not Smith's. Let me have a shot with it first though.'

Saunders handed him a cartridge. The Sniper took aim and fired. All eyes stared at the target. A white disc stole up to the centre.

'A bull!'

Every one of the watching snipers spoke the word simultaneously, so that it sounded across the range as though a giant had roared it through a megaphone. Then each one looked at the other significantly, and wondered what was going to happen. No one doubted but that Saunders had tried to shield Smith.

'The rifle is more erratic than I thought,' said the Sniper innocently, handing it back to its owner. 'Take it to the armourer when you get back, Smith. Section! Fall in!'

The snipers fell in and marched off. A few of the younger men commenced to snigger in the rear. The Sniper smiled grimly as he heard Old Dan's hoarse whisper. 'Shut up, ye dawm eediots. Dae ye think Maister Jackson is as saft in the heid as yersels?'

'I hold you responsible for Smith turning out all right, sergeant,' said the Sniper meaningly after dismissing parade.

'There'll be no fear about that, sir,' replied the sergeant. 'The lad was only a bit nervous. He's one of the best shots in the regiment.'

It was a flash of inspiration that had led the Sniper to act as he did. He had seen at once that both the sergeant and Saunders considered that Smith ought to be passed into the section, and he had avoided the difficult situation which would have arisen if he had denounced their subterfuge. Thereafter none of the Five ever hesitated to let their officer know what their opinion was, though they generally used the sergeant or Old Dan as their mouthpiece.

Goo-Goo's treatment of the new-comers caused great amusement. She recognised their presence the first night of their appearance in the estaminet. For a few minutes she stared at them doubtfully. Then she gravely placed Bi-Bi in Mackie's arms and Fi-Fi in Smith's, and watched the two men solemnly to see how they treated her pets. They soon became uncomfortable under her earnest scrutiny, more especially as the other snipers chaffed them slily; and Mackie tried to get rid of the doll by handing it to the sniper nearest him. Goo-Goo determinedly replaced it, and watched him the more earnestly to his greater embarrassment. After half an hour of this business she was apparently satisfied, for she calmly annexed them as her playfellows, and insisted on their joining in a game with Bi-Bi and Fi-Fi and herself, until the time to sidle up to Old Dan to go to sleep in his arms.

At the end of the rest period the battalion marched off to a ruined village two miles behind the firing-line, which was held as a British reserve position for the sector. Goo-Goo stamped her feet angrily and yelled outrageously when she understood that they were leaving her. Madame had some trouble to prevent her running after the section.

'Pity we couldna take her wi' us,' the Sniper heard young Geordie Smith say to Old Dan.

'Ah wish the bairn was further away frae the line,' Old Dan replied, looking back anxiously at the estaminet.

Several times the Sniper noticed the corporal give the same anxious look backwards, and he wondered a little at the old man's anxiety.

During the week of their stay in the new position, Old Dan's wish regarding Goo-Goo was echoed more than once by every member of the section. The very devil of mischief itself seemed to have seized hold of the enemy gunners, and they shelled camps and billeting areas which never before had received a single shot. The British quickly retaliated on like points behind the German lines, and soon the whole Salient was ablaze with a regular pitched battle between the rival artilleries.

The struggle seemed to wax more terrible after darkness, and every night the battalion was called to the stand-to, ready to take cover in the shelter trenches should the brigade receive attention from the enemy. Sometimes the snipers would hear the noise of big shells travelling high overhead, and they would listen anxiously for the burst, lest they should be bound for Poprinbusch. But save for an odd shell or two the town seemed to be outside the scope of the German activity.

One night the order came to man the shelter trenches. The enemy were barraging the roads at one end of the village. Any moment their shells might descend on the village itself. The crisis had evidently been reached in the artillery battle, and at times the night was as bright as day from the flashes of the guns. Every now and then a broken fragment of Ypres would leap into startling silhouette against a blood-red horizon. Each road of the district could be identified by the line of pin-point shrapnel bursts sparking above it. Overhead the air was full of the snoring passage of long-distance shells, travelling in a direction which filled the hearts of the snipers with a common anxiety.

'Gode! Ah doot they're efter it the nicht,' Old Dan murmured. He was standing beside Ronald as he spoke. A low cry of dismay from someone distracted the latter's attention. Away in the direction of Poprinbusch the glow of a conflagration was reddening the sky. When he turned to look at Old Dan again the corporal had gone.

He had slipped quietly away into the darkness. Nobody had seen him go. But everyone knew his objective, and prayed that success might attend his mission. The Sniper was glad that the old fellow had gone without asking permission, sparing him the pain of having to withhold his sanction. News came in that only one district of the town was being shelled. But that was the district where Goo-Goo lived, and all night they anxiously watched the glow of the blazing city, their thoughts with Old Dan and the little girl whom he had gone to save.

He came back in the early forenoon, exhausted, almost broken. One glance at his grief-seamed features confirmed the worst of their fears. 'She's deid,' was all he would tell them. But gradually as the days went by they heard a little more from him. Yet it was not until the Sniper met a certain gunner major who had brought his battery through the town when the shelling was at its height, that he got the full account.

The quarter near the station was blazing when Old Dan reached the out-skirts. The roads were blocked by panic-stricken fugitives, but by main strength he fought his way through. The air was full of the crash of falling buildings, the screams of the wounded, the hoarse calls of British ambulance men salving among the ruins. Old Dan passed them by unheeding. Crossing an open space the artillery major caught him by the shoulder. 'My guns!' cried the major, pointing to a derelict train round which a few men were working heroically.

The corporal shook himself free and darted down a side-way, the major following him in fury. The nearer end of the street where Goo-Goo lived was a furnace, and the major recoiled from its fiery breath. But Old Dan raced on. The hot air blackened his lips and singed his hair and clothing. His senses swam from the noxious fumes, and their bite at his throat was like the grasp of a red-hot hand of iron. But the greater pain growing in his heart made him blind to his bodily torment. For ere he had raced a dozen paces he knew that he had come too late.

A shell had burst in the street in front of the estaminet. The outer wall had disappeared. Inside the little kitchen bar Madame lay dead across the still form of her husband. And in the far corner, with Bi-Bi and dead Fi-Fi clutched to her breast, lay Goo-Goo. She was still alive when he bent over her, and at his touch she looked up at him and smiled. 'Goo-Goo tired,' she murmured drowsily. Gathering her up in his arms, he raced madly away from the inferno.

The artillery major ought to have put Old Dan under arrest when he met him next morning. The corporal had disobeyed the officer's order and deserted him in his need. But in the British Army extenuating circumstances wash out many a technical crime, and instead of enforcing the regulations the major ordered his men to look after the old man. For he had come on Old Dan sitting by the roadside, crying softly to himself, the dead child in his arms.

CHAPTER VIII

Cissie's Romance

A THICK FINE RAIN was falling when the battalion marched away from the reserve village for their tour in the trenches. The men's waterproof capes glistened wetly in the light of an occasional gun-flash. Liquid mud swilled inches deep on the worn-down surface of the road, and the noise of the treading feet was softened down to a low shuffling swish. Now and then a sudden splash and a deep-toned curse would come from somewhere up the line, as a leading file slid off the roadway into a brimming shell-hole. Save for this, and the low whispering conversation, heard in pauses of the marching, the sound of the battalion's progress was like the sluggish rush of a deep-laden stream; the faint intermittent murmur of the early transport, the roar of its distant rapids.

It was one of those miserable times, so common in the lot of the trenchman, when he walks blindly forward, heedless of the stray bullets and splinters filling the air with their whinings around him, so utterly disgruntled with existence that the news of an attack is welcomed for its promise of excitement and change.

Of all the battalion units the snipers were the most sombre. The death of Goo-Goo had affected each one of them just as much as if she had been their own child, and they slouched along in silence, grieving for the little girl who, for more than two years, had brightened their dreary sojourn in the Salient. The Sniper stumbled gloomily forward at their head. The sergeant followed a sullen pace or two behind. Old Dan and John Brown brought up the rear. Any time the Sniper stepped aside to prove his straggling files, he would hear those two muttering to each other as though they were discussing plans of revenge. Often he felt inclined to go over and join in their murmuring.

C Company was marching immediately in front of the section, Big Bill Davidson in command, Captain MacMichael being away on a staff course. The Sniper saw someone detach himself from the dark moving mass of the company, and fall into step alongside of him.

'That you, Ronald?' said Cissie Rankine's voice.

'Hullo, Cissie!' the Sniper grunted. 'Beastly awful fug, isn't it?'

The two squelched on together in silence for a few minutes.

'Jove, you have got a grouch to-night,' Cissie said at length. 'I came down for some cheerful society, and I find you're as surly as a bear with toothache.'

'What's the matter with you, Cissie?' asked the Sniper, struck with something pathetic in the boy's tone. 'Feeling down in the mouth?'

'Just a little,' Cissie admitted. 'I've been marching with Davidson all the way up, and his irrepressible spirits have jolly well got on my nerves.'

'I compree. The habitually cheerful person on a night like this is too tragic for words. Makes you want to tip him into the nearest shell-hole, doesn't it?'

The Sniper tried to carry on the conversation for the rest of the journey, but it cost him more than an effort. By the time the headquarters village was reached he was feeling more depressed than before. C Company were taking over the billets of the village. He parted from Cissie and led his men on to their usual quarters.

He saw them settled down comfortably, got them their rations long before any of the other battalion units, himself standing out in the pouring rain 'managing' the police sergeant and shamelessly suborning him into releasing an extra bag of coke, before he entered his own dug-out to await his dinner. But something had gone wrong with the Primus stove, and his servant sorrowfully produced the whisky and soda to soften down the announcement that dinner would be delayed. Drinking alone did not appeal to the Sniper, and he struggled back into his wringing trench-coat, and made off towards the cellar where C Company headquarters were located.

As he went down the cellar stairs he heard voices raised in dispute. On his entrance the voices were instantly hushed, but he saw at once that a quarrel had been taking place. Big Bill was sitting on his bed, back against the wall, the customary ironical twist about his mouth, but with the twinkle which usually softened his sallies absent from his eyes. Cissie was standing in the centre of the floor, his face flushed, his hands clenched, shaking from head to foot with excitement. Jimmy MacLauchlan was sitting in the further corner from the door, shifting uneasily about in his seat, his whole attitude indicating distaste for the scene which had been going on.

'What's the matter, Bill?' enquired the Sniper.

'Nothing very much, Jacky,' Bill replied with apparent indifference.

'Rather funny that you and Cissie should be sparring over nothing. Have you been leg-pulling again?'

'No, I haven't,' Big Bill protested. 'It all arose over a simple remark of mine. We were discussing a poor beggar of the first battalion, who has just been killed a week after his marriage. And I simply said that judging by the way some soldiers' girls and wives were behaving, perhaps he was lucky. What must Cissie do but fly into a temper and call me a cad and a rotter!'

'You meant it for me. You know you did. Ever since I met you you've been hinting away about Ella' – Ella was Cissie's girl – 'I know you have, Davidson,' burst out Cissie excitedly.

'I tell you I did not mean it for you, Cissie. My remark was quite simple, and you had no cause to take it to yourself, just because you are engaged to some fancy woman who—'

'You cad!' exclaimed the boy, and, rushing past the Sniper, he struck Big Bill full in the face.

Davidson made no effort to protect himself. He just sat and looked at Cissie. He was a full ten inches taller than the boy, but he was merciful in his strength.

'I am very sorry, Cissie,' he said slowly, 'that any remark of mine should have brought you to striking a brother officer.'

Cissie turned very white. Without a word he swung round and ran out of the cellar. He was very young, and very much in love, with all the young boy's faith in the divine perfection of his girl. The Sniper and he had come up the line together, and some trait of sympathy in the former's character had led the boy to make a confidant of him. He had spoken of his engagement – she was a chorus girl in a minor touring company – and shyly shown him her photograph. 'Isn't she a stunner?' the boy had said. And the Sniper, looking at the sensuous beautiful face, had inwardly congratulated Cissie on his translation from her immediate sphere.

'Have you been chipping him about his girl, Bill?' he asked, when Cissie had disappeared.

Bill raised himself forward to the edge of the bed. He was a good fellow, and, now that Cissie had gone, he did not trouble to hide his distress.

'Yes, I have, Jacky,' he admitted. 'Though I did not mean him to take anything out of what I said just before you came in. You know he is engaged to an absolute rotter of a girl, and the dear little chap won't hear her name mentioned. She's simply plucking him bare. Before he came out he had to sell his motor-bike and compass and things to clear his feet, and now he's sending her the better part of his pay. How do I know? Why, she boasts of it. Some fellows I know are pretty thick with her in town, and from what they have told me, I know she's little better than a street girl. It's awful to think of a good little chap like Cissie being in the tow of such a woman.'

'I had suspected as much, Bill,' said the Sniper. 'But it won't do the slightest bit of good for us to try and open his eyes. You know what we were at his age.'

'But things can't go on as they are. She might simply ruin the boy's life. If the young blighter would only take a hint!'

'No, she won't. She's not the kind of girl who would marry him, and as for the rest, it will be a lesson to Cissie when he finds out. And he'll find out for himself before long. He's not a fool.

'It's just this, Bill,' the Sniper continued after a pause. 'Cissie has been a regular mother's and sisters' darling before the war, and he was flung on the world and among older men before he was fit for it. The army is making a man of him fast, and now that he is safe over here, I think we should leave him alone. Poor kid! It will be an awful shock to him when he finds out.'

Big Bill shook his head doubtfully, but said no more, and the Sniper hurried out of the cellar in search of Cissie. He found the boy leaning against a broken wall which separated the road from a willow-sown outlet of the monastery moat. His face showed a trace of tears. He looked so girlish and fine that the Sniper's heart thrilled with sympathy.

'Poor little kid!' he murmured; then aloud – 'Come and have dinner with me, laddie. I've a whole lot of things I want eaten to save me the trouble of taking them back.'

The boy eyed him doubtfully. 'I'll come if you want me to, Jackson,' he replied.

'Of course I do, you silly young devil! Come along,' said the Sniper heartily, and off the two went together.

The Sniper was old for his twenty-four years. Over in the Argentine he had been early accustomed to responsible duties by his father, and his business relations with the native Argentinians had given him a wonderful tactfulness and knowledge of human nature. He used his talents to the utmost in soothing the wounded spirit of the boy, searching skilfully the while for some opening which he might take to account in weakening Cissie's attachment towards the redoubtable Ella.

He led the boy on to talk of his home, of the retired general, his father, of his two sisters. He was man enough to be interested in the sisters, especially the one older than Cissie, when he heard that she was out in France as a driver to a private hospital unit. 'What a topping girl she must be,' he thought, 'if her brother's looks are any criterion!' He learned that the boy was not on writing terms with his people. There had been some row with his father about money. He thought he saw his chance here, and quickly intervened.

'How in the world did you manage to get into debt?' he enquired. 'You've got a decent allowance, and your pay as well.'

Cissie tried to avoid a direct reply, but the Sniper guilelessly brought him back to the point. At length the boy rather shamefacedly admitted that he had been obliged to send money to Ella.

'You see, Jackson,' he said, 'she has had several illnesses, and she has to support a mother and two sisters.'

The Sniper had got the opening he had been searching for. Very tactfully he proceeded to take advantage of it.

'Look here, old man,' he began, ' I take it you intend to get married some day.'

'Yes,' the boy replied. 'I wanted to get married before I left for France, but Ella said her mother could not spare her yet.'

'Well, laddie,' continued the Sniper, 'you ought to write to Ella, pointing out that if she does not let you save some money, you will never be able to set up house with her. You ought really to do it for her own sake. You know, my boy, the man has always to think for the girl as well as for himself in these affairs.'

What the Sniper said evidently impressed Cissie with its reason, for when the boy rose to go shortly afterwards, he shook his friend's hand warmly.

'You've made me feel what a self-centred little ass I am, Ronald,' he said. 'I'll write to Ella immediately I get back to camp. And I'm going to write home also. I'll tell Maimie about you. She's great. You'd like her.' Maimie was the elder sister. 'And I'm going to apologise to Big Bill. Jove! The cheek of me hitting a man like him!' He blushed at the remembrance of his conduct. Then he walked bravely back to the village.

'I wonder if I've acted properly,' thought the Sniper as he watched him go. 'It's sure to end in a bust-up.'

As the Sniper went down to headquarters that evening in response to a summons by the adjutant, he noticed Cissie parading his platoon for an advance-wiring fatigue. It was to be the boy's first experience of No Man's Land, and he hurried through his conference with the adjutant in order to accompany Cissie to the firing-line to give him confidence. He managed to catch up with the platoon just before it reached his quarters, but instead of joining Cissie at its head he turned down towards his dug-out. Big Bill Davidson had forestalled him, and the Sniper had approached the two near enough to see Big Bill's hand resting fondly on Cissie's shoulder.

CHAPTER IX

The Laugh

WHAT THE ADJUTANT HAD told him very greatly interested the Sniper, and for a long time after entering his dug-out he sat thinking over the matter. Men had been disappearing from patrol parties on the divisional sector during the previous week, and the adjutant had warned him to be very careful of himself and his men when out in No Man's Land.

The report book in which the sniper officer of the battalion in the trenches set down the history of the tour for the benefit of the sniper officer relieving him also had a mention of the affair. He had the book before him now, open at the place where the entry had been made. The report briefly stated that such and such a sniper was missing when the patrol returned, and that a night-long search had failed to discover him. But what specially interested the Sniper was that the last line of the entry had been carefully blotted out.

'Healey has noticed something else about the business,' he murmured, 'but the beggar was afraid that he might be laughed at, and so he has scratched it out. Wish I'd been able to have a talk with him about it.'

But Healey, his brother sniper officer, had been sent on some course of instruction the day before the relief, and though the Sniper used his imagination strenuously to fill in the words between the few decipherable letters of the erasure, no satisfactory result would present itself.

'I'll go up and see how Cissie is getting on. Perhaps there will be something doing,' he said, pulling on his trench-coat and leaving the dug-out.

The rain had ceased to fall, and a ghastly moon was striving to pierce a way through the mantle of mist which still clung to the earth. The line had wakened up to much of its usual turmoil, as if the nightly contestants had come out from lairs where they had been sheltering from the weather.

From all quarters Verey lights were shooting up and describing their flaring curves, and the clatter of machine-gun and rifle fire was steadily growing in volume.

The machine-gun on the Wytschaete shoulder began to search the road which the Sniper was following, and about four hundred yards from the firing-line he was forced to take cover behind a house which stood by the roadside. It struck him at the time that the house would make an excellent observation post, but he did not tarry to investigate its possibilities. His mind was too full of the other idea. He found the place where Johnny Rankine's party were working and climbed out over the parapet. The men were strengthening the outer wire belt, and he came on Cissie sitting beyond his covering party more than a hundred yards from the firing-line.

'Hullo, Ronald!' said the boy. 'Have you come out to father me now? Davidson has just left me. He is a topping chap. Do you know, he would not listen when I tried to apologise to him. He insisted on apologising to me, and he's been up all night with me to break me in to No Man's Land.'

'Yes! He's a great fellow, Old Bill,' replied the Sniper.

'I've also written to Ella, as you suggested,' Cissie added shyly.

He settled himself down at full length on the wet grass as a bullet whined close overhead, and the Sniper got down beside him. The enemy fire-trench was now on the sky-line, and the dark forms could be seen of several Germans working on the parapet. The sound of their labour was quite audible to the Sniper. He could even hear the N.C.O. charged with the duty of firing Verey lights walking up and down the trench.

'Is that one of your party, Cissie?' he asked suddenly, as the figure of a man carrying a burden moved past a few yards from them in the direction of the British line.

'I suppose so,' said Cissie carelessly. 'You would not expect it to be a German?'

A Verey light rose from the German trenches at the same time as one flared up from the British firing-line, both curving directly over where the two were lying. The Sniper noticed that the boy did not seem to pay any attention to the illumination, even when one of the flares fell, still sputtering, quite close to him. The expression on his face was unusually thoughtful and tender. 'Thinking of Ella, I suppose,' thought the Sniper.

The lights died out as suddenly as they had flashed into existence. The sounds of labouring Germans and British, momentarily stilled because of the star-shells, began to float out over No Man's Land again, mingling with all the strange rustlings and murmurings and creakings which go to make the battle-area chorus when nights are normally quiet. A rat or two came snuffing around them. The Sniper heard the little squeaks of disappointment, and the pit-pit-pit of tiny feet, as a slight movement of his foot frightened the small scavengers away. He lay beside his silent companion listening to all the subtle stirrings around him, gradually sinking into that semi-hypnotic state when the senses transmit without the mind perceiving, when naught but subconscious processes are at work, and the human being becomes as much under the influence of instinct as an animal.

It was the cold contracting feeling of the flesh above the spine, the physical discomfort accompanying great fear, that woke the Sniper out of his trance. His hair was standing on end, the muscles were drawn taut all over his body, his lips were twisted back, he was actually snarling. As in a dream he seemed to have heard someone laugh in No Man's Land, someone who was mad and cruel, whose laugh was devilish and triumphant.

As soon as consciousness reasserted itself, his muscles relaxed, he found himself shaking from head to foot. It took his will some time to recover the physical control which instinct had held so lightly yet so completely. The feel of his revolver gave him confidence. He sat up and began to peer into the darkness. Cissie was lying quietly in the same position. Evidently the boy had not heard the sound which had disturbed himself. A conviction that he had been the victim of some nightmare prank began to grow in his mind, and Cissie's growling remark almost confirmed him in this opinion.

'Whatever are you raising such a hustle about, Ronald?' said Cissie. 'You're like a dog messing about treading down a bed for itself.'

The Sniper nearly explained the reason for his restlessness, but fear of being ridiculed, and his companion's evident displeasure at being disturbed in his dreams, quelled the desire. He was glad, though, when Cissie started to crawl back towards the working party. Somewhere in the night there was a lurking menace which made the Sniper nervy in spite of his will control, and as soon as he had seen Cissie safely behind the covering party, he crawled over the parapet and made for his dug-out.

All the way down the silent road his hand never left the flap of his holster. Every dark nook and shadow blob around him seemed to hold a staring spectre. He was frightened in spite of himself, and though his reason mocked at his fears the spectres seemed to mock back.

A new idea struck him when he reached his dug-out. Taking down the report book, he studied the page intently where the sentence had been blotted out. 'I believe Healey heard it also, and was afraid of letting it remain for fear of being laughed at,' he murmured. 'Someone did laugh. It was real. I wonder what it was?'

This thought was uppermost in his mind when Cissie rushed into his dug-out, just as he was preparing to go up the line for the watch after next morning's stand-to. The boy's face was drawn and white. He was shaking as though in a fever. His fingers could hardly hold the glass of spirit which the Sniper immediately poured out for him.

'I've not been asleep yet. Only just come down,' he replied when the Sniper enquired the reason for his early appearance. 'One of my lance-corporals – Garvie – was missing when I got the party in last night. Someone said he saw him go on ahead of the covering party. We searched No Man's Land without finding him. And I nearly got killed. Oh! It was awful!'

The boy could not go on because of the quivering of his jaws. He was labouring under some very great horror, and though the Sniper practically forced another tot of spirits into his mouth, his nervous excitement was so great that the alcohol had scarcely any effect. But the ague gradually exhausted itself, and he was able to continue.

'Someone sprang out at me from a shell-hole, and tried to stab me. I flung up my arm in time. The knife struck against my revolver. See! There's the mark.'

He drew out his revolver, and showed a long dented scratch on its barrel.

'The thing stumbled past me into a shell-hole. I fired, but missed. It got away and laughed at me out of the darkness. Oh God! the awfulness of that laugh! It was not human.'

'I know,' said the Sniper excitedly. 'I heard it too, when I was with you. I thought I was dreaming. He must have just knifed poor Garvie.'

'He!'

'Yes, of course. It isn't a spectre. It's a German right enough. No other being would make patrol work into assassination. He's been at it for some time now, lying in wait every night to stab lonely patrollers or stragglers from working parties. Several men from other regiments have gone missing in the same way. Here, Cissie! pull yourself together now, and get your report off to the colonel. Mention that I heard the laugh also. Write it down here, if you like. I've got to clear up the line mighty quick, or I'd stay and help you.'

The boy had recovered himself by this time, so the Sniper hurried away. The dawn was already breaking, and he had to sprint up the road to reach the firing-line in time. The last hundred yards was more than an effort. He arrived so blown that he was glad to sit down on the fire-step to rest for a while.

A sniping post was located a yard or two on his right. Matthew Oldheim was on duty. Matthew had been a little late in taking up position, arriving after the Sniper, and he sneaked past his officer with such a hang-dog expression on his comical little face that the Sniper could not resist smiling. The smile became broader as he heard the American bustling about the post with more than usual hustle, as if to draw his officer's attention to the fact that he really was a businesslike fellow in spite of being late. The loophole panel went back with a snap. Such a yell of terror and astonishment followed that the Sniper leaped to his feet in dismay. Oldheim came tearing out of the post, wrenching the door-sheet off bodily in his haste.

'Oh, Gotalmity!' he gasped. 'Dere's a fellah lookin' t'rough my loophole wit' his t'roat cut from ear to ear.'

The Sniper raced into the post and looked through the loophole. His heart nearly stood still at what he saw. A man was looking through at him, a dead man, whose head was tilted up slightly, as if to show the great oozing gap which severed his throat almost to the medulla. A horrible stench of blood filled the Sniper's nostrils. In spite of the many surgical operations which he had witnessed in his student days the sight turned him sick. The man was Lance-Corporal Garvie.

'That must have been poor Garvie's body that we saw being carried past us last night,' said the Sniper to Cissie Rankine after the colonel had heard both their stories. 'Have there been any other cases where the bodies were brought to our firing-line, sir?'

'No, Jackson!' the colonel replied. 'It looks as if the low-down swine is getting emboldened by his success. You must get him, Jackson, before this goes any further. The whole firing-line seems to have heard the devilish laugh that you speak about.'

A conference of unit commanders was called to discuss the matter. The brigade major himself attended from headquarters. It was decided to place strong patrols in No Man's Land to try and intercept the marauder. But the Germans seemed to have anticipated this move, for during the early part of the night No Man's Land was swept by a heavy machine-gun fire, and the patrol suffered several casualties.

The night passed without any other incident. No German was seen nor any sound of one heard, and just before dawn the watchers returned empty-handed. Hardly had the last man climbed over the parapet when the laugh rang out again. A minute or two later a trembling orderly sergeant reported that when he had gone out to bring in the garrison of one of the usual battalion listening posts, he had found the two men on duty dead, with their throats cut. The doctor maintained that the throat-cutting was not the cause of death. The men had been stabbed first and then mutilated.

Had the order for attack then been given, the battalion would have gone over the top as joyfully as if they were going to a championship football match. But as the day wore on and darkness fell, the men became nervous and restless. The night held hid from them that unknown terror in No Man's Land, and they grouped closely together in the bays, fearful of going anywhere alone lest something might lean out from the shadows and stab them.

The laugh came some hours before the watching patrols returned to the firing-line. The section musters were instantly called to see if any man was missing. But all were present. At stand-to the numbers were again proved, with the same result. The German had laughed without cause, at least so far as the Eastshires were concerned. The adjutant got into communication immediately with the neighbouring battalions.

When it became known that no one had disappeared from their establishments, much speculation took place amongst the men as to what the laugh might mean on this occasion. The discovery soon after dawn by one of the snipers that a dead German was hanging on the enemy wire increased the speculation tenfold. But the general opinion was that this was the German who had been responsible for the stabbings, and that he had been killed by a stray bullet in the act of getting through his entanglements. The terror of darkness immediately took wings, and the normal night life of the trenches again came into being.

But instead of being solved, the mystery steadily deepened. Frightened stragglers from the next night's working parties came back to their brethren with the news that they had heard the laugh again, and soon there was not a man in the firing-line but had heard it. Some even swore to hearing it three times. But none of the Eastshires were missing. It was the Germans who had suffered from the mysterious assailant, and the morning disclosed three blue-grey forms hanging on the enemy wire. Next night the laugh was reported again, and the following morning showed two more Germans hanging on the wire.

'Whatever do you make of it, Jackson?' asked the colonel of the Sniper when the latter reported the incident. 'It looks as if some homicidal maniac was loose in No Man's Land.'

The Sniper did not attempt to suggest another explanation, but the germ of one was already growing in his mind. He was convinced that the laughter of the past three nights was different in quality to the laugh which had frightened him when out with Cissie Rankine. It was ghastly enough, but neither devilish nor cruel. Besides it sounded familiar. And the sudden change in the demeanour of Old Dan and John Brown helped him further in his conclusion.

During the days immediately following the death of little Goo-Goo, the two had gone about silent and depressed, all their actions evincing a bitterness against the Germans which grew because of the insufficient sniping opportunities to slake their thirst for revenge. Now they were still silent enough, but their depression had vanished. They somehow impressed the Sniper as being more satisfied. Moreover he knew that both of them had been included each night in one of the watching patrols.

He lost no time in putting his idea to the test. As soon as darkness fell he sent his servant with an order for the two men to report to him. The servant came back with word that the two had gone up the line. The sergeant followed hard on his heels to explain that the repair of a sniping post was the object of their visit. The Sniper let the sergeant imagine that he was satisfied with the explanation, and sat himself down to watch for their return. Early in the morning he heard them creep past his dug-out to their quarters. A few minutes later he stole out towards the smaller dug-out, which the sergeant had built for himself and the rest of the Five.

The light of a candle enabled him to see the interior. In one corner the two Saunderses were fast asleep. Sitting round the small box-table were the sergeant, Old Dan, and Brown. On the table he noticed a curiously shaped dagger which Brown had just been cleaning. The three were discussing some point of sniping to be put into practice next morning, but the start which each one of the three made at his entrance restored his confidence in the truth of his conviction, slightly shaken as it was by the fact that the men had not been discussing what he had expected to hear.

'This game of yours has got to stop, men,' he said abruptly.

'What game, sir?' asked the sergeant.

'Good Heavens, sergeant! You have the nerve to ask me that, with this dagger lying here?' The Sniper had noticed an inscription in German on the dagger blade which had at once told him nearly the whole story. 'I have the mind to clear you out of the section. What do you mean by keeping me in the dark about Haggarty and Brown knifing these Germans every night?'

'Hoo did ye get tae ken, sir?' said Old Dan, quite coolly.

'How did I get to know? You surely don't think that there are two men in the world with a laugh like yours.'

'Well, sir, I hope ye willna blame Andra here. We would have tellt ye, but we kennt ye would put a stop tae it.'

'You were quite right, corporal,' said the Sniper curtly.

'Well, sir,' put in Old Dan, 'ye mustna be surprised if some o' us canna think o' a German noo as an or'nary ceevilised cratur. Ah've seen ower muckle o' him. Ah could gae on killin' him forever withoot ever thinkin' Ah was daein' wrang. Yet any bairn'll run tae me tae get a kiss. Besides if we've put the wind up them as muckle as they did us, we'll have done some guid.'

'It was my idea entirely, sir,' put in John Brown quietly. 'I hope you will understand, sir, that no disrespect was intended to you. We simply regard the German in a different light, and ventured to act accordingly.'

'I have already considered the matter, Brown, from the point of view of Haggarty and yourself. The incident is closed now, so far as I am concerned. The less you say on your part the better,' said the Sniper abruptly, leaving the dug-out.

That was the end of the laugh in No Man's Land. Old Dan and his comrades maintained a discreet silence. The episode soon passed into the limbo of things which have been remembered only as one of the great insoluble mysteries of the line. No one ever suspected the part which the Eastshire snipers played in the affair.

CHAPTER X

A Voice in the Night

TROUBLE BROKE OUT IN the northern half of the Salient before the end of the week, and a brigade was moved from the Sniper's division to a reserve position behind the disturbed sector. The normal arrangements for relief of battalions inside the division were temporarily upset, and instead of marching out to their new camp for the usual rest period, the Eastshires were ordered back to the ruined village as brigade reserve.

Their stay was uneventful enough, though not without its anxious moments and alarms because of the hurly-burly going on north of Ypres. But the greatest trial was the weather, which broke down completely, and made the last day or two a period of chronic discomfort. The dilapidated houses leaked like sieves, the cellars got flooded, and the journey back to the trenches was carried out under conditions even worse than the previous march-up from the village.

Warned by his former experience the Sniper sent his servant on in advance to take over his own and the section's quarters before the occupants departed, so that the man would be able to keep the fires going, and have everything prepared and comfortable for the reception of the new-comers. The servant fulfilled his mission nobly. The Sniper's soaking trench-coat and boots were steaming before the glowing brazier of the kitchen annexed to the dug-out before he had finished the soup course of his dinner, and within half an hour of his arrival he was tucked under the sacking which formed his bedclothes, well fed and comfortably warm, what time less provident officers and men were striving to light the damp new fuel in their sweating braziers. He fell asleep thinking of Cissie Rankine. He rather suspected that the boy had heard from Ella.

The glow of the kitchen fire was still shining faintly through the doorway when the Sniper awoke. He found himself sitting up on his bed staring into the darkness. Something had wakened him; what it was he did not know. He had a vague memory of hearing somebody come rushing into his dug-out calling him by name. But he could see nothing. A rat was sniffing about on the table a foot or two from his head. He flashed on his electric torch; the brute leaped to the floor and scampered off under the foot-boards. No other living thing was to be seen. The rain was pattering down on the roof. The wind rattled the loose glass in the flimsy window-frames.

'Damn!' he said. 'Think I was a kid again.'

He shut off the light and lay down. Almost immediately he fell asleep. But again he found himself sitting up on his bed staring into the darkness. The thing had happened a second time. He had felt, rather than heard, someone rushing up to his side, someone who had called him by name, much more distinctly this time, and the voice had sounded familiar.

'Mac!' he called out softly.

'Yes, sir!' said his servant, popping his head in from the kitchen, where he slept.

'Are you trying any fool's tricks?' asked the Sniper.

'No, sir!' said the man wonderingly. 'What way dae ye ask?'

'You haven't been calling out, or anything like that?'

'No, sir! No' that Ah ken o'.'

'Umph!' grunted the Sniper.

'Shall Ah make ye some hot toddy, sir?' Mac enquired.

'No, thank you, Mac. I'm sorry I disturbed you. Turn in again.'

The man silently withdrew, and the Sniper settled himself down among his sandbag coverings. A disturbance had broken out up the line, and he could not fall asleep so readily. A storm of rifle fire was going on. Bullets were cracking above the dug-out. With a wicked 'Wumph!' a shrapnel burst over the road a hundred yards away. The electric-blue flash of its burst shone through the windows, and lit up the interior of the dug-out. The roof was leaking in the far-away corner, and he could see a little rivulet of moisture streaking down the smoothed-out surface of the unrevetted clay wall. The water glittered like crystal in the illumination. Streams of condensed vapour were running down the flutings of the corrugated-iron ceiling and collecting in large pendulous water bulbs on the under side of the storm porch above the dug-out entrance. A lull in the firing enabled him to hear the steady plonk! plonk! as the full-fed drops detached themselves and fell into the puddle outside the doorway. To this sound he at length fell asleep.

He was half-way up the road to the firing-line when next he came to his senses. The rain was descending in torrents, swishing on the cobble-stones as the wind dashed at it savagely. Bareheaded and in his stockinged feet, he was racing madly through it all up the road towards the support position. For some being had come to his bedside, called him by name, and bade him to hurry at once to his friend's dug-out in the support lines.

He drew himself up as the improbability and absurdity of the whole affair began to dawn on him. Cissie Rankine was stationed alone with his platoon in the supports. Had it been anyone else he would have returned at once to his dug-out. But Cissie! The boy had been very queer on the way up to the trenches. A vague uneasiness concerning him impelled the Sniper to go on.

He slipped off the road into the beginning of the support trench and hurried along it. The trench bottom was a foot deep in water, and many times he bruised his unprotected feet against unexpected projections from the revetting and boarding. On a stretch of duck-boards raised above the level of the water he trod on a large buck rat. The animal bit him savagely and wriggled itself from underneath his foot. The trench rat for its size is the strongest animal in the world.

A ray of light streamed out from a chink in the waterproof sheet which did duty as door for young Rankine's dug-out. Wondering greatly that the boy should be awake at such a time, the Sniper stole up to the entrance and looked in. Cissie was sitting on his bed writing a letter at the rude dug-out table. What immediately attracted the Sniper's attention was the service revolver lying ready to the boy's hand. Even as he looked the letter was finished, and the revolver was taken up in a manner that admitted no doubt as to its owner's intention. The Sniper burst through the entrance and wrested the weapon away.

'Cissie!'

'Jackson!'

The boy shrank back from his friend's questioning look. But he quickly pulled himself together. The Sniper could not but admire his pluck as he turned on him and tried to bluff matters out.

'What the deuce do you mean, Jackson, by barging into my dug-out like this?' he said angrily.

The Sniper's reply was to snatch at the letter Cissie had been writing.

'Give me that back,' demanded the boy. 'Give me it back,' he repeated, as the Sniper made no movement to comply. 'I'll shoot you if you don't.'

'See here, Cissie,' said the Sniper sharply. 'You surely don't think I came up in this stew just to pay you a joy call. You know what you were going to do. You know I know also. So don't try to bluff me. I'll see it every time.'

During the short period when the Sniper had been with the regiment, his forceful character and capacity to handle men had gained him a place in the estimation of all the ordinary ranks second only to that of the colonel himself. Cissie's offensive broke down completely before the quiet authority of his manner. The boy cowered back on his bed and gazed weakly at him.

'You can either treat me as a friend,' the Sniper continued, pressing his advantage home, 'and I'll do what I can to help you; or you can treat me as your superior officer, in which case I'll call in a file of men and put you under arrest. This letter, I fancy, will give me all the evidence I require.'

'You would not dare,' gasped Cissie.

He flung himself down on the table and burst into sobbing. The aluminium canteen set, left standing from the last meal, rattled at each racking breath that he drew. His whole body shook with emotion. The Sniper sat down beside him and gripped both his arms, until by main force he held the boy steady.

'I take it that you've heard from Ella,' he said gently. 'She's thrown you over?'

The boy's sobbing had become more normal. He reached over to a pile of papers and pushed one towards the Sniper. It was a reply from Ella to the letter which Cissie had written on the Sniper's suggestion after the quarrel with Big Bill. From the first the Sniper had guessed the cause of the trouble. He had been inclined to reproach himself for the part he had played. But as he read the letter every trace of such a feeling disappeared. It was the sort of letter that makes decent men and women wonder why civilised communities do not make Ishmaelites of their Ella-types and drive them beyond their bounds. The harpy had scornfully rejected the boy's offer of marriage, reviled him for what she termed his meanness, brazenly set down her infidelities, and mocked him throughout for a fool.

'That's not the worst of it,' said Cissie, when the Sniper had finished. 'She called on my people and made a terrible scene. I've had a letter from the guv'nor. It's too awful. I can't show it to you.'

He broke down again, and for a long time he seemed totally insensible to anything the Sniper could say. But the older man's tactful sympathy gradually quieted him.

'It's no use worrying about me, Jacky,' he murmured brokenly. 'It's just the end of everything for me.'

'It's just the beginning, you mean,' said the Sniper. 'Surely the letter she wrote you has shown you what Mademoiselle Ella is?'

'It's not that,' the boy replied. 'I'd been doubtful about her for a long time. That's what made me so touchy when Big Bill tried to chip me. It's not me being such a fool that hurts so much. It's the thought that my people, that all the fellows here, know it. Why did you stop me? I can never face anyone again.'

Again he had broken down, and again the Sniper was soothing him.

'My people will cut me. But I'm far away from them. I won't have to see them again, so that doesn't seem to matter so much. I simply can't face the fellows here. Big Bill and all the others. They all knew. If only I could get away!'

'That's a bit low down, Cissie,' said the Sniper firmly. 'Your people ought to matter more than the fellows here. And it was rather selfish of you to forget the disgrace you would bring on them by getting out of things as you intended. There's the good name of the regiment also.'

He did not spare the boy once he had got this opening. When he had finished Cissie could not look at him for shame of it all.

'What a little cad I am!' he said. 'The best thing I can do is to go over the top and get killed.'

'You are not a little cad,' said the Sniper. 'It's your darned sensitiveness that's knocked your thinking out of gear. And as for your going over the top, what in all the world are you worrying about? Why should you be afraid to meet the fellows here? Of course most of them know you were engaged to that damned harlot, and every one of them thought you were the damnedest fool in creation – for that, but for nothing else. They will change their opinion when they hear you have chucked her.'

'But she has chucked me,' interjected Cissie.

'That's so,' replied the Sniper. 'But I'm going to announce it my way, and they'll all believe it. It's the natural thing to happen. If anyone chips you, tell him to mind his own business.'

'It sounds all right,' said Cissie doubtfully.

'Well, laddie,' said the Sniper paternally, 'take it from me, every one of us can look back on an episode at some time or other where the girl worsted us and made us squirm. Even though the fellows here knew the whole story, they would think none the less of you. Men are very considerate to each other in regard to their girl scars.'

'You always seem to know the right thing to do, Jacky,' said the boy.

'Um! I don't know,' replied the Sniper ruefully. 'There's one or two black-eyed, black-haired witches in the Argentine, who must chuckle every time they think of how they did me in. It's always puzzled me, but at some period in our lives a woman can do what she likes with us, man or boy. I often think that Xenocatl's wife must be living up in the stars, constantly demanding the sacrifice of a male heart or two. However, my boy, the women give us enough amusement, even though the end of it all is the altar, Mrs. Xenocatl's or Brompton.'

He had got the boy smiling now. He soon had him searching for Perrier to take the edge off the whisky.

'Jove! Jacky, I don't know how I ever came to think of that,' said Cissie, looking at his revolver.

'Seems funny now, doesn't it?' said the Sniper, clinking his empty glass significantly.

'Do you know, laddie?' he continued, 'I knew Ella would chuck you. I bargained on it when I got you to write to her suggesting marriage. You see I thought you were too good a little man to be made a fool of. You don't mind, do you?'

'Mind! Rather! I'm more than grateful to you, old man. It's finished now. And so is this,' said Cissie, manfully drinking down his third whisky.

'I didn't bargain on the row with your people though. I've got to put that right somehow.'

'You won't manage that very easily,' said Cissie dolefully.

'You're an only son, aren't you? And therefore a sister's darling. Oh, I know. I'm one too. What do you say to my writing to Maimie? I think she could manage things,' suggested the Sniper.

'I wish you would,' said the boy eagerly. 'She's just the one to do it. She can manage things. I was thinking of doing it myself. Only I don't like.'

'Neither do I, for that matter. You see, your sister does not know me.'

'Oh, yes, she does,' Cissie exclaimed. 'I've told her all sorts of things about you.'

'What!'

'Yes! She thinks you a right good sport. She told me to bring you over if ever I could get to see her,' said the boy, anxious to remove his friend's diffidence.

'The devil she did!'

'Yes! Really. And I sent her your photograph. The one in which we were taken together in Pop. She said you looked quite nice.'

'You little demon!' said the Sniper, more than pleased, however. 'I suppose you add the last bit to avert my righteous anger. But I want bigger compensation than that. Don't be so mean with your whisky.'

'Oh, Jacky. You've had nearly half the bottle, and it was to last me a week,' Cissie expostulated. But he poured out the Sniper's seventh, nevertheless.

'How did you manage to drop in here to-night?' Cissie queried presently.

'I dunno, my lad. Might have been a guilty conscience. Might have been telepathy. Only it was rather a pretty woman who handed me the message,' replied the Sniper lightly.

'You're getting fuddled,' said Cissie shortly. 'Here! What are you doing?' he demanded a moment later.

The Sniper had risen to go, and was busily pocketing a photograph of Maimie Rankine which stood on a little bracket in the corner of the dug-out.

'Fair exchange, my boy. Fair exchange,' said the Sniper, going on with the pocketing.

'You might as well take this also,' Cissie said sarcastically, holding out the forlorn whisky bottle.

'Keep it, laddie, keep it. It's not worth carrying away. Send your man down to my dug-out when it's finished. I've a bottle to spare, in spite of commanding twenty of the greatest droughts in the regiment. Good night, old man.'

Though only two hours of sleep remained to him, the Sniper sat down immediately on reaching his dug-out to write to Maimie Rankine. He propped her photograph up before him and considered it minutely. It was the picture of a well-set-up girl with a clear-cut, determined face. The driving kit she was wearing made her look more like a man than a girl. It was scarcely the sort of picture that he had expected to see, and he felt rather disappointed. His taste inclined more to fairy girls with small feet, small hands, and dainty figure – not that his taste resulted from a very wide experience. Cissie looked more girlish than ever compared with this strapping wench, with her stout knee-boots and big, bunchy gloves. But he liked the straight, wholesome look about her.

'You may be wearing a large size in gloves,' he said, beginning to square the paper into comfortable writing position. 'And if those knee-boots weren't so misleading I'd have doubts about your feet. But you've got the kind of mouth and eyes a man can raise the limit on. I guess you can deal a sure get-out for your brother.'

And she did.

CHAPTER XI

Tragedy

OUR DAYS WAS THE period allotted to the battalion for its stay in the trenches on this occasion. At the end of that time the normal divisional arrangements were expected to be in force. But so far as any sniping was concerned the tour at first promised to be a blank. The weather took a curious turn, fog replacing rain, and for the greater part of the first day the German lines were invisible. The snipers availed themselves of the opportunity to get out on the other side of the parapet to repair the exterior of their loopholes, and the Sniper had the unique experience of seeing how his sniping posts looked from the enemy point of view. It said much for the skill of his men that at a first glance he could not detect any one of the posts even from so short a distance as the first entanglement.

Towards the late afternoon the mist still hung thickly over the land, and the Sniper set out to examine the house which he had noticed on a previous occasion a short distance behind the firing-line. The Germans held the high ground in the sector, and his dearest wish was to find some observation post lofty enough to counterbalance their advantage. He hoped that this house would suit his purpose.

It was the larger of two ruined houses which stood by the roadway connecting the two villages. The road came up from the tree-clad hollow, and ran along the top of the ridge which sloped upwards to meet at its highest point the ridge on which the Germans were entrenched. Hence the reason why the road could be enfiladed so easily. The tree-clad hollow almost hid the lower village from view, but the high ground on which the other village stood crept up beyond it and tilted up one end, as if determined to compromise the little cluster of cottages with the publicity its more reputable neighbour shunned.

The house had belonged to a man of some substance, for it was built in a far more solid and pretentious style than the average Belgian village dwelling-place. And as if to give further evidence of this fact, a large steel safe, whose capacious inside could have tucked away comfortably many fat wads of banknotes and securities, lay on its side in the garden, whither it had been carried, perhaps, for more systematic looting.

The size of the garden also pointed to the affluence of its owner. But it gave an impression of newly acquired wealth and position. No containing walls bounded it from the surrounding fields, and its ungravelled paths, bordered by dwarf shrubs and yearling fruit trees, wandered unchecked into a maze of down-trodden wattle stems. In the corner beside an unpainted summer-house stood the poles of a swing; and in the Sniper's fancy instantly appeared romping youthful forms, and his ear almost caught the echo of merry childish laughter.

Some attempt had been made to put the building into a state of defence, and sandbags filled the lower windows, while the front door was loopholed and inhospitably closed against the visitor. The top of a sandbag barricade peeped from the shattered fanlight. But the defenders had long since departed, and the uncared-for sandbags were slowly disgorging their contents in little trickles of soil from ever-widening rents in the rotting sacking. A small walled court had evidently been judged a sufficient protection for the back, and the door here was open and undefended.

The Sniper entered by this doorway, and found himself in a small hall which ran from front door to back. Bits of plaster and broken bricks carpeted the floor, and, remembering the unfinished garden, he could almost fancy that the house was still in the builder's hands. The new marble fire-places of the front rooms strengthened this impression, and though the ceilings were broken in places, disclosing patches of smoke-blackened laths, the plaster-work of the walls and cornices was firm and white with the clean-cut edges of newness. In one of the back rooms a shell had burst close to the ceiling, burying a big spring bed in a mass of bricks and mortar.

'Some poor devil has had a good house-warming,' he murmured.

A stair led down from this room into a deep, strongly built cellar, an excellent refuge from hostile shell-fire, and he duly marked it down as funkhole. The upper floor was reached by a narrow stairway from the hall, and another flight led up to the top of the roof. The roof itself was gone, but at the head of the stairs there were chinks in the broken brickwork which he shrewdly imagined would give him the outlook that he desired. But the mist hid the German firing-line, and prevented him from coming to a definite decision about the place. Making up his mind to return at a more suitable time, he started on his way back to the firing-line.

But the novelty of walking over ground which hitherto he had only trodden by night tempted him to extend the scope of his investigations. The fog had grown less dense in places, and he noticed the cautious way in which several men out souvenir hunting kept scurrying back, as soon as their wanderings took them an appreciable distance from their trenches. Nevertheless, he decided to risk a little and push further afield, trusting to be able to find some hiding-place where he could lie up till darkness fell, should the mist suddenly rise.

He swung along over the rank fields with all the delight of a townsman out for a morning walk in the country. The loneliness and desolation of his surroundings did not appal him. It was the open country. He could step out as he pleased. No need to worry over the footing as in the narrow trenches with their insecure duck-boarding; and even though he heard the crack of an occasional bullet as some German sentry fired blindly into the mist, the sound did not disturb him. He knew that it was a thousand chances to one against the bullet coming his way. It was glorious to wander where he liked, and coming on a turnip field whose first crop had seeded and reproduced another, he experienced all the joys of a mischievous schoolboy in plucking one or two of the larger roots, peeling and eating them.

While engaged in this occupation he heard a sound of laughter. The mist had thinned slightly in the direction of the headquarters village, and, looking over the hedge which bounded the field, he was able to see, only twenty yards away from him, Big Bill Davidson, Cissie Rankine, and Jimmy MacLauchlan. Jimmy was doing 'Charlie Chaplin stunts' in the centre of a stretch of meadowland, to the great amusement of the other two. In the light of what had happened the night before, it was good to the Sniper to hear Cissie's gay laughter.

Jimmy's imitation was exceedingly good, but a totally unrehearsed effect was funnier still. A bullet cracked suddenly over the Sniper's head. It seemed to go very close to Jimmy, for he stopped short in the midst of a grotesque pirouette, a startled look on his face, all the gay humour completely evaporated. The quick change of expression made him look so comical that from behind the shelter of the hedge the Sniper laughed mockingly. The trio started at the sound and looked questioningly in his direction. Not wishing their company at the time, he slipped quietly away.

On the other side of the turnip field were the ruins of a farm; he made his way towards them. The farm was of the usual French type, built in the form of a quadrangle. The walls were still standing, but fire had burnt out the interior of the buildings. In the centre of the courtyard was a farmer's wain, surmounted by the remnants of a Cape hood. Inside were a few rags of clothing, a wooden shoe or two, and a large shattered chest. It looked as if the farmer had been preparing to leave with his family when the violence of war had overtaken them; and in between the shafts, still saddled and hitched to the cart, was the decayed body of a horse. At the approach of the Sniper two large rats slipped out of the throat cavity and stole away into the ruins of a barn.

The Sniper strolled round the melancholy place, letting his imagination reproduce the picture of that little homestead ere the red hand of war had knocked at its door. His senses could almost feel the terror of the inhabitants when they knew that the Uhlans were approaching. He had heard too much of what the Uhlans had wrought in that district to doubt that this was another specimen of their handiwork. Had the inhabitants escaped? The dead horse in the courtyard, the disordered contents of the wain, seemed to suggest an interrupted flight. What atrocity had these silent walls witnessed?

There were indications, however, that the Germans had been disturbed in their evil work. In the garden behind the farmhouse lay the skeleton of a French cavalryman. The Sniper nearly tumbled over the remains as he left the house on his way back to the trenches. The Frenchmen had evidently driven the Germans off, as the body had been laid out decently on an unhinged door, and the half-dug grave beside which it lay showed that preparations for the burial had been begun. None but comrades would have troubled themselves about such a matter. But something had interfered with the interment, and the spade stood in a corner of the grave where the hand of the digger had left it.

The Sniper had often heard of dead Frenchmen being stumbled on, lying alone or in twos and threes, in unfrequented spots behind the line, where no man could go with safety during the day. This was the first time he had come on such a body, and it brought home to him, more clearly than any of the stories told in the battalion by the older men, the gallantry and self-sacrifice of French Territorial and cavalry units, who, in little detachments, and in countless unknown struggles, had kept Northern France clear of the German flying columns while the main actions of the Marne and the Aisne were being fought.

The Sniper jumped into the unfinished grave, took up the abandoned spade, and commenced digging. He had no intention of leaving that gallant corpse to remain any longer at the mercy of the weather and the rats. But he dug furiously, for the mist was gradually thinning, and the nearest trench was some distance away. At length he completed the digging. Reverently he placed the corpse in the grave and replaced the soil. He had no time to make a cross. But at the head of the mound he drove the spade deeply into the earth, and over the handle he placed the Frenchman's helmet, wrapping the long black horsehair plume around the haft to give it anchorage.

One moment he paused at the salute, and then he tore madly out of the garden and across the open. For the German line was clear to view and the range was only five hundred yards. Breathless and exhausted he tumbled into safety over the parapet of the main communication trench.

After resting awhile he set off towards headquarters. He moved quickly and easily as the trench was broad and well duck-boarded. Swinging round a traverse near the end of the communication, he came to a dead stop. A shell had fallen there, and men had been killed. The duck-boarding was shivered, the sandbag revetting dismantled, and down in the trench bottom, calf-deep in the bloody drainage, four white-faced stretcher-bearers were busy with ropes and waterproof sheeting.

All day under shelter of the mist men had been skylarking outside the trenches. Yet those who had chosen what they considered the safer route had found death waiting for them there. Such is the fickleness of the god of the trench area.

The Sniper silently climbed out of the trench and completed the rest of the journey in the open. At headquarters he learned what had happened. A strange officer was sitting there, a young boy, his face white and twitching, his wide-open eyes staring unseeingly into the dug-out wall. He was a brother officer of the two who had been killed. He had come up with them to take over a neighbouring sector of trenches. Some chance had delayed him at headquarters while his comrades had gone on. He had overtaken them, to see what the Sniper had seen.

No place in the whole line has seen so many tragedies as the Ypres Salient. One of the dead officers had been setting out that night on leave to be married. Over in England a tender-faced girl would be dreaming of the happiness about to be hers. Up the main communication trench the stretcher-bearers were busy with ropes and waterproof sheeting.

The Sniper stayed some time with the boy, talking to him, and trying to wean his mind away from its tragic memories, and presently he recovered himself sufficiently to be able to set out for his sector. The Sniper accompanied him the greater part of the way. But he hurried back to his quarters again, for he knew something was awaiting him there which had to be tackled immediately.

CHAPTER XII

A Surprise for the Staff-Major

A NEW SET OF aeroplane photographs had come in that evening and the Sniper pounced on them eagerly. Certain activity at a part of the enemy's line had lately been exciting his curiosity. During the previous week the Germans had been building two large bombing posts, about fifty yards apart, well outside their wire entanglements, and he wanted to know if the photographs contained anything interesting about them. At the first glance he gave a little crow of delight, and at once he sent his servant off in search of Sergeant Ferguson.

'Look at this photograph, Ferguson,' he said, when the sergeant entered. 'You see the two posts we were looking at to-day? All nicely finished and in order. What do you make of that blurred line between them, as though the photographer had drawn his finger over the wet negative?'

'Footprints, sir,' the sergeant exclaimed. 'Why, the Germans must be patrolling the ground between the posts.'

'Exactly, sergeant. Two men to a patrol at most, I expect, and here is the division simply gasping for prisoners for identifications. Are you game to try it?'

'Right, sir,' said the sergeant readily.

A few minutes later the two were climbing out of the firing-line. They both carried knobkerries, and the Sniper had borrowed Big Bill Davidson's revolver for the sergeant. The mist had completely disappeared, and a rising new moon was dimly lighting No Man's Land. Crawling carefully forward, they worked their way between the two German bombing posts, and, finding a convenient shell-hole, they lay down in it to watch.

A few yards from them the dark festoonery of the German wire showed up dimly against the sky, and further back still was the enemy parapet. The sounds of Germans moving about the trench came to them quite clearly, with often a snarling exclamation as an N.C.O. rated some unfortunate member of the garrison. Presently the Sniper heard the muddy swish of men approaching from the right. Out of the darkness two stumbling forms appeared – the German patrol.

The sergeant began to edge himself up the side of the shell-hole ready to spring. The Sniper stopped him with a touch. On the German parapet an officer was standing. He hailed the patrol and received a low reply. He was still standing there as the patrol skirted the rim of the shell-hole and disappeared into the darkness towards the second bombing post.

'We'll get them next time,' whispered the Sniper.

Another long wait, and the sound of the patrol's approach was heard again. This time the German parapet was clear; the sounds from the trench itself had even ceased, as though the occupants were slumbering. First one, then another dark form appeared above the shell-hole. The Sniper rose and drove his fist straight against the point of the first German's jaw; he heard the thud of the sergeant's blow striking home on the head of the second German. Both Germans fell without a sound. They dragged them into the shell-hole to recover a little, and then at the point of two long Webley revolvers the prisoners were conducted into the British trench.

A staff officer from the division was seated at the table with the colonel, the second-in-command, and the adjutant, when the Sniper entered the headquarters.

'Ah! Jackson. I sent for you some time ago,' was the colonel's greeting. 'We want some information from you about the enemy wire. Major Jamieson has just come down from headquarters to arrange for a raid to-morrow night to secure prisoners for identification. Major Jamieson, this is Mr. Jackson, my sniping and intelligence officer.'

'I have two Germans waiting outside, sir,' said the Sniper calmly. 'Shall I bring them in, sir?'

He opened the door without waiting for a reply, and Sergeant Ferguson prodded the two Germans into the room. The four at the table gaped in amazement at the spectacle. A slow smile spread over the colonel's features, and he turned with a chuckle to the staff-major.

'I suppose we will take it that the raid is very much out of date now,' he said. 'Let us have the story, Jackson,' he added.

The Sniper told his story, getting very embarrassed towards the end at the comments of the staff-major. But the latter at length packed up his papers, and departed with the prisoners to his headquarters. The Sniper wearily made his way back to his dug-out.

'What are you doing with that whisky, Mac?' he roared through the doorway at his servant, who was in the act of helping himself to a stiff glass of the spirit.

'Just drinking your health, sir,' the servant spluttered. 'Lordy, sir! but that's a dawmn guid bit o' work ye've been doing.'

'I'll make you drink it in rat poison if I catch you again,' growled the Sniper, tumbling sleepily into his bed.

Next morning the line had resumed its normal daily activity. German shells were searching the old familiar places, and British high explosive was screaming and rumbling back overhead in more than usual numbers. It was as if the gunners of both sides were bent on firing off as quickly as possible the ammunition which had accumulated during the period of inactivity when the mist was on the ground. Snipers also were on the alert, and every now and then a rifle would crack with that disconcerting isolated sound which speaks of a hidden watcher deliberately choosing a target, no man knows what or whom.

The Sniper was walking down the trench when he heard a sudden rattle of musketry ring out. Clang! Clang! Clang! came the sound of bullets striking a sniping plate. One of his posts a traverse away was being battered at by the Germans, and he raced round the traverse to see what was happening. Sergeant Ferguson was crawling cautiously out of the post into the bottom of the trench.

'Keep away, sir,' called the sergeant hurriedly, as he saw his officer appear.

He drew himself along the duck-boarding to the traverse and stood up beside the Sniper. The rattle of musketry and the clang of the bullets was still going on. The Sniper noticed fragments of metal flying out of the post into the trench. Evidently the steel sniping shield was being cut to pieces.

'They nearly got me, sir,' said the sergeant, noticing the Sniper's questioning look. 'I had been firing at what I thought was a loophole, and then, all of a sudden, four of the beggars opened out at me. They are all together in a new sniping post right in front. Armour-piercing bullets they are using, too.'

'Show me where they are,' said the Sniper, unshipping his periscope and getting into position on the fire-step.

Under the sergeant's directions he at last located the spot whence the Germans were firing. It was a big post on some rising ground behind the enemy firing-line, camouflaged with raw earth, and looking for all the world like any one of the other tangled hummocks with which shells and mines had strewn the vicinity. But his trained eye quickly marked out four small apertures which he knew to be loopholes. The excellence of his periscope even enabled him to see the puffs of unburnt cordite which came from the hostile rifles at every shot.

'They are behind concrete and steel under that surface muck, sir. It won't be easy dealing with them,' said the sergeant.

'It's a case for the heavies, I'm afraid,' murmured the Sniper regretfully. 'Thank goodness you discovered it in time for us to deal with it before the relief.'

'I saw the major of that heavy battery by Dickebusch going by just before you came down, sir,' suggested the sergeant.

The Sniper hurried off down the trench without stopping to reply. He found the major – who was up on a survey of the enemy line for special targets – just leaving the battalion sector. But a hint of what had been discovered brought the gunner hurriedly back to where the sergeant was waiting. A minute later he was in the nearest company signalling dug-out telephoning eager instructions to his battery.

'I am much obliged to you,' he said to the Sniper, when the telephoning was finished. 'That place wants crumping badly. I searched that ground, too, only half an hour ago, without seeing anything.'

The Sniper beckoned the sergeant away out of the major's hearing. 'Put Haggarty and Brown into post 9, sergeant,' he ordered. 'I don't think the Germans have any day communication into that post of theirs, and they will have to bolt for cover over the ridge.'

'I thought you would not have put the gunners on to it, without having some other idea up your sleeve,' said the sergeant, grinning delightedly. 'I think you're right, sir, but I didn't notice it before. The post is right on a slope without a sign of a connecting trench.'

The Sniper went back to where the major was preparing to observe and direct the shelling. Presently the first heavy projectile came rumbling up from the rear. It burst fifty yards wide in a great splash of earth. The major had passed on the correction to the signallers before the débris ceased falling. The second shell burst in the German firing-line right in front of the post, and tore a huge gap in the parapet. The third fell right on top of the post itself. But the concrete of the structure was strong, and the shell actually ricochetted clear and burst several yards away.

'That has frightened the beggars,' exclaimed the major suddenly, as four figures appeared from behind the post and raced madly for the ridge crest. 'Oh, jolly good work,' he added, as a shot rang out and the first German pitched forward on his face. The second fell a yard further on. The remaining two were bowled over as they reached the crest.

'Now for the post itself,' said the major, turning toward the Sniper as another shell was heard approaching. But the Sniper was already walking off to congratulate his men. He had no further interest in the proceedings.

Old Dan buttonholed him immediately. 'Dae ye mind comin' along tae see this, sir?' said the old fellow.

The Sniper followed him along to his post and pointed his glasses through the loophole.

'Dae ye see that coil o' auld wire lying by that shell-hole about half-way across, sir? There's a German ahint it. Ah tried a chance shot at a wee bit o' funny colour Ah saw there yesterday in a blink o' the mist, never really thinkin' that a Boche was there. An' Gode! when Ah looked at it again to-day Ah noticed that that wire had been shifted ower the colour. Ah must have frightened the beggar with my shot, an' the dawmn fool has tried to hide himself a wheen better.'

'How are you going to get him, Haggarty?' asked the Sniper.

'Dae ye no think a wee rifle grenade would shift him, sir?'

The Sniper hurried off in search of the bombing officer, and soon a couple of rifle grenades had been burst close to the German's hiding-place. Before a third shot could be fired the fellow got up and made a bolt for cover. Old Dan's shot killed him before he had gone a yard. 'That will teach him tae shut the stable door after the horse has been stolen,' was his grim comment, as he came out of the post to rejoin the Sniper.

The Sniper had just left the firing-line on his way down to headquarters when the hum of an aeroplane approaching rapidly to close quarters caused him to look upwards with a start. To his surprise he saw a German aeroplane swooping down on the Eastshires' trenches. At five hundred feet its pilot opened fire, but his aiming was defective, and the bullet spray just touched the outside of the parapet. The machine passed so close to the Sniper that he could see the head and shoulders of the German quite plainly, and even observe the intent look on the man's face as he peered along his gun-sights. Out of a sniping post close to the Sniper came Geordie Saunders.

'Well, of all the bluidy cheek!' he heard the man exclaim.

He saw the ex-gamekeeper whip his rifle to his shoulder with that ease of motion betokening long practice with a shotgun, and take lightning aim at the retreating aeroplane. The German was then nearly four hundred yards away. But an instant after the report of the shot the machine shot up to the perpendicular, wobbled a little on its tail, then, lurching forward, came down nose first with a horrible crash just behind the firing-line. The

German artillery at once opened fire on it, but a sergeant of C Company managed to crawl out and bring back with him the body of the German. Saunders's bullet had passed clean through his head.

The pilot was a noted German airman, and the Flying Corps claimed his body, and sent up a party from the nearest aerodrome to carry the dead man off for a special military funeral. One of the two British pilots who came with the party was just a little curt with the Sniper, and seemed to resent the fact that the German had been shot down by one of his men. He apologised immediately when he saw the Sniper's growing irritation, and the explanation he gave made the latter take him and the other pilot off to his dug-out, to extend to them a more than usually hearty hospitality.

It appeared that the British and German pilots had been ancient antagonists, and for the past two months the Briton's sole idea had been to fight the German single-handed and bring him down. The Sniper easily understood his annoyance at another man stepping in, and liked him not a little for the manner in which he spoke of his gallant adversary. They parted the best of friends, with the firm regard for each other of expert for expert.

While making his way back to the firing-line the Sniper had a very narrow escape from being killed by a shell which burst in the trench a few yards behind him, almost at the spot where the two officers had been killed the day before. A little later an engineers' fatigue party were shelled in the same trench, and several men were killed, including an officer with whom the Sniper was very friendly. The stretcher-bearer squads clearing away the casualties were also shelled a little further down the trench, and when the Sniper and Sergeant Ferguson were making their way towards headquarters in the early evening, the shells suddenly commenced bursting around them, and they only escaped by the barest margin.

'What do you make of it, sergeant?' gasped the Sniper as they were resting in an old building after their frantic rush from the trench. 'That's the seventh or eighth time people have been shelled in that trench, all in the last two days.'

'I know, sir. The gunner observing officers are pretty worried about it. They say that the Boche must have got another observation post, but where it is they do not know.'

'It must be pretty near. The stations on Wytschaete could not get the guns on so quickly. By Jove, I've got it.'

He raced away back to the damaged portions of the communication trench, and spent an hour crawling about there, making a careful survey of the district. He ordered the sergeant away when the latter tried to join him, and even after he had finished his examination he said nothing to enlighten his subordinate about what he purposed doing. Early next morning, having left the sergeant in charge of the section, the Sniper climbed out of the firing-line and made his way over No Man's Land.

CHAPTER XIII

The Jackal Rat

No Man's Land was fairly broad at this point, and after walking about three-fourths of the way across, he picked out a shell-hole a few yards behind a battered group of tree stumps, and lay down in its depth. He had rifle and bayonet with him, and a large square of sacking big enough to cover him and his equipment completely. The outside of the sacking had been carefully caked with mud, so that a man could lie under it as securely hidden as though earth indeed had been used to cover him. It was the sergeant's idea, tested on several occasions with complete success. After giving it a little touch here and there to make the camouflage more artistic, he settled himself down contentedly for his long wait until the daylight. Presently he fell asleep.

When he wakened up the sun was high in the heavens. The noise of a working party in the German firing-line sounded alarmingly close to him. He peeped out cautiously from under his cover at the battered trunks ahead of him. What he saw made him want to yell out with satisfaction. His idea had been correct.

From the accuracy with which the Germans had been shelling the communication trench he had come to the conclusion that one of their observers had taken up a position in No Man's Land overlooking it, from which he telephoned all signs of activity to his battery. The only possible position in regard to the communication trench was the battered clump; and there the German observer was, standing on a narrow little platform behind one of the tallest trunks, a broad pollarded giant which gave him ample cover from the British lines.

The telephone wire to his battery actually ran over the shell-hole in which the Sniper was lying. With a subdued chuckle he reached up with his wire cutters and cut the line. And there he lay all day listening delightedly to the German buzzing his futile instructions, and still more delightedly when his victim started swearing at his useless instrument.

With the approach of darkness he heard the German beginning to pack up his instruments; and some time later came the sound of the man's stumbling approach through the night towards his lines. The Sniper rose out of his shell-hole and stopped him on the point of his bayonet. Five minutes later he was guiding his captive over the British parapet, where the sergeant, Old Dan, and nearly all his section were anxiously awaiting his arrival.

'Gode! Ye must have laughed, sir, at that chap buzzin' away on his buzzer and getting no reply,' said Old Dan with a chuckle, when the Sniper gave a brief outline of his adventure.

He kept the German with him in his dug-out while he wrote up his report, Old Dan standing by on guard, the prisoner showing keen appreciation meantime of the Sniper's excellent whisky and Edinburgh shortbread. Then he sent the man on to headquarters under escort, with Old Dan carrying the report of the occurrence to the colonel. He wished to avoid the personal congratulations which he knew the colonel would offer him for this second capture. The Sniper hated such scenes. Early next morning he hurried away up the firing-line to be out of the commanding officer's way.

It was a baking hot morning. The whole countryside was trembling in the heat mist. But the lofty German parapet was clear of the haze, and every line and marking of it was showing up with unusual distinctness. Through his powerful glasses the Sniper could probe every crevice between the sandbags to its depth, even trace the pattern of the material of which the bags were made. Any German showing his head above the parapet on such a day would form an easy target. The Germans were keeping well hid, however, and no sniper's rifle was cracking.

'Ah doot we'll no get a shot the day, sir,' said Old Dan, coming up behind him. 'The Boche line is ower clear, and it's ower hot. He'll be content tae keep doon in the bottom o' his trenches where it's cooler.'

The Sniper went on with his observing. A German working party were busy in the firing-line. He had noticed them for some time, but now they were showing signs of greater activity. The thud of a mallet forcing down revetting stakes sounded louder and louder, and every now and then a lump of débris would be tossed out of the trench. He could trace the party's progress by those débris lumps. Sometimes a whole sandbag even would appear, flopping heavily on the outside slope of the parapet and bounding down into the wire, flung by someone too weary or careless to carry it off to the usual dump.

The Germans were slowly working along to a shallower portion of the trench, and the head of the mallet began to bob up and down above the parapet. More and more of the mallet appeared, until the Sniper was able to see the user's hand where it gripped the haft. It was a big hand, the biggest he had ever seen, and he felt some curiosity about the size of the owner.

'I wish he would show his head,' he murmured, turning to Old Dan.

'Ay. He's a big lump of a chap,' Old Dan replied slowly. 'He'd make a rare target.'

He left the Sniper and walked off down the trench. The Sniper went back to his glasses. So interested did he become in the sight of that bobbing mallet and the monstrous hand which swung it, that he grew oblivious to everything around him. Someone touched him on the shoulder, and he turned to find Old Dan and the sergeant behind him.

'Ah thocht it was a job for Andra,' said Old Dan. 'Will ye let him have a keek at that pairty, sir?'

The Sniper stood aside and let the sergeant get down to the loophole.

'Pretty big fellow, that,' said the latter, looking up after his examination. 'Will you observe for me, sir?' he added.

He had rested the muzzle of his rifle on the loophole lip and was squinting along the sights. The range was nearly four hundred yards, and the hand appeared for a fraction of a second.

The Sniper hastily shoved the horns of his periscope over the parapet and carefully focussed the lenses on the spot where the mallet was showing. He wondered at the sergeant's audacity in attempting such a shot, a shot which even such a fine sniper as Old Dan had preferred not to take, and took all the more trouble in getting a good view. So powerful was his instrument that he could see the veins standing out on the German's hand, swelled as they were to abnormal proportions by the man's exertions.

The mallet swung up above the trench, higher than before, with hand and several inches of wrist and arm showing. 'Now!' thought the Sniper. Crack! went the sergeant's shot. Down toppled the mallet. A yell arose as though it had fallen on someone. The hand remained upraised for just a second longer. There was blood streaming from below the knuckles, down over the wrist and the white of the forearm to where it met the parapet top. With a jerk it disappeared, and howl after howl came echoing over No Man's Land.

'Great Heavens! what a shot!' exclaimed the Sniper.

He turned to congratulate the sergeant, but the latter was modestly disappearing round a traverse.

The moon came out that night with a splendour which had not been witnessed in the district for many a long day. A feeling of peace was abroad in the land, and trenches and rifles and all the equipment of war seemed more atavistic than ever. The Sniper climbed out of the firing-line, picked his way over the wire, and lay down in a shell-hole just beyond, to look up at the beauty of the heavens and dream about home.

For long he lay there, drinking in the mystic beauty of the night, and all around him the trench area slept. The sudden swish of machine-gun bullets over his head woke him rudely from his dreams, and he peered angrily over the edge of the shell-hole to see whence the gun was firing. But no centre of flashes showed in the German lines, though the bullets were still whizzing above him. After a time the wicked rattling and whizzing ceased, and he settled down to his dreaming again. But his former peace refused to come to him, and he rose disgustedly to make his way back to the firing-line.

It was then he saw the rat.

It came out of a shadow blotch and stole stealthily away over No Man's Land, its little hurrying body showing quite plainly against the moon-bathed ground. He watched it interestedly. He had come to realise what useful allies the rats could be in pointing out to him the presence of men – men in unexpected places. For wherever men dwell in the trench area, the rats gather also, to feed from the food scraps to be found there; and this little scavenger, tracking so steadily over No Man's Land, could only be going towards a place where men had taken up a position.

The question instantly suggested itself to the Sniper – What were men doing in such a place? an established position moreover from the fact that they had carried food and eaten there; which they had left but recently, or otherwise the rat would have gone that way before. He got out of the shell-hole and hurried after the rat to find the answer.

For about two hundred yards he followed the tiny dark shape, walking quickly but quietly; for all the noise he made he might have been a night wraith stealing frightfully from shadow to shadow. At length he saw the rat enter a broken-down dug-out more than half-way across No Man's Land, and, getting down into the narrow entrance, he boldly entered after it.

The moon was too bright for any light to show outside, and switching on his electric torch he flashed it round the place. He found the rat making frantic efforts to reach an impregnable shelf on which were lying the remains of a German sausage. The animal faced round at him courageously, its eyes twinkling viciously in the torch-ray, crouching down on its haunches, prepared to dispute possession of the spoils. But, recognising the hopelessness of the struggle, it slipped out of the illumination and scurried through the doorway. From time to time it returned to poke its little snout inquisitively into the dug-out to see if the intruder had finished his examination.

Germans had been in occupation of the place; in a corner, crumpled up between two stout, pointed staves to which it was attached, lay a German army blanket, unmistakable from its melancholy thinness and sickly grey-blue colour. The Sniper examined it carefully. Its centre was riddled with innumerable small holes, as though a child in a fit of spleen had driven a pair of scissors through it repeatedly. The Sniper laid it back as he had found it, and left the dug-out. But first he tumbled the sausage off its perch to the floor, as a reward for the part the rat had played in leading him to the place.

Next evening, accompanied by the sergeant, Old Dan, and the rest of the Five, he set out for the firing-line. They had to take to the communication trench, as a machine-gun was sweeping the road with deadly and unwonted accuracy. In the firing-line they found a worried machine-gun officer eagerly searching No Man's Land for a trace of the gun which was causing the annoyance. But it was a mystery gun, which gave no visible sign of its presence, though the bullets went whizzing viciously overhead, making the roadway impassable.

The Sniper led the way over the top and in a wide detour round behind the old dug-out. There the mystery was explained to them. The blanket was erected a little in front of the dug-out, suspended between the two staves driven into the earth, and behind it was a German machine-gun, with a German gun-crew, firing through the blanket, the loose material offering no obstacle to the passage of the bullets on their deadly mission, but totally obscuring the flash of the exploding charges from the eyes of British observers. The gun stopped its firing; the gun-crew threw up their hands and surrendered, as they saw the sheen of five ready bayonets and their officer felt the Sniper's revolver driven hard in against the small of his back.

Late that night the battalion machine-gun officer dropped into the Sniper's dug-out to get fuller details of the capture. He had hardly seated himself when a huge grey rat stole in at the doorway. The gunner had never seen such a large rat before, and he reached for his revolver to shoot it. The Sniper stopped him with a gesture. Picking up a large lump of bully beef he flung it into the entrance. The monster pounced on it greedily and with a squeak of gratification scuttled away.

'He has been coming in here every evening lately,' he said, noticing the gunner's surprised glance. 'He's the patriarch of the tribe round about here.'

'But why do you encourage such a brute about the place?' asked the gunner.

'Partly because he is old, and I don't think he can forage quite so well for himself. And also because of the help his great-grandsons and great-grandnephews give me sometimes,' said the Sniper; and then he told the gunner the story.

'It's jolly good work, anyhow,' said the gunner when the story was finished. 'It's just like you to put the main credit down to a beastly rat. Always anyone or anything but yourself. You are getting the M.C., by the way.'

'Who told you that?'

'I've just heard from headquarters, and the colonel told me. He is awfully pleased. It's the brigade recommendation for those first prisoners you brought in. Ferguson is getting the D.C.M. also.'

'Ferguson should have had the D.C.M. long ago,' said the Sniper warmly. 'That's the worst, or rather the best, of all old line battalions. Your old regular colonel is mighty slow with his recommendations. Is it settled that we are being relieved to-morrow?' he enquired.

'Yes. The rest camp is finished now, and we go straight to it.'

'Then off you go, my boy. I have a good deal to write up, besides going round to drink Ferguson's health,' said the Sniper firmly, showing the gunner to the door.

CHAPTER XIV

The Hidden Hand

THE GOOD NEWS HAD come at last that the rest camp had been completed, and the battalion marched expectantly out of the trenches to its new quarters. The expectancy was not doomed to disappointment. The quartermaster had certainly laid out a model encampment. The situation stood high, thus obviating all chance of flooding, and the amenity of the site had been further secured by the raised brick roads which intersected it. An expansive brick square in the centre held the cookers, so that food could be distributed quickly and in good condition to the occupants of the surrounding huts and tents. Timber had run short for hutments, and half of the men were lodged in tents. But a tent with a raised wooden floor, connected by wooden gangways to the raised causeways, was a very excellent habitation in the worst of weathers, and the men were more than content with the shelter provided for them.

The officers' quarters lay at one end of the camp, a hut being allotted to each company; and in C Company hut a merry crowd assembled after the first morning parade. There were four subalterns from other companies, the doctor, the Roman Catholic padre attached to the brigade, and the Sniper's brother sniping officer, Healey of the Midshires, who had been left behind for some reason when his battalion had relieved the Eastshires. Big Bill was in his most sparkling humour, and his sallies were setting the whole hut roaring, the padre being the object of most of the remarks.

This padre R.C was a most extraordinary fellow – a priest, yet with all the knowledge of a man of the world. He had been on nearly every race-course in the United Kingdom, could play a good hand at auction or poker, and drink a specially stiff glass of spirits. For the good things of the table he had the keenest relish, with a self-confessed weakness for tinned peaches which formed the subject of many a joke. Nor was his portly appearance – his height of five feet six corresponded to a weight of over sixteen stone – suffered to pass without many scathing remarks. But his store of repartee seldom found him without a ready answer, and his invariable good humour made him a firm favourite. His popularity was founded on other things besides, not least of them a complete selflessness in the face of danger; and though he had none of his creed among the officers of the battalion, each one of them regarded him as a personal friend.

'Good business this morning, padre?' Big Bill had just asked.

The padre's reply was a broad, uncomprehending stare.

'Oh, come on, padre,' urged Bill. 'I'm not going to ask you to pay your last bridge losses, so let's hear how you got on. How many candles did you sell to your deluded flock?'

Bill had often rallied the padre on his supposed sale of candles, and the latter had always met him in the greatest good humour. He thought the time had now come to administer a sterner rebuke, especially in the presence of so many officers.

'Davidson,' he said, while an expression of pained surprise ruffled his usually mild countenance, 'I am surprised that a person of your supposed education and up-bringing should ask such a ridiculous question. You know that I do not sell candles to any of my communicants.'

'Not holy candles?' asked Bill in an awed whisper.

'Certainly not!' replied the padre. 'I'm surprised at the abysmal ignorance you display.'

'Ignorance!' yelled Big Bill. 'Abysmal ignorance too. Holy Moses! do you hear him?'

His face became solemn. With a great show of dignity he began to interrogate the padre.

'Padre,' he said, 'have you read Cardinal Lonzino's "Exposition of Church Law"? Or Bishop Allodani's "Treatise on Doctrine"? Or Father Petrolius' "Commentaries"?'

The titles and names of the authors of these works were, of course, wholly fictitious, but at each negative of the increasingly mystified padre, the tone of Bill's voice became more pitying and reproachful.

'Padre,' he said sadly, after an impressive pause, 'do you mean to say you have not read the works of these pillars of your church? And yet you accuse me of ignorance! I do believe, padre, you left seminary before your education was completed. You've been making eyes at the milkmaid or something, and got excommunicated by the brethren. You're not a priest at all. Oh, padre,

padre!' he wailed. 'Think of the disgrace! think of the scandal! What will your poor wife say?'

The worthy father could do nothing but gape at Bill in wonder. As his tormentor paused, he prepared to say something, but Bill had continued before he had managed to utter a word. A new thought seemed to have occurred to him. His expression of reproach gave place to one of sly understanding.

'Ah, padre, my lad, I've got it,' he began. 'You're not as stupid as you look. You haven't sold a blessed candle this morning. That's what it is. Not a holy candle, not one. It's the disappointing trade that's made you so forgetful. But never mind, old Friar Tuck. I'll buy out your whole stock. It will be fine to light up our dug-out with holy tapers.'

He rose from his seat with a wild, jubilant 'Yahoo!' and charged down on the chaplain. The latter tried to get out of his way, but before he could rise, the box on which he was sitting had been kicked from under him, and Big Bill was rolling him barrel fashion along the floor. The spectacle was so irresistibly funny that the whole company yelled with laughter.

'Davidson,' gasped the padre, when he at last managed to scramble to his feet, 'you are really incorrigible. Come and help me to get the dust off my tunic.'

Davidson's big hand came down with a thump on the padre's back that sent dust and priest flying.

'That's cheered you up, padre,' he said amidst his mighty thumps. 'You'll not need to . . . go bankrupt. . . . You'll be able to . . . stock . . . a more fetching design of . . . Ow!'

The padre's fist took him between wind and water. He sat down on the floor with a bump, his shoulders banging against the wall with a force that shook the whole hut. There he sat for a moment or two in silence, gazing sorrowfully up at the padre.

'Oh, Father, Father!' he said plaintively. 'That you should demean your cloth in such a way! Especially after I went to the trouble to order peaches for lunch for your particular benefit.'

The padre gave a little crow of delight. 'Davidson! You splendid fellow!' he exclaimed.

He ran to help his benefactor to his feet. But Big Bill swept him down beside him. His strong arms circled round the chaplain's neck, nearly choking the reverend man, while his great head buried itself in the priest's shoulder. Mournfully reproaching his would-be helper for his base ingratitude, Big Bill sobbed bitterly on the padre's best tunic.

The acting was perfect, and the others roared their appreciation, the padre himself nearly exploding in his efforts to laugh against Bill's strangling pressure. But a summons from Captain MacMichael, who had lately returned from his staff course, stopped the clamour and the whole company sat down hungrily to lunch.

In the afternoon the Sniper had to ride over to a neighbouring town to draw money for the battalion pay-day on the morrow. He asked Captain MacMichael for the loan of the company charger, a fine big black colt of which he was very fond. Though everyone knew the errand on which he was bound, the spirit of gaiety, born of Big Bill's baiting of the padre, led them all to chaff the Sniper sorely as to where he was going. Big Bill would have it that he was off to meet a girl, and besought him tearfully for an introduction. Healey, the Midshire sniping officer, told him of another girl whom he could go to see if his lady friend did not turn up. 'She's at the chocolate shop above Moulin Rouge. Mention my name and you'll be all right,' he shouted as the Sniper galloped away.

The fields were bare of crops and almost hedgeless, and once clear of the camp he headed over the open country. His horse was an unusually handsome animal, and, unlike the average present-day infantry subaltern, he himself was a splendid rider, having spent most of his boyhood in the saddle. Many a group of officers sitting anyhow on a scratch lot of transport animals pulled up to watch him enviously. No more pleasing sight can be seen than a good horseman on a good horse in full career over the open country.

He slowed his mount down to a walking pace as he struck the high road leading towards his destination. About half a mile away a side-track left the road, and wound away round a hill towards Moulin Rouge. He smiled as he recollected Healey's parting injunction. A mounted officer was coming along the road towards him. As he drew nearer the Sniper was astonished to see that the rider was wearing kilts. He recognised him as an officer of a Highland regiment in the same brigade. Before they met the Highlander swung into the side-path. Even though some distance still separated them, the Sniper marked the curiously intent expression on the Highlander's face, and wondered at the haste with which he was spurring his horse.

'Jove! I wonder if he is off to see the girl Healey spoke to me about?' he said to himself.

Arrived at the Field Cashier's office, he presented the company requisition notes and received in exchange various packets of paper money. The money was done up in prearranged amounts, and he stuffed it away without examination in his haversack. Had he only known the guileful ways of the

Field Cashier when notes of small denominations are short, he would not have taken the money so carelessly. The adjutant showed him the error of his ways before he was back five minutes in the rest camp.

'Mr. Jackson,' said that worthy with the weary smile of a kind wise man rebuking a wayward child. 'How much money do you think we pay each man?'

'Ten to twenty francs,' said the Sniper readily.

'Then how do you suppose we are going to pay nine hundred men ten to twenty francs each out of fifty hundred-franc notes, ninety fifties, and three hundred fives? Take the hundreds and fifties away, Mr. Jackson. I don't want them. Get me five-franc notes in exchange.'

'Where?' gasped the Sniper helplessly.

'I don't know,' said the adjutant cheerily, walking out of the orderly-room to his quarters.

Big Bill roared with laughter when the Sniper met him outside and explained his plight. But, for all his practical joking, Davidson was a kind-hearted fellow of a truly wonderful resourcefulness. On his advice the Sniper rode over to a little village and enquired his way to a certain grocery store. To his great astonishment – for he had still a lingering mistrust of Bill's advice – the Belgian shopkeeper eagerly agreed to change the notes, and did so to the full amount. The desk in his private room was literally snowed under with five-franc notes, the proceeds of many sales to customers from the surrounding rest camps, and he even enquired if the Sniper could relieve him of any more.

'You pay de men to-morrow, Monsieur. Den it all come back here,' he said pathetically. 'An' so mooch leetle paper, it ees so deeficult.'

The Sniper rode back rejoicing, no longer wondering why the British soldier was so popular a stranger within the gates.

Darkness was falling when he reached the rest camp. The lamps were lit in the officers' quarters, and little streams of light were playing out over the camp. Cissie was sitting in C Company hut laughing merrily with two other Sandhurst boys, but as soon as the Sniper entered he rose and drew him aside.

'I've had a letter from Maimie,' he said. 'She's quite near St. Omer. We'll likely be able to see something of her when we go out for long rest.'

'That should be jolly for you, Ciss,' remarked the Sniper in a tone in which he meant to convey neither polite interest nor indifference. Miss Rankine had not acknowledged his letter about her brother, even though she had acted on it and put things right with Cissie and his people.

'She's mentioned you quite a lot, Ronny,' Cissie continued.

'That's rather flattering,' remarked the Sniper much more interestedly.

'Yes. She thought an awful lot of the letter you wrote about me.'

Tired by his extra journey, the Sniper soon retired to his sleeping-bag, but during the night he was aroused by the sound of heavy gun-fire. He struggled up from within the folds of his valise and listened. The other occupants of the hut were awake also. All the heavy batteries around them seemed to be engaged. The rolling thunder of the bursting shells came down from the line.

'It looks as if someone had got the wind up pretty badly,' said Captain MacMichael.

'Blast his teeth, whoever he is!' grumbled Big Bill from his corner. 'Ought to be hamstrung for disturbing the sleep of overworked subalterns like this.'

'Do you think the Germans are trying to break through?' asked Cissie rather excitedly.

'Sure thing,' replied Bill. 'Von Kluck has heard of your arrival and he wants to catch you before you do any harm. I'd run for it if I were you. Shoo, kid!'

The talking gradually ceased, and the tired officers fell asleep again.

'Have any of your fellows heard what the row was about last night?' asked Big Bill after next morning's parade. 'They say that Healey's crowd were raiding the German trenches.'

'I heard that too,' said Jimmy MacLauchlan. 'All the camp seems talking about it.'

'Have you heard if it was a success?' Captain MacMichael enquired.

'Some say it was, others say it wasn't,' Big Bill answered.

The adjutant settled the matter at a meeting of junior officers which he called before lunch.

'I have called you fellows together,' he said, 'under instructions from brigade headquarters. I have to warn you specially not to speak about any matter, outside your own quarters, concerning the doings of your battalion, company, or platoon. They have reason to believe that German spies are very active just now all along behind our lines, and they wish you to be on your guard. For example, last night the Midshires tried to raid the German trenches. Lieutenant Healey, who left us yesterday afternoon, was in charge of that raid. No one was supposed to know anything about it, outside brigade headquarters, the colonel, adjutant, and Healey himself. Even the men were picked only at the last minute. Yet when they went over the top, the Germans were lying ready for them, and practically mopped the party up. Poor Healey himself was killed. The gun-fire last night was the finish up of the affair, and the Midshires have suffered so badly that it looks as if we might be due for the trenches again before our time.'

The news of Healey's death saddened everyone. The bright, merry-hearted Irishman was genuinely liked wherever he went. But more disquieting intelligence came in within an hour afterwards. It seemed only an ugly rumour at first, but a message from brigade headquarters to the adjutant confirmed it – Kenneth McBain, a young Highland officer, had been shot while out riding. His horse had returned to camp alone, its saddle and withers covered with blood. A search party eventually found him in a ditch, shot through the back. The sinister feature of the case was that his body had been completely covered over with leaves and ditch rubbish. It was his dog, a little French bull-pup which he had rescued from the ruins of Ypres, that found him; and but for it, leading the searchers to the spot, he might have lain undiscovered for days or even months.

McBain was the Highland officer whom the Sniper had met out riding, and he immediately went and reported the matter to the adjutant. But the information threw little light on the affair. The body had been found a long distance from Moulin Rouge. He returned to find C Company and the officers who messed with the company discussing the matter.

'Funny that McBain and Healey should be killed about the same time,' said Jimmy MacLauchlan. 'They were such pals.'

'Do you infer that there was any connection between their deaths?' queried the padre.

'No!' said Jimmy dubiously. 'Only it's funny.'

'They say that McBain's dog whined when he would not take it with him. And went on whining all the time he was away,' ventured Cissie.

'And why shouldn't it whine? Did you ever know of a dog not whining when it was chained up?' asked Big Bill scornfully. 'There's always a lot of stuff tacked on to any strange happening. Your true blue Briton likes a mystery. If he does not get it ready made, then he will manufacture it.'

'I would not dismiss the story like that, Bill,' said Jimmy. 'Dogs are queer things. My guv'nor once told me that he had seen a dog go crazy with fright for no apparent reason whatever. It was in a room in my uncle's house, and my father was alone with the dog. The room was supposed to be haunted, that's all.'

'That might be easily explained, though,' said the Sniper. 'A dog is always terrified at something it can't understand. A professor of mine once told me that he had known of a dog fainting at the sight of a bone drawn across the floor by an invisible thread.'

'True, Jackson,' said Jimmy. 'But take it from me, dogs are kittle cattle.'

'Oh, shucks, Mac!' said Big Bill. 'You're giving me the creeps.'

'There are more things in Heaven and Earth than are dreamt of in your philosophy, Horatio,' quoted MacLauchlan.

'What are you calling me Horatio for?' queried Big Bill innocently.

'What the deuce are you all cackling at?' he asked with great dignity, when the laugh over his supposed ignorance had ceased.

'Oh, Bill, you did look a fool,' said the padre gleefully.

'Which just shows what a fool you are, padre. Just bear in mind, my little fat boy, that there is no art to read the mind's construction in the face,' said Bill, quoting Shakespeare in turn, neatly transferring the laugh on to the padre. Bill's general education was really surprising for a Sandhurst boy.

'But look here, you fellows,' he added. 'What's the good of moping over poor Healey and McBain? We've seen our pals go under before. It may happen to us any day. Let's stop talking about the whole ghastly business. Who says four at auction? You, Jacky? Mac? MacMichael? No, Skipper? All right. We'll let the padre play, if he'll only promise to remember to lead his highest up to his partner's call in "No Trumps", and not go trumping tricks already taken, even though the master card is only an eight.'

This latter sin the padre had committed only the night before, and he blushed under Bill's home-thrust. Without further discussion the four sat down to their game.

Before the end of the rest period Healey and McBain were only memories. The trenchman must quickly push tragedy behind him, otherwise life in the battle-line would be unbearable. The Sniper even led his section past the spot where McBain's body had been found without the thought of the ghastly discovery entering his mind. He was too much interested in the reality of the subject which he was discussing with the sergeant and Old Dan. That night he intended to transform the house by the road – the house which he had visited during the fog – into an observation post. The three of them were working out the details of the project.

CHAPTER XV

Spies behind the Lines

S AY, SMIT',' SAID MATTHEW Oldheim to Geordie Smith, 'what you tink of de officer's idea?' The two were in the cellar under the house by the road, which the Sniper and his section during the night had equipped as an observation post. Telephone wires had been led from the trenches and headquarters, and fitted up to a transmitter on the top of the stairway leading to the roof. An observer stationed there could immediately send a message either to the snipers in the trenches, or to the colonel and so on to the artillery. A second transmitter had been connected up in the cellar. It now stood on the top of a large-scale map of the district, spread out on a table formed of trench-boards laid across neatly built-up piles of sandbags.

Much had been done to make the cellar habitable. Two upturned empty oil-drums cushioned with sandbags did duty as chairs, and a rough couch, built up in the same way as the table, stretched along one side. On the other side was a safe with the door wrenched off. Its shelves were well filled with tins of jam, butter, bully beef, and other oddments. In the centre of the floor was a glowing charcoal brazier with a steaming dixie on the top; and two bubbling canteens were suspended from hooks on either side in contact with its hot surface. Oldheim was bending over the dixie busy with preparations for an early breakfast.

'Ah dunno,' replied Geordie. 'Seems a guid sort o' a place for a direct hit.'

'Wal, dat's so. Guess Mr. Jackson is prepared to take de risk,' said Oldheim. 'But what you tink of de idea?'

'What dae ye think o' it, yersel'?'

'I've enquired dat from you, George.'

'But Ah'm askin' it back o' you,' said Geordie dourly. 'What have we got tae dae wi' it? It's the officer's funeral, no' oors. Ah dinna believe in askin' ower muckle.'

'Dat's your way, George. It don't stand for me,' replied the American. 'Ef you don't ask questions you cut no ice.'

'Oh!'

'Yep! When I started my time wit' de Pennsylvania railroad, de first job I got was shaving two-inch solid iron from de base of a wheel standard. Dey gave me chisels an' hammer, an' told me to get busy. I got under de car. In one hour de edge was off all my chisels, and de skin off my back. De older boys come along. "How you getting on?" says one, an' goes off to laugh wit' de oders. "My, you doin' fine," says anoder, an' goes off to laugh wit' his gang in de power-house. Dat job took me a week. When it was finished, dey show me how to edge an' harden my chisels. Ef I had asked at de beginning, job would have been over in a day.'

'But hoo is it that you Yankees swank so much aboot things ye dinna ken, if ye ask sae many questions?'

'Don't know dat 'Mericans swank more dan óder people. Some do. So do some Englishmen. Possibly more, possibly less,' replied Oldheim. 'Swankin' 's no good, George. When I'd been tree monts wit' de Pennsylvania, boss says to me, "Take dese gentlemen roun' de shops." Dey ask me all sorts of questions. I tell dem what I know 'bout my shop. 'Bout de oders I tell dem plain blank lies. 'Cos I know noding about dem. After a real fine lie dey begin to smile. I turned all red. Sort o' guessed dey smelt somet'ing. Den one said:

'"Boy, you got derned good imagination. But I'd better introduce myself. I de president of de Caldwin Locomotive Company, an' dis is my chief engineer, Mr. Wilson. Ef you want to know anyt'ing 'bout engines, guess he'll be able to tell you." Gee! I could have jumped in de furnace. Dere had I been swankin' about engines to de biggest railway pots in de States. I never swanked again. Started askin' questions.'

'Gode, Matthy! what a fool ye must have felt,' said Geordie.

'Yes, George. Questions pay better,' Oldheim agreed.

'Is breakfast ready, Oldheim?' said the Sniper, entering the cellar. 'The mist is thick on the ground, so we might as well eat while there's nothing to be seen.'

Oldheim immediately laid out the food on a trench-board. The bacon rations for the three of them had been stewing in the dixie. Cooked in this fashion it made a splendid dish. There was plenty of bread and butter and tea, with two tins of skippers, a boiled tongue in glass, and a tin of peaches to finish off with. Several of these items had been furnished by the Sniper, and Geordie's eyes glistened as he watched each extra being produced.

'Gode, sir,' he said. 'Ah wudna mind bein' on this job a' the year roun'.'

'Well, Smith, you'll be here just as long as the Boches let you stay.'

'Dawm the Alleyman!' said Geordie.

'You forget de Alleyman brought you here, George,' said Oldheim.

'Humph!' said Geordie.

'See who is on the line, Oldheim,' said the Sniper, as the transmitter began to buzz.

Oldheim picked up the receiver. 'It's de colonel,' he said, first carefully disconnecting. 'He wants to know if you can see anyt'ing, sir.'

'Oh, tell him it is misty, and there's nothing doing,' said the Sniper. 'Jove,' he added when Oldheim had resumed his seat. 'The colonel's as keen as a two-year-old over this post. That's the fourth time he's rung up to ask the same question. We'll have to tell him something the next time, or he'll be coming up to see for himself.'

Smith went up to the observing station when the meal was over. The Sniper stayed behind to do some map work, while Oldheim cleared up. The clearing up was only half-finished, when Geordie's voice sounded down the stairway.

'Sir, sir!' he called. 'Come up and see this.'

Both the Sniper and Oldheim rushed for the stair. Smith was standing gazing out of the first-floor windows.

'Did ye ever see the like o' that, noo?' he said, pointing away to the right of the line where the sector held by the Canadians began.

The firing-line was still wrapped in mist, fast thinning, however, and the ground behind the trenches, towards which Geordie was pointing, was quite clear. Down a narrow track from their trenches a group of Canadians were escorting a large two-horse wagon. None of the three had seen a wagon so near the firing-line before, and the sight took their breath away.

'Gee! Dey are some boys, dese Canadians,' said Oldheim admiringly.

'There's the colonel ringing up again,' said the Sniper, as the transmitter began to buzz. 'Tell him about the wagon, Oldheim.'

'I tink de colonel is coming up to see for himself,' said the American, returning hastily from the transmitter.

'Go and tell him the wagon is nearly out of sight,' said the Sniper hurriedly.

'I tink I just stop him in time,' reported Oldheim when he returned.

'Oh, look, sir!' called out Geordie.

But the 'hoomp!' of distant shrapnel bursts had already attracted the Sniper's attention. German observers on Wytschaete Hill had seen the wagon in a thin patch of the haze, and had turned their guns on to its course. The group of soldiers scattered over the fields at the first burst. But the driver whipped up his horses, and though some of the shell-splinters must have whistled very near him, he succeeded in racing into safety behind a slight rise where he was hid from view.

'It's just like Canadians to bring their stores up to the firing-line in such a fashion,' said the Sniper. 'They are the limit.'

Followed by Geordie, he climbed up the stairs to the observation station. There was comfortable room for them both, and through several discreet spy-holes in the broken bricks they could overlook a wide sector of the enemy trenches to a goodly depth behind his lines, until the Wytschaete buttress and its continuation toward Hollebeke shut off the view. The mist was fast clearing, and the line of the main German communication trench was momentarily growing more distinct. It looked a mere black ditch in the ground at first, but close examination through powerful telescopes revealed some activity going on at the point where it met the Messines road.

'Do you notice anything in that trench where it crosses the road?' the Sniper enquired.

'Gode! ay, sir,' replied Geordie. 'It's full o' Germans. They're working on the parapet or something.'

The Sniper rang up headquarters and reported the matter to the colonel, giving him the exact map reading of the working party. Within a few minutes the artillery were shelling the spot. The first shell burst in the trench at the end of the working party. The second breached the parapet about the middle of them. Four shrapnel shells followed, just as the Germans were getting out of the trench to scatter over the open, and several of the enemy fell before they could reach further shelter.

'Very good business, Jackson,' said the colonel's voice over the 'phone when the Sniper reported the result to him. 'Don't put the guns on again to-day though, or the Germans will begin to realise that a new observation post is being used.'

The wisdom of the colonel's advice was fully appreciated by the Sniper. If the Germans once realised that their long undisturbed privacy on the further side of the ridge had been broken into, they would immediately start shelling every house behind the British lines which could possibly be used as an observation post. Only the cellar would then be left for himself and his men to retreat to, and a direct hit from a heavy shell would reach them even in that hiding-place. Accordingly he contented himself with noting down every sign of German activity, only reporting now and then to the colonel any specially interesting item of information.

Late in the afternoon he was standing out behind the house watching the setting sun gild with its rays the Scherpenberg, Mont Noir, Mont des Cats, and the other hills in that direction, when out of the ground almost at his feet rose the sergeant. He had crawled up over the open without the Sniper noticing his approach, as fine a demonstration of scout-craft as anyone could have given. It seemed almost uncanny.

'I thought I would like to see the place by daylight,' said the sergeant in explanation of his arrival.

Together they went over the post, not a detail of the arrangements escaping the sergeant's critical eye. At the end of the inspection he was almost genial to his officer.

'You are on a good line, sir,' he said. 'But you will have to be careful.'

Shortly after his arrival the usual evening bombardment commenced. The Sniper went to one of the rear windows on the first floor to watch the shrapnel bursting. Ypres was receiving the greatest attention. The black H.E. clouds wreathed thickly about the shattered towers of the cathedral and Cloth Hall. The line of the roads radiating from the ruined city was marked by intermittent shell-bursts, and Sanctuary Wood seemed on fire. British shells were hurtling overhead in reply. Their slow rumbling course told of a bigger calibre than the Germans were using. The lower village then began to receive an occasional shell or two, and next the turn of the communication trench came. Just where the trench met a road leading into the village a black cloud appeared overhead. Slowly it dissolved away and immediately another cloud took its place. The Sniper could not hear the noise of the shell-burst, and the cloud appeared and disappeared as if by magic.

'The Germans know where the C.T. runs,' said the sergeant, who had quietly joined him.

The Sniper's gaze wandered away to the dark circle of hills behind which the sun was setting. Somewhere among them a light was flashing. At first his mind, drugged by the mystic beauty of those slumbrous gold-tinted mounds, attached no special meaning to its appearance.

'That's a curious light, sergeant,' he said lazily.

'Your compass, sir. Quick!'

The sergeant's rough tones woke the Sniper from his trance.

'God! It's signalling,' he said, as the significance of the flashes dawned upon him.

Three compass readings he took before the flashes ceased. Followed by the sergeant he tumbled down to the cellar to plot out the direction on his map. The map was on a large scale, every house, almost every tree, being indicated. The Sniper's carefully drawn pencil passed through the topmost house of the Moulin Rouge.

'That's the only house on the line, sergeant,' he said. 'But I'm hanged if I can see how the place is visible from here. What do you think?'

'The hill on which Moulin Rouge stands must be invisible from here, sir. At most, only its top can show between the shoulder of these two hills,' said the sergeant, indicating the position on the map. 'I know the place well, and in any case you cannot see the firing-line from any of its houses because of this wood running right over its crest.'

'You're right, sergeant,' said the Sniper, carefully comparing the figures of the contours intersected by his line. 'That would throw us back on any other point of the line But do you know, sergeant, I've got a weird sort of suspicion about that place.'

'So have I, sir,' said the sergeant softly.

'What do you mean?'

'Well, sir, I've heard it whispered that those in the know can get all the spirits they want there.'

'Officers or men?'

'Both, sir. The place is kept by an old shrew with a daughter and son. The daughter is much too pretty to be her real daughter. The son is supposed to be a discharged Belgian soldier, but if ever I saw a man who was dangerous, he is.'

'You are rather good at sizing people up, sergeant,' said the Sniper. 'But I can't report merely suspicions to headquarters. Hanged if I'll report the thing at all! I'll go round and see the place first.'

He was sitting pondering over the matter that evening, when Big Bill rushed into his dug-out.

'I'm leading a raiding party into the German lines tonight,' he said. 'Start off at midnight. Just dropped in to give you the word so that you can be up for the show. Can't stop. Got ever so much to see to,' he added, when the Sniper pressed him for further details.

Sergeant Ferguson entered the moment Big Bill had gone. 'Sorry to disturb you, Mr. Jackson,' he said. 'Is it the case that Mr. Davidson is leading a raid to-night?'

'I believe it is, sergeant,' the Sniper replied, 'I suppose you came to say something,' he added, as the sergeant delayed saying anything further.

'There was a raid a week ago,' said the sergeant slowly. 'It failed. The Germans had got warning of it. We are trying a raid to-night. They may be waiting for us. Those flashes we saw, sir. Might they not have been a warning?'

'What do you suggest should be done, sergeant?' asked the Sniper, fastening on to the sergeant's point at once.

'That you and I go out on patrol, sir. You will need to go,' he added diffidently. 'Because an officer's report will be necessary.'

'Good Lord! What sort of an opinion do you have of me?' exclaimed the Sniper, reaching for his equipment and making for the doorway. 'Come along, man.'

A party of men were already cutting a way through the British barbed wire for the convenience of the raiders when the two reached the firing-line. No preparatory bombardment was intended. It was hoped to take the Germans by surprise. Officer and sergeant made their way through the gap and crawled out into No Man's Land. The Sniper could not but admire the easy way in which the sergeant covered the ground. He could hardly distinguish him from the tangle of shadows of No Man's Land, yet he had to crawl along as quickly as he could to keep in touch with him. Somewhere in front, barely a hundred yards away, was the German line, wrapped in a suspicious silence. Perhaps enemy patrols were watching their approach. A quick bayonet thrust might come out of the darkness. Ugh!

The Sniper shrank away at the touch of the sergeant's hand. In an instant he had recovered his nerve, and crawled up alongside him. The sergeant was staring steadily ahead. The Sniper looked in the same direction. At first he could see nothing other than the dark irregular débris heaps. Then one of the heaps moved slightly. The clue was sufficient for his straining eyes. The focus was readjusted, and into his field of vision leaped the misty picture of two crouching German soldiers staring in his direction. It was a listening patrol.

The sergeant backed cautiously, and the Sniper followed him. They worked round to the right, and again tried to move forward. Again a listening patrol was encountered. A third venture brought the same result. The Germans had listening patrols strung along the whole of the battalion sector.

'Hist!'

The Sniper heard the sergeant's low warning. He saw him disappearing into a shell-hole and quickly tumbled in after him.

'There's a big German patrol coming up on our right,' whispered the sergeant. 'They are making for our lines. See! There they are.'

A number of indistinct forms were crawling past about ten yards from the shell-hole. The Sniper counted nearly twenty of them. His first impulse was to fire his revolver among them, but he at once checked himself. The flash of his shots would have directed towards him the fire of every rifle and machine-gun of the sector.

'They are examining the gap in our wire, sir,' said the sergeant. 'Here they come back again.'

The Sniper marvelled how the man could see so clearly. As for himself, once the Germans had passed him, he had lost all trace of them in the shadows.

'Get down, sir,' said the sergeant. 'They are coming directly on to us.'

The two crouched down in the bottom of the shell-hole. The Sniper could hear the swish of the approaching patrol. A harsh voice whispered something above his head. It was the patrol leader warning his men of the presence of the shell-hole. The Germans passed close by on either side and disappeared into the night. At once the sergeant got out of the shell-hole and walked coolly towards the gap in the wire.

'It's quite evident the Germans are expecting the raid, sir,' said Ferguson when the firing-line was reached. 'If the colonel wants me to corroborate your report, I shall be at the section dug-out.'

'I wonder how the Germans got their information,' said the colonel an hour later. Divisional headquarters had cancelled the raid immediately after the Sniper's report had been telegraphed to them, and the colonel was discussing the matter with the major, the adjutant, and the Sniper. The latter had an idea which might have enlightened the gathering, but he discreetly kept it to himself.

Next night the German listening patrols were out again, and every night after that, until the end of the battalion's spell in the trenches. On the last day of the tour, a large board was stuck up above the German parapet. On it was printed in large capital letters –

WHAT ABOUT THAT RAID?

CHAPTER XVI

Marie of Moulin Rouge

G OOD AFTERNOON, SARE. YOU come in and buy shokolate? Shokolate-au-lait, sare? Ver' good. Then you buy caffee? Ver' good caffee. Yes?'

'Yes, I'll have some coffee, chérie,' said the Sniper, dismounting and tying up his horse to a ring in the wall. He stood outside the topmost house of the Moulin Rouge, and at its door was one of the prettiest girls he had ever seen.

'This must be the girl Healey mentioned to me,' he said to himself, as he followed her into the house.

The street door opened on a room fitted up in the usual estaminet fashion, but it was into a small back parlour behind the bar that she led him. An old woman was sitting here, a shrivelled-up old hag, who glared malevolently at the Sniper as he entered.

'You no mind grand'mère, sare,' said the girl reassuringly. 'She no see much, an' she ver' discrete. Oh, ver' discrete.'

The Sniper laughed inanely. The girl's suggestion was so obvious. Her eyes looked at him seductively from beneath their lowered lids, and when she left the room to bring his coffee, she flicked her skirts brazenly, affording him a generous view of a well-formed silk-stockinged calf. The Sniper had seen that movement before in the dance halls of the Argentine, and he summed her up accordingly.

'She's no green hand,' he decided.

Through the crack of the door the girl looked at him critically. He was still smiling inanely. She shrugged her shoulders contemptuously. 'Oh, these British boys! *Pfui!*'

The Sniper just caught the last word of her exclamation. At least he heard the low hiss of it, a sound more than slightly familiar to his ears. Over in the Argentine he had met many Germans; he had often heard them use the expression, giving it the same contemptuous inflection as Marie had done; to the best of his knowledge it was used by no other race. His heart gave a great bound as he mentally put the question – Why should this girl, presumably French or Belgian, use so characteristic a German term? His original suspicion allowed him but one answer: the girl was a German. Only with difficulty did he restrain his excitement at so early and significant a discovery; but he was smiling as carelessly as ever when Marie returned.

'You Scottees boy? Yes?' she said. 'I like Scottees boys. They gallant. Ver' gallant.'

She had seated herself opposite him; her toe pressed lightly on his foot. She leaned so far forward on her elbows that he could look down the neck of her low-cut gown.

'You from the 2nd Eastshires? Ah yes! What you do? Companee co-mandare. No! What?'

'I'm sniper officer,' replied the Sniper.

'Ah! snipare offiseer,' she exclaimed. 'Ver' interesting. Marie knows. Eef Boche shoot Tommee, you find where Boche ees, and you shoot 'eem. What? You brave Scottees boy.'

She was looking at him with greater interest now. The Sniper's grin grew more inane. He reached out across the table and grabbed clumsily at her hand. She withdrew it quickly beyond his reach. Her eyes glanced roguishly at him from a modestly averted face.

'Scottees boy!' she said reprovingly.

'Jove! you can give the glad eye, Marie,' he said admiringly.

The girl laughed merrily. A customer rapped on the counter at the moment, and with a little shrug of annoyance she rose and went into the bar.

'Healey was sniper officer,' thought the Sniper. 'Jove! So was McBain.'

He swung idly back in his chair. Through the tail of his eye he saw that the old hag was watching him. His mind was working furiously; but on his face was the sensuous smirk of the callow youth about to make his first conquest.

In the yard behind the estaminet someone was sawing wood, and whistling over his task. The sounds floated in through the open window above the Sniper's head. The tune was familiar, and he followed the whistler note by note as a music lover does a singer who is singing a favourite song. But he could not remember the name of the tune or any of its associations.

He got up and looked out of the window. In the yard a well-set-up man in the uniform of a Belgian soldier was busily sawing up logs for firewood, timing each drive of the saw with the tune he was whistling. The Sniper felt dimly that there was something paradoxical about a humble Belgian peasant being able to whistle that tune. But why? He could not answer that question.

Marie returned from the bar and came up beside him.

'Gustave, my brodder,' she said. 'Shell burst near 'eem. No fight again. No right here.' She tapped her forehead significantly and gazed pityingly at her brother.

'Jolly bad luck,' murmured the Sniper sympathetically.

'Yes! Ver' sad,' said Marie, sitting down again and drawing him down beside her. 'You no look at 'eem. Make Gustave ver' angry.'

'Poor little Marie,' said the Sniper tenderly.

He slipped his arm round her waist and drew the girl nearer to him. In spite of himself he thrilled at the feel of her. She was wonderfully made, with every point of seductive beauty which a man pictures – not in his wife, but in the favourite of his harem.

'I am glad you come, Scottees boy,' she murmured. 'Marie so lonely, and sad.'

'Poor old girl,' said the Sniper, pressing her consolingly. 'Don't you know any other nice officers?'

'I once know nice boy. He dead now.'

'Healey,' thought the Sniper. 'Or McBain.'

'Marie ver' sad when he dead. Ver' good to Marie.'

She had slipped one arm round his neck and drawn herself up closely to him. The Sniper could feel her breast against the soft of his under-arm. Her face was close to his. Her chin dimpled against the first button of his tunic. Her eyes shone through a veil of tears with the brilliance of diamonds in the half-light; and the Sniper felt that a man might well sink his soul in their glorious depth with never an afterthought for the price he had paid.

'If he was good to you, Marie, he must have been a Scotsman,' he said jestingly.

'No! No! No!' exclaimed the girl vehemently. ''E no Scotteesman. 'Ees friend Scotteesman, an' no like 'eem. No nice. No!'

The Sniper wondered at her vehemence. She had drawn away from him abruptly. There was more than a hint of the vixen in her manner.

'You have not been able to fool McBain altogether,' he thought. 'Don't see why you should make me suffer for one bad Scotsman,' he said aloud.

'Poor little Scottees boy! You no like 'eem. You ver' gallant. Marie likes you.'

Her arm was round his neck again. She was rubbing her forehead against his cheek as demonstratively as a cat eager to make amends for scratching a fondling hand. For the life of him the Sniper could not restrain himself from quivering under her touch. She was a glorious girl.

'Jove! What a girl you are, Marie,' he said, his voice all shaky and high-pitched.

The girl looked up at him languorously. Slowly she raised her face to his till her eyes were just below the level of his own. The Sniper trembled at the passion of them. His hand clutched at the bosom of her dress. She caught it and pressed him away.

'No! Scottees boy. No!' she said.

His right arm was firm round her waist. But she held him off with outstretched arms, arching her body backward so that all the voluptuous rounds of her figure stood the more plainly revealed against the tautened draperies which sought to hide them. For a moment she gazed at him, her lips parted, the tip of her tongue caught tight between her teeth. Then she drew herself up to him again, so closely that her warm breath played on his cheek and throat.

'Not here, Scottees boy,' she whispered.

The door leading on to the yard rattled against the wall as someone whose hands were engaged in holding a burden, pushed it clumsily open with his foot.

'Sh! Gustave!' said the girl, springing clear of the Sniper.

The brother entered the room bearing an armful of firewood. He took no notice of the Sniper, but walked straight up to the fireplace and slid the logs into a corner of the large open hearth. In spite of the cramped stoop which his awkward burden gave to his shoulders, the precision of his every movement spoke of years spent in military training. He still softly whistled the tune which had puzzled the Sniper. The latter was on the point of asking the girl its name when her brother gave him the clue.

He had poured himself out a glass of home-brewed beer from a jug which stood on a dresser in the corner, and was holding it up against the light examining the translucent fluid critically, when the closed door in the Sniper's memory suddenly opened. Once in Buenos Ayres he had been present at a dinner in a German club. Four German students, lately out from the Fatherland, had sung that song – a song to the glory of beer – ending up with raising their glasses against the light, as this pseudo-Belgian was doing. The fellow was a German, too! The Sniper came to the decision the instant that he identified the song.

Quickly he built up the case in his mind to include the old hag also: she would be a German agent planted in the district years before the war. The Sniper had often heard of such persons; he had regarded them as some rare species of beings, little likely to come within the scope of his personal experience, even if they existed at all. But now that this concrete case had presented itself, he realised how easily such a thing could be done. Madame's long settlement in the district would relieve her of any suspicion in the minds of her simple neighbours, and a hint of absent grandchildren would serve to explain the later appearance at the estaminet of Gustave and Marie, or any others for that matter, even if they too had not been 'planted' before the war. How to pierce through this web of camouflage which the years had woven was the problem awaiting solution by the Sniper, and his agile mind marshalled and remarshalled the facts of the case as he already knew them, so that he might the more readily place any fresh fact in its proper context.

'Scottees boy!'

Marie's voice interrupted his meditations. Looking round, he saw her standing by another doorway, beckoning to him. He immediately rose and followed her.

The door opened on a narrow stairway leading to the upper floor of the house. At the top were two rooms, one of them Marie's bedroom, into which she led him. Two windows lightened the place, one looking down the road towards the village, the other on the front of the house facing the road by which the Sniper had come and commanding it for over a mile of its length. The position of the windows was the only point to which he paid any attention. The furnishings of the room did not interest, or surprise him unduly; even though the place was no modest retreat of an ordinary country wench, but rather the luxurious boudoir of a successful metropolitan *grande cocotte*.

'You like my room?' said Marie, looking at him with that age-old look of Woman in the presence of Man.

The Sniper shuddered under her glance, not this time from the response of sense to sense, but at the thought of the brave men whom this siren had lured to this room, tricked of their secrets, and sent to their deaths.

'Thank God for the Argentine dance halls,' he thought.

Marie tripped daintily over to her bed and flicked back the quilt coquettishly. She laughed at him as he remained motionless, as though overcome by his feelings. In an instant she had glided up to his side and kissed him. Just as swiftly she slipped away from him and flung herself down on a couch which stood along the wall opposite the bed.

'Come near Marie, Scottees boy,' she said.

He went over and knelt down beside her. She flung her arms round his neck and pulled his head down tight on her bosom.

Someone rapped impatiently on the bar counter. 'Marie!' shrilled the old hag's voice.

'Huh!' said the girl in annoyance. 'Gustave one big pig. He might watch estaminet. Marie back in one leetle time,' she added, slipping off the couch and hastening towards the door.

'Marie one leetle fool,' murmured the Sniper ungallantly, when the girl had gone.

As lightly as a cat he crossed the floor and slipped into the other room. As in the room which he had just left, there were two windows, one with the blind tightly drawn. He drew the blind aside and looked out. What he saw gave him the last link in the chain of evidence he had been slowly building.

The window was set in the eastern wall of the house, and looked out on the lofty pine-forest which Sergeant Ferguson had mentioned as hiding Moulin Rouge from the firing-line. But directly opposite the window a narrow lane had been cut through the top of the trees, unnoticeable from any place but the window, through which the Sniper caught a glimpse of the distant firing-line. It was from this window that the signal lamp had sent the flashes which he and his sergeant had seen from the observation post; the flashes which had warned the Germans of the raid Big Bill was leading. Thus had warning been sent out of the raid in which Healey had lost his life – Healey who had been 'good to Marie!'

The sound of Gustave's whistling came to him through the other window. He crossed over and looked out, and immediately cursed himself for his want of caution. Gustave was standing in the yard looking directly up at the window. The Sniper saw suspicion at once leap into the man's eyes. He stopped his whistling and glared up at the intruder.

'Good afternoon, Gustave,' said the Sniper inanely.

'Good afternoon, Gustave,' he repeated, as the man still continued silently glaring at him.

'I no spik Anglees,' growled Gustave.

'Really, Gustave; how funny,' brayed the Sniper.

He heard Marie mounting the stairs, and her quiet entrance into the other room; then her quick agitated steps as she came in search of him. He stole over to a bed in the corner of the room and seized a pillow. When she appeared in the doorway he was stealthily tiptoeing back to the window. He saw her quick nervous glance at the blinded window, but before she could say a word he had stopped her.

'Sh! Marie. Come and see this,' he said.

She crept up to the window and watched him. Gustave had resumed his wood-sawing. The Sniper hurled the pillow, striking the man squarely between the shoulders, nearly toppling him over.

'Haw! Haw! Haw!' he roared.

Marie joined in his laughter, as Gustave looked angrily up at them. He took no notice of his sister. It was on her companion that he centred his gaze. The Sniper read the menace in his glance, and realised that only the readiest wit could get him out of this house in safety. The man was no fool, and not to be deceived as readily as Marie.

'Come away, Scottees boy,' said Marie, tugging at his sleeve. 'You naughty boy. You make Gustave angry.'

'Jolly good shot, wasn't it, Marie,' he said, grinning fatuously.

He suffered her to lead him back to her room, and draw him down beside her on the couch again. But he had no intention of resuming any philandering. Pretending suddenly to notice the time, he leaped to his feet in dismay.

'Jove, Marie!' he exclaimed. 'I must be going. I had no idea of the time.'

Marie stood up and looked at him steadily. When she spoke he noticed the threat in her tone.

'You no go, Scottees boy,' she said.

'I must, old girl,' he replied. 'The colonel has called a meeting of all the unit commanders for six o'clock, and there's only half an hour to go.'

'A meeting?' queried the girl.

'Yes! It's beastly important. We've got to discuss preparations for a raid that we are going to make next week.'

He saw the gleam of interest appear in her eyes at this statement. 'A raid! Yes. Ver' important. You must go,' she said quickly.

He looked down on her hesitatingly. Then as if overcome by his emotion, he knelt down, and covered his face with the edge of her skirt.

'I don't want to go, Marie,' he said. 'You are so beautiful. I want to stay. I can easily tell the colonel my horse went lame, or something like that.'

'No, Scottees boy,' she was pulling him gently to his feet. 'You mus' go. Marie no get you into trouble. But you come back to Marie,' she whispered.

'Back, Marie!'

'Yes. You come to-night. Stay wit' Marie. Marie wants you. You come! Scottees boy? Eh?'

'God! Marie, if you'll let me, I'll come.'

His arms were around her, pressing her savagely to him. But she gently disengaged herself from his embrace and moved him off to the door. She was all eagerness now to get him away in time.

'Au revoir, leetle boy,' she said, opening the door of the bar parlour to him. 'I no come to the estaminet door wit' you. Better no people see. You come back, eh?'

'Yes, little girl, I'll come back,' he promised.

Outside in the road he fussed about his horse for a little; he dared not depart at once. A quick upward flick of his eyes as he left the estaminet door had disclosed Gustave at the upper window with something in his hand which looked very like a rifle. He had not the slightest doubt that the fellow intended to shoot him as he rode down the long stretch of road in front of the estaminet. It would be so easy. No houses near, thick trees on every side through which the assassin could drag his victim to some place of concealment, while the horse went home riderless, with a bloody saddle to tell of the tragedy which had happened – 'As McBain's horse went home,' thought the Sniper.

He fumbled away with his saddle-girths, and listened for the signal which would tell him he might depart in safety.

If it did not come there was his revolver, and then it would be either Gustave or himself. Marie's voice sounded chidingly from somewhere above him. He heard Gustave growl out a reply. Then Marie spoke again. No reply came from Gustave. The Sniper leaped easily on to his horse and rode away down the road.

'I expect the little b— is telling her brother how the poor fool of a Scottees boy is coming back with extra special information for the friends on the other side of the line,' he murmured.

The colonel listened grimly to him as he told his story. Half an hour later he was telling the same story to four grim staff officers in divisional headquarters.

'We are very much obliged to you, Mr. Jackson,' said the general when he had finished. 'Your investigations could not have been more thorough, and your services will not be forgotten.'

They made him dine with them at the headquarters mess; kept him there till the spies were brought in, and safely locked up in the provost-marshal's prison.

'Scottees boy!' murmured Marie reproachfully, as he left the cell with the identification party.

A fortnight later his name appeared in the Honours List among the D.S.O.s.

CHAPTER XVII

The Section on its Mettle

IT WAS A VERY apologetic sniper officer who met the Sniper at the beginning of the next trench tour, to give an account of the previous week's doings in the line. He had only succeeded Healey a few days previously. He was also very young, and very, very inexperienced. And though what he reported annoyed the Sniper exceedingly, he said nothing about it to the boy. What had happened was this.

As in duty bound the Sniper had told his brother sniping officer about the new observation post by the road, admonishing him strongly to take every precaution in using it. The latter had promised to be careful, but the first morning of his occupation someone of his party had allowed the brazier to smoke. Only a wild rush down the road saved them all from the shells which were quickly screaming around the house; and the house itself was totally destroyed.

'It is annoying,' said the Sniper, after communicating the news to the sergeant. 'But we shall just have to build another. Warn the Saunderses, Brown, and Haggarty to be ready in an hour's time, and we'll get busy.'

He had decided to convert a ruin which stood at the head of the main communication trench into an observation post to replace the one destroyed. The place was only a one-storey building, with all but the rear portion of the roof blown away; and was nothing like so secure from observation as the house by the road. But it was the next best position in the sector, and all night he and the Five laboured to transform it to their purpose.

They made as little outward change as possible. But by a judicious rearrangement of the roof-beam, a space was made where a sniper could comfortably command the German line, and yet be hid from German observers. The post could not be made bullet proof; only cover from view could be attempted. There was this advantage, however, that ready access could be had to it during the daytime by a ladder placed against the rear wall, the wall itself being broad enough to screen the approach to the post from the communication trench.

In the early grey of the morning, the Sniper stood in front of the house and examined his handiwork. John Brown was already in occupation. Short as the intervening distance was, he could not detect the man's presence, nor did there seem to be anything to indicate the change which had been made. Yet he was not satisfied. Somehow or other he felt that the post was not safe. He had been warned that the opposing German snipers were a resolute, efficient set of fellows, and not the slightest precaution could be overlooked in dealing with them.

'Tell Brown to come out of the post, sergeant,' he said at length. 'We shall not use it to-day.'

When he returned to the firing-line after breakfast, a group of snipers were standing in the trench critically examining the old house, and he hastened to join them. A glance showed what was attracting their attention. The woodwork fronting the post had been cut to pieces by machine-gun fire.

'They turned the gun on it half an hour after daylight, sir,' said the sergeant. 'It was lucky you took Brown out of it.'

'Ta fox will leave its hole just ta night before farmer comes to dig him out,' said Adam Saunders.

'Gode, yes, sir!' said Old Dan. 'It's wonderful hoo snipers get a warnin' at times. Dae ye see that stretch o' parapet just ahint the hoose? The communication trench Ah mean. It's solid enough the noo, but aboot three months ago, the top o' it was as saft as a rotten tattie. Naebody kennt that. But we got uneasy aboot comin' up it. Why, we didna ken. Every one o' us used tae bend oor heids when passin' it. The other men laughed at us, but dod! they were wrang. One day the Boches turned a machine-gun on it whiles a fatigue pairty were comin' by, an' a wheen bullets went richt through and killt fower o' them. They built up a new parapet after that.'

The detection of the observation post was only the first of a series of checks the Sniper and his section were to receive from the Germans. During the rest week a new German division had come into the line, and their snipers were of a very different class to those previously in occupation. Before the first day of the tour was over, the nature of the struggle before them had been fully realised by the whole section.

'They've scrapped all their old loopholes,' the sergeant told the Sniper after the first examination of the line. 'You'd better pass the word through the companies for the men to be careful, sir, until we find where their new posts are located.'

'Ay, sir. They're ower quate for me,' remarked Old Dan. 'When ye get men shootin' at onything at a', ye ken that it's only foolbuddies agin ye. When they're quate, ye ken they're up tae the business, waitin' for a certain chance. Ah dinna like it at a'.'

All day the Eastshires lay quiet in their trenches. The men took every precaution when moving about, and every tendency to carelessness was rigorously checked by the N.C.O.s. They knew that such a man as Sergeant Ferguson would have given no such public warning without due reason. But when the day had nearly passed without a single shot being fired from the German side, some of the less experienced men began to jib at the restraints placed upon their freedom of action. The older men did not relax their vigilance. They read danger in the continued silence, and many a gloomy prophecy was uttered by them when some young stripling out with the last draft showed signs of recklessness.

The trouble started next morning at breakfast time. Two of the men in the act of throwing empty tins over the parapet were shot through the head. Then the second-in-command received a bullet in the shoulder at the head of the main communication trench when coming up with the colonel to go the morning round. An hour later a subaltern of A Company was shot through the body actually while walking in the fire-trench. A feeling of disquiet settled down on the battalion; there was no need to issue a second warning. The men stuck to their cover like rabbits to their warren when the guns were near at hand, and the day saw no further casualties.

The success of the morning broke the enemy silence. The Germans always seem to know when a relief takes place in the British trenches, and it was just as if their snipers had been holding their fire until they had measured the quality of their new opponents before conducting a vigorous offensive against the sniping posts located by their observers. All day they kept up a systematic fusillade on several of the posts, and so accurate was their fire that one or two of them had to be abandoned. The enemy used a type of steel bullet which easily penetrated some of the older loophole shields, and more than one of the section had a narrow escape from these dangerous missiles. A second shield was hastily fitted to each loophole, and the double width of metal proved sufficient to stop the armour-piercing bullets. But the snipers had to be very careful about opening their loopholes, and in the posts subjected to the heaviest fire the protecting panels were only slightly lifted so as to leave the narrowest of chinks through which observation could be carried on.

Over-confidence is a vice that will lead the best of snipers astray, and the Germans sinned grievously. They had summed up their opponents as of little account, and the lack of any reply to their shooting encouraged them in this idea. But the section was working strenuously. It was no longer a case of morning and afternoon watch. Every one of the snipers voluntarily remained on duty all day. The Sniper divided up the German line into narrow sectors of observation, putting a sniper in charge of each, with instructions to carry out the minutest possible scrutiny, inch by inch. The plan yielded immediate results, and one after another the new sniping positions were found and noted down.

'We'll gie them somethin' tae put in their pipes and smoke the morn,' the Sniper heard Old Dan remark as the section filed down the trench that evening to their quarters.

The sniper who had shot the subaltern of A Company was the first to suffer. From the manner in which the casualty had occurred it was obvious that the fellow must have been stationed above ground-level. A clump of tall trees stood some distance behind the German line a little to the left of the point, and only from one of them could the shot have come.

It is a fairly simple matter to detect a sniper in a tree if the tree stands by itself. But where it is one of a number grouped closely together the detection is extremely difficult. All that the Sniper could do was to put a man on to keep the trees under constant observation. He chose Matthew Oldheim for the job because of the American's proved capacity for accurate observing, and gave him the best telescope of the sniping outfit to help him.

There was a clearness in the atmosphere of Oldheim's first day as watch-dog which boded the near approach of a rainy spell but gave great assistance in observation work. The Sniper happened to be near the spot where the subaltern had been killed, when he heard a shot from Oldheim's loophole. He immediately fixed his periscope in position and looked towards the German line. Near the top of one of the trees under observation a German soldier was struggling. He was holding on by one of the branches and trying to swing himself behind the trunk. Another shot came from the loophole, and the German ceased struggling. He released his hold on the branch and crashed to the ground, falling across a tree which had been cut down by shell-fire. The crack of his breaking back whipped like a rifle-shot across No Man's Land.

'I done in dat fellah,' said Oldheim coolly, as the Sniper approached him. He was peering out into the trench from the low entrance of the sniping post, nursing his rifle as though it were a child, a sodden unlit fag-end drooping from the corner of his mouth, his dirty ugly face puckered up in the smile of a man who has just carried out the achievement of his life.

'Jolly good work, Oldheim,' exclaimed the Sniper delightedly.

'Yes, sah!' said Oldheim, straightening himself up. 'I was lookin' at dese trees wonderin' where de devil could be hiding. When somet'ing went sparkle, sparkle in one of de trunks. I see anoder higher up, an' den anoder. It was de ol' sun shinin' on spikes in de trunk. I says, "What are spikes for but for climbin' on?" So I waits until de silly devil goes and sticks out a foot. I says, "Dat's good enough for me." So I fires. Guess you saw de rest, sah.'

Oldheim's success was hailed with great delight. No more dramatic snipe had taken place in the history of the battalion. One after another of his comrades slipped along to congratulate him, and so many of the officers took him away to their dug-outs to give him a 'reviver', that the sergeant had to spirit the gallant fellow quietly down the communication trench and put him to bed. Everyone felt that it was the beginning of the end for the German section.

Shortly after noon young Geordie Smith reported that he had seen what looked like a red handkerchief waved low down in the German parapet. The report was an extraordinary one, but the Sniper had no intention of dismissing it as ridiculous without first closely investigating the matter. Both he and the sergeant settled down by a loophole and began a thorough examination of the German parapet.

The sun had just passed its zenith and was pouring down an unwonted radiance from a cloudless sky. Every detail of the German line showed up with added clearness, and suddenly the Sniper saw what looked like a red handkerchief flicked for a moment near the base of the German parapet. At first he thought it was an illusion of his overstrained eyes, but the phenomenon was repeated, and the second appearance enabled him to discover the explanation. A small hole had been made in the parapet and surrounded with sandbags of different colours, so cleverly arranged that, even after the spot had been indicated, very intensive observation was required to make out its outlines. The flash of colour was the red healthy face of the German observer, revealed all the more clearly by the high visibility of the day. Evidently a careless movement of the German's head had drawn aside the curtain behind the loophole, allowing the brilliant daylight to shine through for an instant, thus giving him away to the watching British snipers.

Young Geordie was given the opportunity of taking the shot. His bullet went clean through the loophole. Three shrill screams of agony came from the German line, the third scream cut off sharp in the middle as though just at that instant Death had laid his hand on the man's throat and choked him.

Geordie was very white when he came out of the loophole. A death-cry is always a terrible thing, and it was his first success as a sniper. A stiff tot of spirit from the Sniper's flask pulled him together, and he grimly went back to his post to search for another victim.

After this second casualty the German snipers began to see the mistake they had made in under-estimating their opponents, and their firing ceased entirely. Their silence was even more menacing than their activity, and a second warning was issued for the men to be very careful. A sniper of all people was the first to neglect it.

He was a man who had come out from the depot a few months previously with a recommendation from his musketry officer that he should be taken on as a sniper. As this recommendation is never given unless the recipient is a very promising shot, he was immediately attached to the sniping section. The new recruit had had some experience of shooting before the war, and was a very efficient rifleman. But because his skill on the range matched that of even the oldest and most crafty sniper in the section, he was inclined to think himself above taking the advice of men who had been engaged in sniping more months than he had been a soldier. And soon his carelessness in the trenches, endangering both his own life and the lives of those associated with him, brought it to a question as to whether his undoubted success in killing Germans made it worth while from the point of view of general efficiency to persist with him as a sniper.

Late in the afternoon the Sniper caught him standing by a rather lofty loophole with the covering curtain tucked into a cleft in the sandbags above the loophole, thus taking away the dark background which ought to have been behind his head, and rendering both himself and the loophole conspicuous to any German observer. The Sniper sternly reproved him, and the man at once adjusted the screen in accordance with the recognised practice. It turned out afterwards that the sergeant had already checked him earlier in the day. But the two reprimands were not sufficient, and as soon as the Sniper was out of sight the curtains were tucked above the loophole again.

The Sniper was only a traverse or two away when he heard the thud of a bullet striking home. Running back, he found his man lying dead in the bottom of the trench. A bullet had come straight through the loophole, a tampered bullet, and the man's head was shattered. It was the first casualty of its kind for the tour. All the other casualties had received clean wounds.

'It always happens, sir,' said the sergeant, who had hurried along on the report of the happening reaching him. 'Once the German suffers a reverse, he at once turns to dirty tactics.'

The method by which their comrade had been killed raised a very ugly feeling in the section. The more experienced men had to watch the younger snipers very carefully to prevent them from beginning a wild fusillade on the enemy loopholes, and otherwise exposing their positions in their eagerness to mark down the hiding-places of the enemy sharpshooters. Old Dan went raging up and down the line like a wounded bear. The sergeant followed him, but his manner was as imperturbable as ever.

'Gode, Andra!' the Sniper heard Old Dan say, 'Ah dinna ken hoo ye keep your temper. If Ah'd caught young Wattie Finney keepin' his loophole open as ye found him, in spite o' a' the tellin's, Ah'd have wrung the young deevil's lugs off.'

'Possibly, Dan,' replied the sergeant quietly. 'If you find young Wattie doing the same thing again you can wring his ears off if you like. But you won't find him.'

The sergeant was right. The section stood in awe of Old Dan's rough and ready manner of enforcing an order, but they had even more respect for their sergeant's subtler methods. The two men made an excellent combination for securing discipline – Old Dan, tremendously strong and prepared to use his strength without the slightest hesitation; the sergeant, infinitely inflexible of purpose, and of a personality so compelling, for all his impassive ways, as almost to hypnotise a man into obedience.

It was the Sniper who discovered the post sheltering the German responsible for the vacancy in his section. He spent most of the following morning in searching the German parapet opposite with minute care. There were many suspicious blotches of colour purposely made by the Germans to camouflage their posts, but the excellence of his prismatic periscope enabled him to decide on one particular point as the most likely to be the exterior of a loophole. Both the sergeant and Old Dan after a careful examination agreed with him, and it only remained to test the suspected spot.

The method of testing for a suspected loophole was quite simple. A shot fired against a steel plate gave a distinctive metallic clang, altogether different from the noise of a bullet striking the parapet or even a stone; and if the plate was there, no matter how skilfully camouflaged it might be, a bullet would prove its presence.

'Will you try a shot, sir?' said the sergeant, looking at the Sniper expectantly.

The invariable custom of the section was that the man who discovered an enemy sniping post should take the first shot at it. The Sniper at once took Old Dan's proffered rifle, and went into the nearest loophole.

'Look out, sir!' he heard the sergeant yell immediately after he had fired.

A long rectangular panel had opened in the German parapet. The daylight shone through the opening, and revealed the extent of the loophole quite plainly. He saw the long barrel of a German rifle appear in the gap and swing about uncertainly from one end of the sector to the other. Then a little puff of cordite smoke came from the muzzle and a shot rang on his shield within an inch of the loophole.

'Two inches low left,' called the sergeant, as the Sniper fired again.

The Sniper corrected his aim. His finger was pressing full on the trigger when a second shot from the German struck the shield. The shock made him involuntarily complete the pull.

'Damn!' he said in disgust.

'Gode! ye've hit him, sir,' yelled Old Dan triumphantly. 'Your bullet sliced the wood off his rifle and slappit him clean in the face. Ye can see the chip lyin' below the hole. Gode! Look at his rifle.'

Somehow or other the Sniper had retained his aim in spite of the accidental pressing of the trigger, and the bullet had gone home. He could see a large white splinter from the wooden casing of the rifle-barrel, lying below the loophole, and the rifle itself was cocked up in the air by the weight of the butt and slowly slithering out of sight into the trench.

'Well shot, sir!' said the sergeant, shaking him warmly by the hand.

Old Dan nearly twisted his hand off in his delight. One by one the two Saunderses and Brown came along the trench to add their congratulations. Discipline restrained the younger men from doing likewise, but they were every bit as pleased at his success. It was his first snipe. He had brought it off at considerable risk to himself. They were proud of the pluck and skill which their officer had displayed.

But this taking of a man's life shook him considerably. He could now understand young Geordie's white face after shooting his first German. A pull at his flask cured him, however, as it had cured young Geordie, and he was soon as busy as ever supervising the activities of his men.

CHAPTER XVIII

The T.M.O. Takes a Hand

A COUNCIL OF WAR took place in the Sniper's dug-out after the evening stand-to. Sergeant Ferguson, Old Dan, and the others of the Five were present. They listened to what the Sniper had to say, studied the aeroplane maps of the sector very carefully, and went back to their quarters very greatly impressed by their officer's ability. Half an hour later, armed with picks and shovels and reinforced by several members of the section, the council set out for the firing-line. With the first flush of dawn their task was finished.

A small sap had been dug out from the firing-line to a slight rise in No Man's Land, and here a four-loopholed sniping post had been made, carefully camouflaged with all the skill which the Five had garnered from many months' campaigning in the Salient. The rise at best was only a foot or so above the level of the parapet. But in the low rolling swamps of Flanders an elevation of a foot may represent the difference between observing and being observed. From the aeroplane maps, the Sniper had seen that the rise was directly in line with what apparently was the German main communication. Dawn found him, along with the sergeant, Old Dan, and Adam Saunders, peering through the loopholes almost into the bottom of the trench. They commanded nearly twenty yards of it, and even behind the first traverse or two the head of any German passing up the trench would be visible to them.

'You were right, sir,' said the sergeant. 'It's now only a question as to whether any Germans come by before we are discovered.'

'How long do you think they will take to find this place?' asked the Sniper.

'Half an hour, sir,' said the sergeant laconically.

'Gode! Here's a workin' pairty,' exclaimed Old Dan suddenly. 'Doon ahint the fourth traverse.'

'Hold your fire till the trench in front is full of them. You and I, sergeant, will take the fore half. Haggarty and Saunders cover the rest. Be ready to switch on to the heads behind the traverses,' said the Sniper quietly.

Round the traverse into the exposed portion of the trench swung a German officer. The early morning sun shone on the shiny peak of his hat and lit up his red healthy face. Behind him came a string of grey figures, burdened with mattocks and digging tools. The heads and burdens of the others could be seen appearing above the parados behind the intervening traverses as the working party moved forward. The front-line parapet was creeping up to the officer's neck. Behind him the trench was a-wriggle with waving spades and heads.

'Fire,' whispered the Sniper.

Five rounds rapid rang out. The sergeant's first shot took the German officer in the forehead and he disappeared beneath the falling forms of the men behind him. There was a dishevelled grey-blue mass in the trench like a heap of sandbagging dislodged by a shell from the parapet. Before the Germans in the rear of the party knew what was happening, a scattered volley flicked away the heads from above the parados behind the traverses as cocoanuts go down before the throws of a group of schoolboy experts. Four men who had escaped this latter shooting burst helter-skelter round the corner of the near traverse, and went sprawling over the bodies of their comrades. Four shots rang out and they ceased sprawling.

The German officer at the rear of the party climbed out over a traverse to see what was happening. Old Dan stretched him lifeless across the parados. His black peaked cap fell off, and but for the white shiny bald spot in the centre of his crown he would have been indistinguishable from the dull grey background of the sandbagging on which he was lying. From amongst the silent forms in the fore trench a man suddenly uplifted himself. A shot took him in the spine. His legs, jammed tight by the fallen bodies, remained upright, and his body bent backwards on them like a broken reed. His death roar reverberated across the muddy levels like the bellow of a bull seeking its mate among the meadows. Twenty Germans had been slaughtered in almost as many seconds. The cries of dismay from the survivors were fading away down the trench.

'We had better clear out, sir,' said the sergeant quietly.

The Sniper crawled quickly after his men along the shallow sap into the firing-line. A hasty explanation to the officers in charge got the garrison cleared out of the firing-line on either side of the sap entrance. A few minutes afterwards the German shells were screaming round the spot, wreaking a vain revenge on the empty sniping post and its empty surroundings.

'You had better mention this, Jackson, as confirmation of your report to divisional headquarters,' said Colonel Stewart an hour later, pointing to the damage from the bombardment.

'I'll mention your battery in my report,' he added, turning to the big forward observing officer. 'I think they must have created a record for speed in retaliation.'

The blow seemed to knock all heart out of the German snipers. They did not fire a shot during the rest of the week, and seldom opened a loophole. The section was able to go on methodically tracking down the enemy posts and dislodging the shields as far as rifle fire could do so. At one portion of the line, however, where a perfect nest of posts was discovered, all such efforts broke down, and the Sniper soon saw that he would have to employ more drastic methods if the sector was to be cleared of the Jaeger pest.

The place where these posts were located was a strong point in the German line. It was an entrenched mound standing immediately behind the German fire-trench, and at its base was a solidly built sandbag breastwork. In this breastwork the enemy snipers had built their lairs.

They had been very difficult to detect, because of the small size of their loopholes; and the mound rising sharply behind formed a natural dark background, which prevented any light showing through and so disclosing the loopholes when they were open. The steel of the loophole shield defied any attempt to smash it, and when the surrounding sandbags were ripped away in an effort to dislodge the plates, it was found that they were embedded in concrete quite impervious to a rifle bullet. Careful observation showed that the posts were always occupied, and it was evident that the Germans were only biding their time till they were confronted by weaker opponents.

'We've got to shift those fellows somehow, sergeant,' said the Sniper on the last day of the tour. 'They will make as great a hash of the Midshires next week as they did the week before, and when we come in again we'll have the same old struggle to fight over again.'

'How are you going to shift them, sir?' enquired the sergeant. 'Raid or artillery?'

'Neither. A raid means permission from the brigade, and the gunners with their super-knowledge of trench conditions would wonder what sort of a section we possessed if we asked them for their help. I think I know a better way.'

The Sniper paid a call on the commanders of the companies in the firing-line, and after a short discussion with each, departed towards the headquarters village in search of the trench mortar officer who covered the sector. This worthy had won the well-deserved reputation of being an artist with his guns. He was an American Scot, McAllister by name, and he lived in a cellar of a ruined convent in the village.

'Mr. McAllister is in, sir,' said the gunner's servant.

But the Sniper stumbled down the narrow stairs to find the cellar empty. Much to his surprise, a large oak coffin stood on low trestles along one of the walls.

'Jove, if I were McAllister I'd have that shifted,' he murmured.

'Mr. McAllister is not here,' he called up to the servant.

The man came tumbling down the stairs. There was a sly smile on his face when he entered. Going up to the coffin, he tapped softly on its lid.

'Sir! Sir!' he called. 'There's a gentleman to see you.'

A muffled snort came from the interior of the coffin. Its lid swung back, and a blanketed sleepy-eyed youth sat up in it.

'Good afternoon, Jock,' said McAllister cheerfully, flinging his blankets aside and climbing out of the coffin. 'Bring along that bottle,' he yelled after his disappearing orderly.

'Finest bed I've had for years,' he remarked, seeing the Sniper's amused surprise. 'What can I do for ye, ma braw lad? Man, Ah like your wee bit bonnet,' he added, breaking into the Doric, as Scot will do the world over when he meets a brother Scot.

Over the Glenlivet the Sniper explained.

'Have you got your colonel's permission?' asked McAllister.

'No!' said the Sniper. 'He would never grant it with the relief due to-night. He's got the other colonel to consider. That's why I came direct to you. You've got pretty much a free hand.'

'Sorry,' said the T.M.O. sadly. 'It can't be done, then. You know what you infantry fellows say when our little beauties start barking and their German brothers bark back in reply.'

'I've got the permission of the company commanders in the line though,' said the Sniper. He might have added that he was leaving the battalion next morning on a fortnight's intelligence course behind the lines, and so did not care whether the colonel was annoyed with the bombardment or not.

'You have, have you? That will save me from physical violence, anyhow,' said McAllister much more cheerfully. 'Guess you're some boy. Don't mind the strafing as long as you get the goods. All right, I'm with you. Gee! I've been praying for a target for weeks. Come along, my boy, and we'll get on to it right now.'

The two hurried up towards the firing-line.

The news of the approaching bombardment spread like wildfire, and the whole trench garrison rushed to the spyholes in the parapet and every other vantage point from which they could get a glimpse of the fun. Nothing interests British soldiers more than to witness a thorough punishment of the German lines. It is such a concrete example of Britain's growing munition resources. Every man knew the importance of the strong point opposite, so that even those who were off duty and supposed to be asleep, roused themselves and hurried out of the dug-outs to the firing-line. It was just as if they were crowding to see a boxing or football match behind the lines. There was a rare scramble for periscopes and shaving-glasses among those who arrived too late to get a place in the spy-holes. But though the excitement was intense, not a sound was made to give the Germans warning that anything unusual was about to take place.

A dull 'poop' was heard, the well-known sound of the sixty-pounder trench mortar in action, and everyone looked upward with a jerk. High overhead, twirling its central stem round and round, the shell could be seen ascending. It reached a point where it appeared no larger in size than a small rifle grenade, and then plunged down the other side of the curve, towards the German trenches. Right behind the mound a spray of earth rose, but no explosion followed.

'Dud!'

The word went down the line in a harsh whisper. As if to accentuate the failure a jeering shout came from the Germans.

Another poop and another shell flew into the air. This time the gunner had shortened the range, and the shell fell right in front of the German trench. A huge splash of earth shot up. A wailing note of agony followed the sound of the explosion. When the débris had subsided a great gap could be seen in the parapet and the wire in front of it. Another shell fell into the trench. A cluster of timber baulks, veiled in earth and sandbags, rose into the air, carrying above it all the spread-eagled figure of a man. The shell had fallen into a dug-out or a mine-shaft. Again that wailing cry came over No Man's Land. Four more shells burst at intervals along the German trench, and the bombardment was finished.

The German parapet had been blown in along the front of the mound, and the whole position looked as if some great beast had stamped on it and rent it. It would take the Germans at least a month to make good the damage done, and the men shared the openly expressed delight of the Sniper and McAllister at the result of the bombardment. But a watchful look was on every face, and quick glances were cast towards the darkening evening sky. All knew what was coming. And suddenly it came.

A warning shout arose, and a small black object was seen travelling rapidly from the German trenches. It struck the outside of the British parapet and burst. But the explosion did no damage. It was only a small hand-bomb thrown by a spring gun. Only an earnest of the coming storm, however, for now all along the sector these missiles were soon hurtling over from the German line, and louder explosions indicated the presence of some light trench-mortar bombs. But no heavy stuff came over, and the men laughed heartily as they dodged about the traverses to escape the flying fragments. It was a grim game, this dodging of death, and many narrow squeaks occurred. But no casualties were suffered, and the greatest good humour prevailed.

The poop of the British gun was heard, and the roar of a sixty-pounder bursting in the German lines drowned the medley of lighter sounds arising from the explosion of the enemy bombs. It was a hint of the power the British had at their disposal, and the Germans were not slow at taking the hint. The rain of bombs ceased, and a tense silence settled down as darkness hid the lines from view.

'Good shooting, eh?' said McAllister cheerfully, getting down from the fire-step where he and the Sniper had been observing. 'Thirsty work, though.'

'Ay. Thirsty work,' said the Sniper, leading the way towards Captain MacMichael's dug-out.

'Here, Jackson,' said the adjutant, entering the dug-out a few minutes later. 'You had better do a scoot. The colonel is up the trench looking for you. He's got you booked for the next strafe.'

The Sniper silently faded into the darkness of the trench.

'Jackson! Jackson!' wailed McAllister, stumbling after his vanishing form. 'Don't desert me in this confounded ditch maze.'

After the relief, when the Sniper was leading his men through the village past the headquarters, the colonel's voice boomed out from the darkness.

'Ferguson! Where is Mr. Jackson?'

'Gone on ahead, sir,' said the sergeant coolly, adroitly placing himself between the Sniper and the colonel until the danger zone was passed.

CHAPTER XIX

Maimie

THERE ARE MANY FORESTS in France, large forests and small, with trees of oak, or elm, or fir, but all with the same peculiar characteristic – compactness. The French are a nation of small-holders. No fewer than six million of them have a share in owning the soil of the fatherland, and multiple ownership spells intensified cultivation. The last ear of wheat, the last beetroot or parsnip, has to be forced out of the last square yard of ground that the owner of that square yard and his kindred may live. Hence the compactness of the forests. Their sombre green bulks appear in the distance as clearly outlined from the surrounding country as though a draughtsman had drawn their limits and a painter splashed in the colour between his lines.

Near at hand the cultivated land can be seen sweeping right up to their margin with never a sentinel tree or outpost clump abutting. But as if to make up for the lack, their ranks are packed as close as a Roman phalanx. There is a hint of aggressiveness in their solid formation, a suggestion of defying the open country to advance any further. But the close-planted trees are only another example of the French landholder's thrifty instincts, which decree that, whatever the nature of the crop – cereal, tuber, fruit or timber – the soil must be cultivated to the utmost of its productivity.

Once inside any of those forests the stranger can wander for hours without finding his way out again. Fine French highways run through some of them, and the wanderer has merely to strike such a road to extricate himself eventually from the maze of trees. But broad expanses exist untraversed by these highways, where not so much as a footpath may be found, and the narrow tracks of the forest creatures only serve to lead the stranger further away from the thoroughfares of men. He may count himself lucky to find the winding path of a ranger, but even with its guidance the dense undergrowth, arching rankly over the perennially sodden surface, makes his progress laborious and painful. The mud clutches at his feet, or cunningly slides him into some unsuspected bog-hole whose concealed stepping-stones are unknown to him; and the withes and runners of the brushwood displaced by his advance whip back on his unprotected face, slashing it cruelly.

Down one of the narrowest and muddiest of these paths, in one of the largest and most trackless forests of France, wandered the Sniper.

He was covered from head to foot with the mud of many falls. His tunic and breeches were torn. His hands and face were scratched and bleeding through their outer casing of slime. His cap was gone, and his mop of hair was sodden and sorrowful, tousled in places, with patches plastered down flat by the mud. He looked as battered a specimen as ever came out of a Flemish crater-fight in the depth of winter. He was pushing along a dilapidated bicycle, the wheels of which refused to go round because of their mud-blocked hubs. But, using it as a ram, he was crashing through the undergrowth in search of the highway which would take him back to his billet.

His billet lay in a little French town, not far from St. Omer, where he was attending the intelligence course with his brother sniper officers of the division; and that day he had been out on a road reconnaissance, the report of which had to be handed to an officer stationed some miles away at a point previously indicated on the map. He had completed the report and found the collecting officer in record time. His present predicament was the result of an ill-fated desire to find a short cut home through the forest.

A map and a compass are apt to create a feeling of over-confidence in one's ability to get across any sort of country. Before he had travelled a mile the Sniper began to realise the difficulty of his task. The path he had been following soon proved impossible for cycling, and another mile on foot made him fervently wish that he had never left the road. The path had disappeared in a maze of willow stems, and, breaking through in an endeavour to pick it up again, he only found the maze getting denser and denser. When at length the willows thinned into an open space, he found it necessary to set his map and find his proper bearings.

It was no easy matter to get the map laid out level on the muddy uneven surface, but at length he succeeded. The needle of his compass swung evenly on either side of the line of magnetic north. He was fast working out his bearings and direction, when one of those mysterious forest winds lifted the map into the air and whirled it away among the undergrowth.

He spent half an hour vainly searching for it, and nearly an hour in getting back to the place where he had left his bicycle. His compass had disappeared into the mud. He discovered its whereabouts by the crunch of its breaking under his foot. Thereafter he was completely lost. For over an hour he dragged his useless bicycle through the clinging swampy undergrowth, now falling into the mud with the bicycle on top of him, now tripping over it and crashing against the trunk of a tree. But for the discovery of his adventure which would ensue, and the fear of the ridicule of his companions, he would have flung the machine into the undergrowth and pressed on without it. A man in less fit condition would have adopted this course long ago. But the Sniper, though thoroughly disgruntled, was just as thoroughly obstinate, and, viciously lunging the hapless machine forward, he at length struck the path down which we found him descending.

'Thank Heaven! There's the road at last,' he exclaimed as he saw the trees thinning in front of him.

'Oh! – Alfreda!' he yelled, a moment or two later.

He heard a metallic snap under his foot. Something had sprung up from the slime and struck his leg a violent blow just above the ankle. Looking down, he found the front wheel of his bicycle and his left leg caught together in the jaws of a man-trap. It was fortunate for him that the wheel warded off one of the jaws and his stout trench boot took much of the force from the other. But as it was, his ankle was numb from the blow, and he had enough medical knowledge to know what that numbness meant. If he did not reach the road quickly he would not be able to reach it at all.

Bending down, he searched for the spring of the trap, and, quickly releasing it, he extricated himself from its hold. Without waiting to examine his foot he pressed forward through the undergrowth. A few painful steps brought him to the edge of the wood, and, hopping across the containing ditch, he lay down thankfully by the roadside.

His only hope now of reaching his billet was to wait for some passing transport. His ankle was too painful to carry him any further, and his bicycle too clogged up with mud to move without a thorough cleaning. But the worn condition of the road spoke of the passing of many heavy lorries, and he had no fear about getting the lift he desired. Just at the time he was fully equal to commandeering a general's car if necessary.

From round a distant bend of the road he heard the hoot of a car. A few moments later the car swung into view. As it approached him he saw that it was an ambulance.

'Just the very thing,' he thought.

Two persons were sitting in the driving bench, a girl driver and a man in the dress of a private hospital orderly. They were laughing heartily together, and seemed very pleased with each other's company, even to the extent of ignoring his signals. He rose painfully out of the ditch, rage in his heart and a huge clod of mud in his hand. As the car passed him be savagely hurled the mud against the back of the mud-screen. The missile burst into slimy fragments, spraying impartially over the mechanism and the occupants of the car. The ambulance drew up with a jerk. A regular R.A.M.C. orderly looked out of the rear flaps and grinned. From the driving seat stepped down the girl driver and a very irate private orderly.

'What the deuce do you mean, fellah?' demanded the orderly, blustering up towards him.

The Sniper looked him over sourly. The man's appearance annoyed him. He had the viciously handsome face of the successful woman hunter, with the long glossy hair plastered back over the crown and delicately manicured finger-tips of the bounder about town. His uniform was elegantly tailored, with those little officer touches about it designed to show that the wearer was not an 'ordinary Tommy'. He was the sort of fit young masquerader in khaki whom every honest trenchman abhors, and the Sniper almost wished that he had another clod of mud in his hand.

'Pick up that bicycle, and put it into the car,' he said curtly.

The orderly looked at him viciously before taking a hesitating step or two towards the bicycle. He had just recognised the Sniper's muddy stars.

'Did yer hear that order?' demanded the R.A.M.C orderly, edging up to him. 'A little spryer on yer pins, me lad.'

The pukkah man had apparently long resented his connection with his superior inferior, and was only too glad of the chance to tell him off before an officer.

The orderly picked up the bicycle and slammed it into the car.

'A little more care with guv'ment property, me lad,' sang out the R.A.M.C. orderly. 'Take it out again, and put it back as guv'ment property ought to be treated. That's better, me lad,' he added, as his instructions were carried out.

The Sniper caught a faint twinkle of amusement in the girl's eyes at the sight of her late companion having his comb cut. It was quite evident that she had her own ideas about his character, even though she had been quite willing to be amused by his company.

'Where are you going to, driver?' he asked her.

'Zutkers!' she answered shortly, a trace of the old annoyance in her tone.

'Good! I wish you to take me to Nordes.'

'Really!'

He heard the sarcastic ring in her tone, but quietly ignored it, and turned towards the ambulance. At the first step his long-suffering leg sent such a thrill of agony through his frame, that he staggered and would have fallen had not the R.A.M.C. man darted forward and caught him.

'You have hurt your foot,' he heard the girl exclaim.

Immediately she was down on her knees in the mud, busy untying his boot. Her touch sent more agonising twinges through his foot, and when she pulled off his boot he nearly swore. But he watched her with interest nevertheless. She looked so pleased at the opportunity to show off her knowledge of first-aid treatment.

'You poor boy,' she said when the foot was at length laid bare.

Even the Sniper was surprised at the discolouring and swelling which his ankle displayed. She ripped open his field-dressing and began bandaging his leg. The R.A.M.C. expert looked on doubtfully. From his non-interference the equally expert Sniper deduced that the girl had a personality which demanded and secured the respect of those in contact with her. But her bandaging was too dreadful for an ex-medical student to tolerate. It secured no support for his ankle, and when he stood up the folds collapsed over each other like a badly-rolled puttee.

'Excuse me,' he said, and, putting his foot on the car step, he began to unroll the bandage.

'Here, you!' he ordered, holding out the gauze pad to the private orderly. 'Soak that in water.'

'Look slippy, me lad,' said the pukkah man. 'You'll find a water-bottle in the van.'

The orderly took the pad surlily, and drenched it. The Sniper wrung out the excess water, and started to apply a cold compress to his ankle. The girl had drawn away from him, abashed at his rebuff. But he noticed as the bandaging proceeded that she took more and more interest in his work.

'My, you can bandage, sir!' said the R.A.M.C. man admiringly.

'Simkins,' said the girl, with all a woman's anxiety to reassert her prestige, 'please clear out one of the stretchers.'

'It is quite unnecessary. I am going to ride in front,' said the Sniper quietly.

'But that is Mr. Hatch's place.'

'Mister,' repeated the Sniper in a tone of voice which made R.A.M.C. gurgle with laughter.

Hatch had already climbed up to the driving seat and the Sniper hobbled up to him grimly.

'Get down,' he said.

Hatch made no motion to obey.

'Get down,' the Sniper repeated, thus putting the fellow technically as well as morally in the wrong.

Again the latter made no movement. Without more ado the Sniper gripped his tunic collar and slung him into the middle of the road.

Hatch scrambled to his feet and rapped out an exclamation – a filthy oath which made the girl bite her lip with vexation. In an instant the Sniper had hobbled across and had him by the scruff of the neck.

'You little swine,' he growled, shaking him until the teeth chattered in his head.

'Aw, leggo! You're murderin' me,' yelled Hatch. He collapsed in the road as soon as the Sniper released him.

'Stand over there! At attention! You may stand at ease, or do anything you like when I'm gone,' ordered the Sniper.

'Now,' he said, motioning the girl to her seat.

'You are not leaving Mr. Hatch behind?' demanded the girl.

'I am.'

'But it is a fifteen-mile walk.'

'Well, he can choose for himself. But if he comes along with the car, I shall clap him in the guard-room as soon as we arrive for gross impertinence and insubordination. Both very serious offences out here.'

'Don't worry about me,' said Hatch hastily to the girl.

'I shall not go either, if you leave him behind,' she said rebelliously.

'I'm afraid I must ask you to go, driver,' said the Sniper quietly.

The girl climbed up to her seat and hid her burning cheeks in her preparations for starting. The Sniper climbed in after her. She jerked in the clutch so quickly that he listened for the C-r-r-p! of the stripping gear. The car lunged forward and threw him on to his seat. The unexpected movement twisted his leg, and the pain of it nearly made him faint. He saw the girl's quick glance of contrition. But he recovered himself instantly, and she at once gave all her attention to the driving again.

The Sniper leaned back in his seat and watched her curiously. The pain had lessened in his ankle, and his irritation over Hatch's insolence was passing away. He began to feel that he had been rather abrupt with the girl, and wished she would give him an opportunity to become more friendly. But the girl drove on without taking the slightest notice of him.

Something in the poise of her head struck him as being slightly familiar. The tilt of her chin, the direct way she had of looking ahead. Where had he

seen it before? He suddenly remembered the photograph he had taken from
Cissie Rankine's dug-out. The likeness was identical. This girl was Maimie
Rankine.

'Good Lord! What will Cissie say?' he murmured.

'Does your foot hurt?' asked the girl, looking round at him.

'No, thank you,' said the Sniper.

He nearly addressed her by name, but something stopped him. He felt
unwilling to disclose his identity. He had annoyed her; she did not want to
speak to him. But to 'Mr. Jackson', her brother's friend, she would have to
be polite. If only he had recognised her at the beginning how differently he
would have acted! He cursed himself under his breath for having allowed
his irritation to make him so tactless.

This was the girl who had written asking her brother to bring him to
meet her. She would not want to meet him now, and he was sorry. A finer
girl he had never seen. She was as lovely as a man could desire, of that type
of beauty which looks good at the wicket or bunker, when a difficult ball
has to be taken and a partner not to be let down; just the sort of girl whom
thousands of town-hardened johnnies would only have been too pleased to
take about with them and show off to their friends.

After a while his sense of humour began to reassert itself. He began to
picture Cissie's amazement when he heard the story. He could see the boy
almost wringing his hands in dismay. Cissie had been so enthusiastic about
his meeting his sister. He gave a chuckle of amusement over the picture.

'Oh, it's too funny!' he exclaimed involuntarily.

'What is too funny?' demanded the girl. She had been watching him for
some time, wondering what was the matter.

The Sniper pulled himself up in confusion. She had such a straight way
of looking at the person she addressed. He saw that her face was splashed
with mud, and before he could stop himself he had muttered, 'You have got
a spot of mud on your nose.'

He could not help laughing again as he realised what he had said. The girl
glanced at him wrathfully.

'I'm not a bit surprised,' she said coldly, looking at the mud-spattered
wind-screen.

She drew out a small mirror from somewhere among the folds of
her leathern kit, examined her face carefully, and proceeded to wipe
off the offending spot with a minute pocket-handkerchief. The Sniper
interestedly watched the proceedings. He was not a bit surprised when
a powder-puff followed. The sight of this khaki-clad girl calmly dabbing

powder on her nose proved too much for his equanimity, and he gave a smothered laugh.

The girl coolly wiped off the excess powder without seeming to notice his amusement. The Sniper checked his ill-timed mirth and began to scrape away the mud which covered him thickly. Looking up, he saw the girl watching him. Her glance wandered from his collar-badges to his D.S.O. and M.C. ribbons. He noticed a look of comprehension growing in her eyes.

'You are from the 2nd Eastshires, my brother's regiment. You are Mr. Jackson!' she exclaimed.

'Yes, Miss Rankine,' he said.

She released her hold of the steering wheel in her surprise, and he caught it just in time to prevent the car running off the road. She resumed her hold of the wheel at once and drove on for a few yards in silence. Then she suddenly broke into a peal of laughter. He liked the sound of it. Her voice was rich and musical, and full of life.

'And you recognised me some time ago, and did not tell me,' she said. 'I agree with you. It is too funny.'

Again she was laughing, and he joined in with her. They seemed suddenly to have become old acquaintances.

'Really, you ought to have told me at once who you were,' she said. 'I wonder what Johnny will say?'

'You mean your brother? We call him Cissie. Yes, I thought about that some time ago. He will be rather surprised.'

He admired the perfectly natural way in which she was accepting the situation. After the first surprise, the scene might have been a drawing-room in London, so collected and calm was her manner. They talked away to each other, he giving her recent regimental history, and she listening, save for a leading query or two. He had tried to talk about theatres and latest revues. But she had quietly pulled him up, and led him back to the regiment. Her father had served in the same battalion, she told him, before graduating into the ranks of the higher staff, and he soon gathered that she considered herself as much a part of the regiment as he was himself. The journey went all too quickly for the Sniper.

'We are almost at Nordes now,' said the girl at length. 'I suppose you will go into hospital with that foot.'

The Sniper had forgotten all about his sprained ankle. 'Good gracious! no,' he said. 'I'll get the doctor to send me back to our rest billets. The course I am on is nearly finished. The battalion has gone into long rest billets now.

I'll be as comfortable there as in hospital. I'm going to share your brother's billet, by the way.'

'Yes, I know. I called in to see him two or three days ago. I often pass quite near you on the Calais road on my way to St. Omer for stores.'

'Do you? On what days, and at what time?'

'As a rule, Fridays and Wednesdays in the afternoon. But why do you ask?'

'I expect to be passing that way very often. I should like to meet you again.'

'I shall be very pleased to see you,' said the girl, quite naturally.

She drew the car up opposite the field ambulance, and the Sniper descended.

'I'm awfully pleased to have met you, Miss Rankine,' he said, lingering by the car bonnet.

'And so am I,' the girl said frankly. 'Having heard so much about you from my brother, I was looking forward to meeting you. I felt quite disappointed at not seeing you when I went to call on Johnny. Au revoir.'

In the dressing station the Sniper listened to the noise of the engine as it faded away down the road, and so disconnected were his replies to the doctor's questions that the latter began to suspect a much more serious injury than a sprained ankle. Only with difficulty did the Sniper manage to escape being sent to hospital. But the cold compress had done its work, and that evening a limber bore him off to the little village where his battalion was billeted.

CHAPTER XX

Rest Period Impressions

L E REPOS WAS THE name of the Sniper's billet. Few houses justified the name more truly. Squarely facing the main road, which forked on either side, the solid appearance of the building marked it out from all the other houses of the village. Even though the war had called away the builders before their work was finished, and composite wooden blinds had to serve in default of glass in some of the windows, not for a moment could the passer-by doubt that comfort, as well as rest, dwelt therein. And Madame who owned the place saw that her home lived up to appearances.

Madame was small, and placid, and old. But her light-treading foot, and bright sparkling eye, made her look twenty years younger than she really was. Madame was young enough at heart to glory in her youthfulness. Though when the Sniper remarked on it, she would protest volubly that she was an old, a very, very old woman. Yet her eyes would shine with almost girlish fire, and her glance become so roguish that the Sniper would say, in mock reproach:

'Oh, Madame! Vous êtes une grande coquette.' And Madame would struggle hard not to appear pleased. But her eyes would betray her by shining the more brilliantly, and sometimes she would let drop a gay anecdote or two of the time when she was belle of the village, fifty years and more ago.

Then the Sniper would tell her. 'Madame, vous êtes très méchante.' And the old lady would rush from the room with a great show of indignation, only to return in a very short time with a bottle of rare red wine, all dusty and cobwebby, as befitted its stay of years in the cellar of her former home. And Madame would drink to the health of her gallant young officers, and they would drink to the light of Madame's eyes, so that the old dame wondered greatly at their 'manières polies'; for never before had she imagined that the British could be so polite.

All through those days of rest and training, Madame tended her two officer guests as though they were her sons. Nothing was too good for them. Nor did she spare her scoldings when they tarried too long about changing their clothes after a drenching. 'They were just her boys,' she told them, when they protested against the trouble she took on their account. And the night before he left, she bent over the Sniper as he sat at some writing, and kissed him. 'Ah, M'sieur Shagson,' she whispered, 'your mother must indeed have been blessed of Our Lady.'

Adam Saunders tapped at the door of Le Repos, and entered.

'Serjent Ferguson's compliments, sir, and would you tell him whaat you will be doing with the section thiss affternoon?'

'Road reporting, lance-corporal,' said the Sniper. 'Fall in 2.30. Help yourself, Saunders.'

'Best respects, sir,' said Adam, raising to his lips a generous tot of the Sniper's whisky.

'Letters for censoring, sir,' said Geordie Saunders, entering the billet after the road-reporting parade was over.

'Thank you, Saunders. Help yourself,' said the Sniper.

'Best of health, sir,' said Geordie a moment or two later.

'Wull ye sign this indent for a pair o' bits, sir?' said Old Dan after tea-time.

'Right, Haggarty. Help yourself,' said the Sniper.

'Here's luck tae ye, sir,' said the corporal. 'Guid nicht, sir.'

'Come in, Ferguson,' said the Sniper as he heard the sergeant's knock just after Last Post had been played. 'Are these battalion orders. Right! You know where the bottle is. Here are to-morrow morning's instructions.'

'Serjent Ferguson's compliments, sir –' said Adam Saunders next day.

Then Geordie would bring the letters, Old Dan his indent, and finally Sergeant Ferguson would come with the daily battalion orders. Poor fellows! They had been accustomed to their daily 'dram' almost from childhood, and whisky was unprocurable for the non-commissioned ranks in France. Therefore they looked on their officer as some merciful dispenser of Providence able to import whisky by the case, and tapped him, each at his appointed time, as regularly as the clock. But John Brown never came.

'Ho! ho! ho!' Madame would laugh scornfully after the sergeant's departure, holding up the attenuated whisky bottle for the Sniper's examination.

'Ah, wisest of women,' the Sniper would murmur. 'Do you think I do not know what they are up to? Do you think they do not know that I know? But they winked at Homer down the road and 'e winked back, the same as I.'

'Monsieur Homer? Qui est-il?' asked the mystified old lady.

The Calais road ran along some rolling high ground about a mile away from the little village. You could just see the end houses peeping out from behind the shoulder of a forest bluff, and even these were hidden wall-high by orchards and saplings, giving the village an appearance of secludedness and quiet, very pleasing to the eyes of tired wayfarers on the high road.

The ground in between was hedgeless save for the tree-studded enclosures of isolated farm steadings, and showed the multifarious nature of its uses by the alternating strips of colour distinctive of the various crops. Patches of brown earth, rain-beaten and ruffled, with long low mounds at each end, spoke of tuber crops grown and stored safely away. Narrow patches of stubble next, bounded by stretches of green, with the clean striated banks of ploughland beyond, showing up in marked contrast to the lifeless blur of the tuber land succeeding.

Wild game, four-legged and winged, abounded here, for the use of fire-arms is severely restricted in war-time to the French civilian. But sometimes the sound of a discreet shot would be heard, generally at early dawn or late evening; and those who heard it would mentally decide that it was sniper Geordie Saunders bringing down a hare on the run with a .303 bullet, to grace his section's – and his officer's – table.

The ground on the other side of the road rose gradually to a long low crest, hummocked here and there by buttes which had once been tree-covered. Only a patch or two was cultivated. The rest was moorland, where cattle wandered loose, and pigs nuzzled under the shrub clumps in company with wilder scavengers. It was fine country for riding, and the Sniper often of an afternoon took the company charger and rode it like a mad thing from butte to butte and down the long slope to the roadway.

But on Wednesdays and Fridays he climbed the highest mound, whence he could sweep with his glasses a long stretch of the stately highway beneath. Always at the same time an ambulance car would swing into view round a distant turn, and the Sniper would come galloping down just in time to straddle the road and force the driver to come to a standstill.

'Good afternoon, Miss Rankine,' he would say.

'Good afternoon, Mr. Jackson. What an exceedingly troublesome person you are! Do you ever do any work at all?'

But the pukkah RA.M.C. man would grin a welcome out of the rear flaps, and Maimie was much more kind than her first greeting hinted.

'Who is that little girl you are always meeting on the Calais road?' asked Big Bill one day, suddenly bursting in on him as he was seated at tea with Cissie.

'What little girl?'

'Why, the little ambulance driver.'

'Shut up, fathead,' said the Sniper with such emphasis that Big Bill instantly took the hint.

'You have not been meeting Maimie to-day, Ronny, have you?' asked Cissie when Bill had departed.

'I have.'

'Oh you rotter! Why didn't you tell me? I've only seen her once. I'm coming with you the next time.'

'You are not,' said the Sniper decisively.

'Oh that's it, is it? But I am coming. After all, she is my sister and not yours.'

'Thank the Lord for that!' murmured the Sniper dream-ily.

The old church stood in the centre of the village about thirty yards from Le Repos. Its foundation dated from the Spanish Netherlands, yet it looked strangely modern to men accustomed to the ruin of the trench area. A chime of silvery bells called the villagers to service, and of an evening the Sniper would hear the rich strains of the organ sounding from the old-fashioned loft beneath the spire, and the tender quavering notes of the aged priest intoning the chants of the Benediction service. The Sniper was not a Roman Catholic, but often he attended these services. More often he visited the church during the day, when the building was empty and he could be alone with his thoughts.

The interior decoration of the church, as with most other country churches in France, inclined to the gaudy. But there was some fine old wood-carving, and the stonework of the apse and the altar itself was a delight to the eye which measures architectural beauty by its simplicity and natural strength of design. The confessional box was a work of art wrought in the time of Parma. One half of the floor-space was occupied by chairs turned away from the lectern, so that the congregation could kneel, facing the preacher, on the low-placed seats and rest their brows reverently on the high-topped backs. The names of the owners were engraved on each chair. There were Allans and Leslies among them. The Sniper wondered if these names were relics of his own regiment when it fought in the French service three centuries before. The walls were adorned with plaster and porcelain saints, with the names of the donors inscribed below them. 'Pour la famille Massemin' read one inscription. 'Yes,' said Madame proudly, when the Sniper mentioned it to her. 'That is the gift of my family. And did you see our burial stone in the graveyard?' About the end of the first week of the rest period another visitor appeared in the church, a private soldier of the Sniper's old company. His visits gradually became longer and longer. Sometimes the Sniper would find him there in the early morning, and on returning in the afternoon the man would still be there. The private always knelt in the same seat, and the Sniper wondered at his piety. He also wondered how the man managed to get so much time off parade.

About the same time strange rumours began to circulate about the Roman Catholic padre. The various messes whispered to each other that he was constantly appearing at meal-times, and always accepting the invitation naturally extended to him to sit down and eat. Moreover, he ate with an avidity which made Big Bill Davidson talk mysteriously about preliminary diabetes symptoms. The padre had a billet to himself, and was supposed to take his food there. Only occasionally did he appear to do so; and his next meal-time appearance at any of the other billets would always set the occupants thinking where they could replenish their devastated food supplies. Certainly something had gone wrong with the worthy priest.

One morning towards the end of the third week the priest entered the church. The Sniper was examining an inscription on the wall behind the reading-desk. The private soldier was kneeling devoutly in his accustomed place. The priest made straight towards the kneeling form, a look of fury on his usually placid face. To the surprise of the Sniper he seized the man by the scruff of the neck and dragged him roughly out of the church. The man's protesting cries echoed through the church from the vestibule – 'Oh! your Riverince! Your Riverince!' Amid the priest's angry denunciations the Sniper caught the one significant word – 'Rations.'

In an hour the story was over the village and the regiment was shaking its sides with glee. The man was the priest's servant. Instead of attending to his duties, chief among which was the drawing and preparing his master's rations he had taken to spending his time in church, trusting to the padre's religious scruples to enable him to continue doing so without molestation. And the poor padre had been reduced to begging in order to escape starvation.

'Padre, Padre!' said Big Bill reproachfully. 'That you should interrupt a poor man's devotions to demand attendance to your carnal desires! I'm surprised at you.'

The shrine of Our Lady of the Cross-roads stood just outside the village, where the two great French highways swept up from the interior to make to Her their united reverence ere sweeping onward to the firing-line on the business of war. The big lumbering British transports passed by unceasingly; and that there might be no mistake as to their mission, often during the morning and evening quiet, the light breezes would bear to the ears of the worshippers the low thudding roll of the guns, and the softer, quicker murmurs which spoke of some distant trench turmoil.

In spite of the low-toned muttering into which the mellowing distance transformed their wrath, these guns had a menace reaching almost to the shrine itself. Not so very far up the roads the disfigured foliage and scarred trunks of the trees showed where the German long-distance artillery had searched for the village. And sometimes a transport down from the trench area, its slate-painted sides spattered with white raw wood scars, the canvas of its hood all torn and slashed from the shrapnel, would pause at the shrine while the driver descended to give thanks to Our Lady for the protection she had afforded him.

It was no ordinary shrine that Our Lady inhabited. Its size, its golden vessels and well-garnished interior, spoke of a munificence on the part of the donor rare even in a country so richly dowered with sacred buildings as France. A tablet on the wall told the passer-by that the donor was Madame la Marquise, chatelaine of the old château whose blue-slated pinnacles appeared above the woodlands a kilometre or so to the right. Then one could understand. For in stately old France *noblesse oblige* is an imperative transcending all other laws.

The tablet stated that the shrine had been built to the memory of Madame's husband, who fell in the War of '71. Perhaps some day she will add another inscription; for in this war of the Revanche, Madame has suffered again. And she to whom the Mother of Women granted consolation in her first bereavement, came but the more often to worship at the shrine that her greater grief might be assuaged.

Many others came also to seek the protection of Our Lady for their loved ones, for many brave men have gone from the village in the service of France. Stacks and stacks of little blue wooden swords fixed to the walls of the shrine gave their number. For each absent one a taper was lit every evening, and placed in one of the many holders before the altar, so that as soon as darkness fell the interior of the shrine was ablaze with light; and those who entered from the darkened roadway were struck with wonder at the glory of Our Lady, and bowed in common adoration with the many silent worshippers who knelt there.

Thither each twilight came Gabrielle, granddaughter of Madame who owned Le Repos, Jeanne her friend, the miller's daughter, and Marie of the farm by Le Temple, the friend of both; to set up their lighted tapers and to pray that Henri, Jacques, and Paul might return safely from the war.

Gabrielle was the light and joy of the Sniper's billet. In the morning when she met either Cissie or himself, she had always a merry quip or gibe to flick at them; and throughout the day, as they trained hard in the fields surrounding the farm, they would hear her singing at her work, so that their men sloped arms to the tune of some old French folk-song, and marked time to the stirring rhythm of the 'Marseillaise'.

They seldom saw her in the evening; only when she came into the big farm-kitchen to write a letter. Then there was a look in her eyes which had made the Sniper half-laughingly question old Madame as to the reason. And she had replied: 'Yes! But for the war Gabrielle would have been betrothed.'

Later she told him that Gaby's fiancé was still in training. 'Just now it is all right. But there will be heart-sickness for little Gaby when Henri goes to the trenches,' she added wistfully. For Madame had felt that heart-sickness. After '71 she had been a widow.

There came a time when the Sniper noticed an anxious look creeping into Gaby's eyes. She still sang the 'Marseillaise' as often; but the other songs not so frequently. Madame told him that Henri had gone to the trenches. From the intelligence reports he knew that there was trouble in Henri's part of the line.

He did his best to cheer the drooping spirits of the little French girl. But what skill can cure an aching heart? Will any trenchman ever forget the feeling of helplessness in his soul at the sight of that terrible heart-sick look in the faces of the women of France when they know that their loved ones are in danger?

Then one morning he did not see Gaby. Cissie told him that he had heard her crying. He noticed that Madame's eyes were red with weeping. Throughout the day he listened in vain for the 'Marseillaise'. Nor did he hear it again for many days.

Dusk was falling over the village. The faint glimmer from the tightly-shuttered windows of the shrine told that the worshippers were already assembling. Thither came Gabrielle, Jeanne her friend, and Marie the friend of both.

Gabrielle was the last to arrive. As she came through the darkening shadows, that quick intuitive sense of disaster which the war has given to the women of France made Jeanne and Marie strangely silent. No greeting passed between the three. For an instant they stood gazing mutely at each other. Another instant and Gabrielle was sobbing in the arms of her friends.

Jeanne gently took the three tapers, and set them up in their wonted niches. Together the girls knelt down on the worn ledge in front of the altar. Only the Mother of Women, who through death agony became glorified, can soothe the aching heart of woman bereaved.

The faint threatening roll of the guns came down the evening breeze. The shadows seemed to draw together more quickly to hide the suffering land from view. But inside the shrine there was light as well as sorrow, symbolical of the greatness and grandeur of the spirit of France, which no trial or sorrow can extinguish, which only shines the more brightly the greater her travail becomes.

CHAPTER XXI

The Section at Home

BEFORE THE REST PERIOD was completed the Germans attacked and succeeded in capturing a portion of the trenches formerly held by the Sniper's division. The rest period was at once cut short and the division was ordered up to recapture the position, all counter-attacks by the troops in the sector having failed to dislodge the Germans. The order came late one evening. Before the morning two brigades of the division were billeted in Poperinghe. The other brigade had gone on alone to carry out the attack. The Sniper's brigade followed as soon as darkness fell, to relieve the first brigade, or to reinforce them in a second attack should the first attempt fail. Six hours before the attack the Sniper's regiment arrived at a reserve position about two miles from the firing-line, where they were to spend the night and the following day.

In taking over a new position keen competition always takes place among the units for the most comfortable billets. It is generally a case of first come first served. The Sniper managed to secure a fine big sandbagged barn for his section in which several stacks of fodder were stored. Much to the delight of his men, he took it upon himself to order the stacks to be served out as bedding, and personally superintended the arrangements for the section's comfort.

He was hurrying away to secure decent quarters for himself before the other officers should commandeer everything, when the signalling sergeant appealed to him to find accommodation for the signallers. This section had no officer in charge of it, and a section without an officer in France is like an orphaned Ishmaelite when it comes to securing a share of the good things in the trench area. It is the officer who always fights the section's battles and secures fair treatment for his men.

The Sniper immediately set about to secure a hole in which to stow the signallers away, and by dint of much insistence he forced another unit to disgorge sufficient of its shelter to accommodate the derelict section. But by the time this had been arranged all the other officers had long ago completed their billeting and settled themselves down for the night, and the only sleeping-place the Sniper could find was a muddy corner of a ruined stable already overcrowded with the horses of the mounted officers. After being twice stamped on by a restless charger, he abandoned the stable and made his way down to spend the night in comfort with his section.

Half a dozen men bade him welcome when he entered the barn. The sergeant and Old Dan had arranged a sleeping-place for themselves apart from the section in a dismantled stall, and they at once surrendered their quarters to their officer. A store of charcoal had been discovered and rifled, and a glowing brazier stood in the centre of the floor, on which the section's rations were cooking. As soon as the Sniper had deposited his kit, he was ushered to the most comfortable seat by the brazier. The section gathered round him in order of precedence. They shared their rations with him, insisting on his having the best of everything, and he leaned back on his comfortable truss of hay thinking slightingly of the sanctions of rank and discipline which had compelled him first to seek quarters apart from his men and had led him – to a muddy stable.

After the meal he withdrew to his corner and dug himself under the fodder. But sleep would not come. His brain was throbbing with thought impulses, vanishing immediately when he set his mind to trace them to their source, but ever renewing their impact as soon as he relaxed his mental control. It was not concern for what the morrow might bring. He had seen too many strong men shot down, not in the heat of fight, but in cold blood; and the sight had hardened him. His unrest was deeper-seated. Right down among the primordial instincts of his selfhood, some unknown influence was working. He was like a man who, listening to a glorious orchestra, feels some kindred chord awakened within him, whose vibrations send through his being thrills of vague longing for an ideal something, something indeterminate and constantly elusive. He gave up trying to sort out the medley of ideas and impulses flitting across his consciousness and, raising himself on his elbow, with head pillowed on his palm, he took to watching the group of snipers sitting round the fire.

The sergeant had retired to his sleeping-place and the majority of the section had followed his example. But Old Dan still sat by the fire with about half a dozen others busily writing letters. John Brown sat a little apart from the main group, the only man not writing. He had just refused Matthew Oldheim's offer of writing materials. His Oxford accent contrasted incongruously with the American's queer dialect and mode of speech, and the Sniper studied him interestedly. Now and then the man looked up from the fire at one or other of his companions. Each time a curious, half-mocking smile played on his twisted features. Evidently some demon of unrest was troubling him also.

'Writing to your girl, Billy?' he said at length to one of the younger snipers.

'Yes!' said Billy, looking up for a moment, and immediately going on with his writing again.

'How did you manage to get a girl, Billy?'

'Ah dinna ken,' Billy replied simply.

The boy did not immediately resume his writing. The faraway look in his eyes showed that in fancy he was wandering down some country road with his simple Scottish lass, and possibly wondering to himself how such a clod as he had ever managed to win so glorious a girl.

'Neither do I, Billy,' said John Brown coolly.

The boy's face flushed as he grasped the full rudeness of the remark. But he kept his temper manfully.

'Ah'm no surprised at ye wonderin' hoo Ah cam tae get a girl,' he said. 'An' if ye saw her, ye'd wonder still mair.'

He fell to with his pen again. Brown turned his attention to the American, who was scribbling on a patent paper block.

'Are you writing to your girl too, Oldheim?' he asked.

'Yep!' said the American without pausing in his task. 'Had her twenty-seven years. My moder. No use for any oder girl. Oh, darn you, Brown fellow!' he added. 'You got me muddled. "We are in rest billets just now at –" How you spell the place we'm just left, Billy?'

Billy spelt out the name to him. 'But we're no there the noo, Matthy,' he said wonderingly.

'Nope!' said Oldheim. 'But you don't tink I one big jay goin' tellin' de old lady dat we'm goin' up to battle. Guess when we'm done, time enough to tell her. Get de ol' lady writin' to King George if she tink I'm in trouble. Sure! An' you, Mister Brown? Ain't you got no moder to write to, 'stead of jollyin' Billy boy?'

'No, Massa Oldheim. I ain't got no moder,' said Brown.

'Den I sorry for you,' responded the American, going on with his scribbling.

There was silence for a minute or two. The Sniper fancied Brown's face grew more bitter. He eyed first one of the snipers and then the other very critically, as if testing each one for his possibilities as a fresh victim.

'Oh, you fellows are the uttermost edge. You're giving me the creeps,' he burst out. 'Here we are on the fringe of an attack. To-morrow you and I may be with yesterday's seven thousand years; by which Fitzgerald meant to say that one tiny blue-rimmed hole in the forehead would let in all the mystery, all the knowledge, that man and God has learned since the beginning of time. And what are you doing? – Writing to women creatures who wear thick boots and woollen combinations, none of them knowing what the feel of silk next their skin is like; none of them with an idea in their heads outside the latest ailment of Sarah Jones' baby, or the latest hat shape in Messrs. Pumpkin, Bumpkin, and Sons' sale of up-to-date, two-seasons-back goods.'

'Look here, Jone, just stop it,' said Old Dan, glancing up from his writing. 'We've heard your opeenions o' weemin before, an' we dinna agree, an' dinna want tae hear them agane. Every wumman isna bad, and each one o' us here, 'ceptin' yerself, has got haud o' the richt kind. Get awa' tae your bed, laddie.'

'Why do you infer that I got hold of the wrong kind, Dan?' asked Brown.

'Ah'm auld enough tae be your grandfather, Jone, an' Ah ken fine. If ye'll tak an auld man's advice ye'll get rid o' your ideas. They're no richt. They canna be richt. Awa' an' lie doon, laddie. Ye'll find a wee drap Scotch in ma flask if ye canna gae tae sleep.'

The Sniper had often noticed the curious bond of sympathy connecting the two men and the influence the elder exercised over the younger. He was not at all surprised when Brown rose and moved off to his sleeping-place. He said good night to Old Dan, but the others he ignored. It was his custom to ignore them, save only when he gibed at their little failings. From time to time the Sniper heard him moving uneasily about among the hay.

'He's an awfy chap. I doot he's a bit crackit,' whispered Billy as soon as Brown had gone. 'He must have gotten in tow with an awfy wumman tae mak' him blether like that. Have ye ever had a lassie, Matthy?' he asked after a moment or two of reflection.

'Yep! William. Some.' Oldheim replied quaintly. 'Once I see one at a window in Noo York City. She called me in. I ses, "Dat a nice gel," so I goes in. Find husband waitin' to hold me up for my dollars. Husband and I in hospital for about a month after.'

There was a little ripple of laughter from the snipers, and Oldheim continued.

'Den I saw a nice gel in a saloon in Piccadilly. Went home wit' her. Soon as I got to her apartment, she puts her arms roun' my neck, an' steals my tie-pin. I gets it back, an' clears out quick. She follows me to de street hollarin' an' hollarin'. I ses, "What you hollarin'? Want police, eh?" She ses, "Yep, you dirty Yank. If you don't give me two pound I give you in charge for assault. I'll let de public know 'bout you bein' in my apartment. What you say now?" "I don' care if de King know I in your apartment," ses I. So I pushes her into de basement an' beat it quick.'

'But have ye never met a decent lassie?' Billy asked when the laughter and chaffing were over.

'Yep! I met decent gel once. Very decent gel,' Oldheim replied. 'Sat next her in de stalls at de Hammersmit's Empire. She ses she take me home. After de show we get somet'ing to eat. Den we get into an automobile an' drive an' drive right de oder side of London. We get out, an' I pays de driver. Near on four dollars. Den we walks 'bout half a mile. Den de girl ses, "You wait here till I see if de coast is clear." I waits for one hour an' she don' come back. Guess I'd be waitin' dere yet for dat girl to come back. Had to walk all night to find de place I was stayin' in. Dat little gel decent, Billy. Sure!'

'Did ye no have anither shot at gettin' a lassie?'

'Nope! Guess I too dam ugly,' said Oldheim calmly.

'Ah'll gie ye a knock-doon tae a sister o' mines if ye like.'

'Can't do dat till after de war.'

'Och, ay, man. Ah'll write tae ma lassie tellin' ye're gaun tae write tae her sister Bella. An' Ah'll tell her what like o' chap ye are. Bella will write ye a' richt. She's just cast oot wi' a lad. Gaun! Write noo,' urged Billy.

'What'll I say?' asked Oldheim, opening out his writing block.

'Say ye are a lonely sodger, an' would she excuse you just dropping her a line for something better tae dae. Say ye've heard frae me that she's oot o' a lad the noo, an' that Ah reckomendit ye tae apply for the vacancy. Tell her aboot the fecht we're noo gaun up tae. Pile it on thick. Lassies fairly like that. Say ye've heard she's a graun' baker, and that ye likit that bite o' one o' her scones Ah gied ye. She'll mebbe send ye some.'

Oldheim scribbled industriously for a minute or two.

'I got a photograph here, Billy?' he suggested hesitatingly.

'Naw! Naw! Dinna send that the noo. It'll dae after ye get the scones,' said Billy hastily.

'Isn't it fine tae have a lassie tae write tae, noo?' he asked when Oldheim had finished his letter.

'Dat's de first letter I sent to any gel,' said Oldheim. 'Do you tink she will reply, Billy?'

'Ay! She'll write ye. Even if it's only for the fun o' the thing. She's a richt game stick, is Bella! A guid lassie tae,' added Billy sententiously.

'Which lassie are ye writin' tae, Geordie?' he enquired of young Geordie Smith. 'The Bedford one or your reg'lar one.'

'Baith o' them,' replied Geordie. 'Ah had tae write the Bedford lassie, for she sendit me a packet o' cigs last week.'

'Ay, ye had tae write her,' remarked Billy cannily.

'Gode! Ah wonder if Auld Dan'l is writin' a lassie. He's takin' a richt lang time over it,' Geordie whispered mischievously.

The eyes of the circle fixed themselves on the corporal. He had finished his letter and was coaxing a huge number of sheets into an altogether inadequate envelope.

'Are ye writin' tae your lass, Dan'l?' asked Billy.

Old Dan looked round him with the air of a man wakened to the realisation of his true whereabouts out of a dream of home.

'Yes, Billy,' he answered.

'Fancy an auld man like you havin' a lassie, Dan'l,' said Billy reprovingly.

'An' why should Ah no', seein' Ah've been maimed tae her syne forty-twa year?' demanded Old Dan.

'Ye've been a fine lang time ower your letter,' young Geordie tactlessly remarked.

'Ye impident young deevil,' roared the old fellow. 'Ye'd be a lang time yersel' if ye had been on the pitheid afore ye were nine, same as Ah was, 'stead o' gaun tae a fancy board-schule till ye were fowerteen, learnin' nithin' better than hoo tae gie lip tae your betters. Ah'll put ye ower ma knee an' gie ye a guid skelpin' if—'

'Ah beg your pardin', Dan'l,' said Geordie hastily. 'Ah didna mean tae gie ye lip.'

'Ye never could mean onythin',' said Old Dan cuttingly. 'Ye're but a puir ignorant boy, George. Only fit tae haud the cuddy by the heid. But turn in, laddies,' he added in a softer tone. 'Ye'll a' be sair put tae it the morn' if things dinna gae richt wi' the attack.'

One by one the snipers disappeared from the firelight. The Sniper heard the hay being tossed about as each man eased it and teased it to suit his comfort. In a very few minutes all were asleep. But still sleep would not come to him. Rising silently, he stealthily picked his way over the forms of his men and sat down by the fire. With a start, almost guilty, he realised that

John Brown was sitting within a yard of him. The dying glow outlined the man's face from the shadows, and the Sniper marvelled at what he saw there. The bitter gibing twist was gone from the features. In its place was a new expression, curiously tender, the look of a man reflecting on a sorrow from which all bitterness has passed away.

'Can't you get to sleep, Brown?'

The man swung round sharply at the Sniper's question.

'Oh! That you, Jackson?' he said, using the surname so naturally that the Sniper did not even notice the slip. 'No, I can't get to sleep at all, to-night. But I don't think I want to go to sleep, at least not just yet.'

He turned to look into the fire again, and for a minute or two there was silence. Each man steadily examined the glowing stove. From somewhere out of the night came the boom of a distant gun. The sound seemed to rouse Brown to a new train of thought.

'Does it not strike you as curious,' he began abruptly, 'that you and I, both school and 'varsity men, should be awake and restless, while the working classes around us' – with a wave of his hand he indicated the sleeping snipers – 'should be sleeping peacefully and contentedly without a care for the morrow? I wonder what conclusions a sociologist would draw! – Sense of responsibility of the classes; the want of it in the masses. Healthy imagination; unimaginative health. What? I wonder.'

'He would envy them their coolness, anyhow,' said the Sniper. 'The sight of these simple fellows coolly writing to their girls and then going quietly to sleep as if they were safe in rest billets! Why! They are simply great.'

'They are,' said Brown, with such feeling that the Sniper faced round and looked at him questioningly.

'Yes, Jackson, I mean it,' said Brown quietly. 'I've done nothing but sneer at them since I came into the section. You heard me to-night. How they've stood it I don't know. It's all come from what happened nearly three years ago. I was engaged then. I left Oxford to join the Army, and while I was away slogging it with Kitchener's mob, a civilian fellow turned up and made all the running with my girl. He had made a fortune in war profits. He offered her a share. She accepted and turned me down. It seemed such a reversal of the scales of justice that I thought the whole universe gone wrong, especially the girl part of it. I've seen things crooked ever since – until to-night. Do you know, Jackson, I think I've got a new soul to-night. I've got just the feeling that Browning must have had when he wrote, "God's in his heaven – all's right with the world"!'

Brown leaned forward and threw some more charcoal into the brazier, poked at the glowing mass with an old bayonet, and interestedly watched each scintillating splinter leaping over the brazier top as the heat disintegrated the parent mass. He seemed to be playing for time to consider how best to explain to an outsider what was not yet wholly clear to himself.

'It's been coming ever since Old Dan began fathering and big-brothering me. Why he should have troubled I don't know. He is just the largest-hearted man I've ever met. Did you see his face to-night while he was writing? No? I did. It taught me things – things that the world would not have expected to see in the face of a rough old Glasgow carter. Forty years ago he married a girl of his own class. To-night he was writing to her, and there was the same look in his eyes that must have been there when he asked her to marry him. Billy, Oldheim, all the others, were the same. I suddenly saw what an irrational fool I had been to imagine everything rotten because I had found one little unit faulty. Did you ever realise, Jackson, how much a man's mental sanity depended on his faith in womankind? It's the basis of faith in everything. Take it away and what has he to fall back upon? Religion? Philosophy? Business? None, nor all of them, will satisfy him. A man's woman is his religion and philosophy, and business is only a means to an end which is Her. The ordinary individual lives for his woman. Most of his kind will die for her. I'm going to live for my woman now. I think I know where to find her.'

A splutter of machine-gun fire broke out up the line, German machine-guns by the slow, ponderous note. The enemy evidently sensed the coming attack, and were nervously searching for patrols. It ceased as abruptly as it commenced. In the tense silence of the ensuing moments a sleeping sniper called out a girl's name. Brown looked at the Sniper and nodded, as if to say, 'You see where his thoughts are.' With a whispered 'Good night,' he rose and disappeared into the darkness.

After that, sleep came easily to the Sniper. All the unrest had left him. The confused tangle of ideas and impulses tormenting his brain had sorted themselves out and become coherent. The conversation of his men, the talk with Brown, had given him the master idea to which all the others had attuned themselves. He too had found a religion, a philosophy, and an end to his endeavours. When the roar of the guns heralding the commencement of the sister brigade's attack summoned him to the 'stand-to' he woke from a dream in which the central figure had been Maimie Rankine.

CHAPTER XXII

The Storm

THE ATTACK OF THE First Brigade was completely successful. After standing to for an hour watching the flaming tumult all around them – the gun-flashes behind, the angry flare of the shell-bursts in front – the Eastshires were ordered back to their shelters. The Sniper was warned to hold himself in readiness as one of a taking-over party. Soon after breakfast the party set out for brigade headquarters.

These consisted of a row of dug-outs built into a steep bank not far from the Ypres–Commines Canal. The natural security of their position had guarded them from enemy shell-fire, but all around were gathered the sweepings of the grim work up the line. In one dug-out, and flooding out of the doorway, was a large pile of abandoned equipment, haversacks, trench tool carriers, kitbags, and straps, all muddy, bloody, and shrapnel-torn. Against the outside wall stood a conglomerate of battered and twisted rifles. Near the dressing station lay several wounded, swathed in blankets, waiting to be carried down to the ambulances by the stretcher parties, who were heroically toiling backwards and forwards, undeterred by the wicked shrapnel-burst blotching the air above their heads. Further away a number of still forms were lying, men long past the surgeon's aid. From this pile of human débris, four grimy fellows were carrying a ghastly something, sewn up in sacking and waterproof sheeting, to an open hole at the edge of a cluster of wooden crosses, where another man was waiting, expectant foot on shovel, ready to begin the work of burial.

A silence fell on the party. No matter how hardened the soldier may be, the sight of a broken corpse always reminds him of the fate which some day may be his.

The embankment stretched along the edge of the canal like a huge rampart, until it merged into the high ground running north to Hill 60.

The sector which the Eastshires were to occupy ran along the crest of this high ground with the canal as its right flank limit. A huge mine crater, blown by the Germans to assist in their attack, cut the position in two, necessitating the use of two communication trenches. One had been dug immediately after the attack on the other side of the embankment. The other was the communication trench previously in use. The Sniper began his tour of inspection with the former trench.

He reached it by a cutting which led over the embankment and down a muddy slide on the other side. The first sight that met his eyes gave him an idea of what to expect in the rest of the position. At the top of the slide, pushed into a side-sap, sat two dead men. They did not bear much resemblance to human figures, but the bloody rags of uniform still clinging to them proved their identity. A few yards along the trench was the body of another man. His leg was fractured below the knee, the break showing clearly through the folds of his puttee. One foot was either gone or buried in the mud. He resembled a broken wax figure, a victim of childish spleen. The trench was so narrow at this point that the Sniper had to step over him.

Up on the high ground above the trench other dead men were lying. They lay among the snow fully accoutred, the red flush of health still in their cheeks, like tired soldiers sleeping. They had been part of a company of Dorsets who had charged over the embankment ten days before, in a brave effort to retake the positions below shortly after the Germans had made their attack. A machine-gun at the end of the embankment had caught them with its fire and stopped their rush.

From the position of the bodies the Sniper could easily reconstruct the picture of that counter-attack – one moment a group of strong men behind the shelter of the bank, the rich warm blood of strength pulsing in their veins; another moment of tense life as they rushed on over the crest; and then the leaden hail, the men dropping out, until there were none left to carry on the attack any further. The getting-in of the wounded from such a difficult situation must have been a rare achievement on the part of the stretcher-bearer squads.

When passing up the muddy slide again on his way back to headquarters, he heard the sound of sobbing coming from behind a traverse in the continuation of the trench rearward along the top of the embankment. Turning down the trench, he came on a man buried to the armpits in loose earth. The usual bit of bloodstained bandage showed that he had been wounded, and he had evidently been making his way down to the dressing station when the sodden trench walls had collapsed on the top of him.

The Sniper hurried off to headquarters, and secured three men to dig the man out. But the poor fellow had been buried so long that the icy cold had numbed his limbs and senses. He was still sobbing quietly when his comrades helped him away.

The other communication trench was even more gruesome. It had lain in the path of the main attack, and the dead were scattered thickly in its neighbourhood. Near its commencement a group of Nissen huts had been constructed in the sparse marginal growth of the trees covering the high ground at this point. The huts had been solidly constructed, and little damage from shell-fire was visible in their structure. But many dead lay in them. In one hut opening on the communication trench two weary-looking men rested, backs against the wall. One had his arm round the other's neck and head on his comrade's shoulder, like a tired child cuddling up to a stronger mate for support. They had been struck down in the barrage, and had crawled under shelter to die.

This communication trench was called Hedge Row, because its upper end skirted a hedge by the side of a field beyond the wood. Its lower end was the main street of a dug-out city, once very prettily laid out with bowers and rustic paths. The dug-outs were surface structures, only shrapnel-proof at best, and the men who had sought shelter in them had paid a terrible price for their folly. There are only two ways in which to treat shell-fire. Go deep under the earth or get out and lie down in the open. The men in these dug-outs had been pinned down beneath the wreckage of the frail structures, and succeeding shells had churned their bodies up into a horrible mixture of matter and humanity.

Just above the dug-outs more dead were lying. The Sniper particularly noticed the appearance of one man. He was a strikingly handsome fellow, and his neatly cropped moustache and curly black hair betokened one accustomed to pay great attention to the details of his personal appearance. Even in death his posture was elegant. He reclined against the broken parados like a great actor resting from his mimic labours. One arm was carelessly hunched over a supporting sandbag, and the fingers of the other hand seemed to be playing with the identity disc slung round his neck. Perhaps he had drawn it out when he felt death approaching, to make sure that he would not be buried unknown. It was difficult to believe that he was not asleep.

Further up near the edge of the wood a heavy shell had burst, blocking the trench with dislodged sandbags and débris. The drainage had collected on the higher side of this barrier, and was pouring over the top in a cascade, gurgling down through the open slats of the duck-boards. There was nothing for it but to plunge boldly over the obstacle and struggle on immersed to the waist.

Just where the water shallowed a man lay dead, half floating, half submerged – a horribly disfigured man, but not with the disfigurement of slashed face and broken limbs. Not the slightest scratch was visible about him. Yet by some freak of the explosion which had killed him, his skull had been shattered so that his head was but a plastic mass held together by the skin. He lay on his back, his face flattened out by the pull of gravity. Every feature could be traced quite easily. But the eyes were ghastly and fish-like, the mouth all askew, the lips bloated and thick as a buck negro's, and the nose but a daub of flesh. The movement of the water as the men swished past made his head bob about like a half-inflated bladder, and the face took on still more horrible grimaces.

The Sniper had good reason to remember that face. He had to pass it four times a day during the next five days. It still appears in his dreams as a hideous nightmare of the past. He felt no surprise that the body should be left so long without burial. The first consideration in the trench area is always the safety of the living. Only by live men can a trench be held, and all the efforts of the survivors after an attack are diverted to consolidation work to provide themselves with sufficient cover. Few people realise the labour and time required to bury a dead man in a restricted bullet-swept area like that of the trenches. In the case of the 2nd Eastshires not a man could be spared from the work of repairing the battered trenches, and soon few were left even with the necessary strength. The dead must ever wait on the quick, though in ordinary circumstances the quick make a show of waiting on the dead.

The Sniper hurried along the communication trench and entered the main position. Rain had commenced to fall heavily, and he was anxious to complete his investigation and get back to look for some shelter for himself and his men. There were four lines of trenches, one of them recaptured from the Germans and two others beyond, originally German, into which the attack had been pushed. The enemy had suffered very severely, but most of their dead had been lifted out of the way and laid along the parapet. The colour of their uniforms so harmonised with the dull blue sandbags that one could easily have passed on without noticing them save for a grey face or hand appearing here and there. But many bodies were still lying in every side-sap and ditch which the garrison had not yet found occasion to use.

One man had evidently been wounded early in the attack. He lay without tunic or shirt, with an unfinished bandage on his breast. Another German was jammed in a gap of the parados where a rush of bombers had poured out into the open. The trampling hasty feet had almost denuded him of clothing, plainly revealing just over his right thigh the two bullet-holes which had killed him. A third lay on his back spread-eagled with a neat little hole in his forehead. How little a thing is required to let the life out of a vital spot! He was a squatly-made fellow, with thick, mulatto-like lips and flat, bestial countenance. His curly hair, the rings through his ears, his deep, broad shoulders, and his long arms finished off with huge knotty hands, gave him a curious buccaneer look. If the original German army contained many of his kind, it was quite easy to understand the atrocities committed in France and Belgium.

There was much in that German trench to interest a British officer, and the Sniper studied thoroughly each detail of its arrangement. The bottom level was excellent, only in the damaged portions had any drainage collected, and the ease with which he could walk about surprised him. The manner in which the Germans obtained a smokeless fire also struck him as very ingenious. In strong cupboard-like boxes let into the parados were stacks of what looked like rabbit-wire-netting ovals, consisting of two pieces of netting about a foot and a half long stuck together by a pitchy substance mixed with shavings. One of these could burn for several minutes, giving out an intense heat.

But the sniping loopholes attracted most of his attention. Those constructed after the Germans had captured the position were built on a very similar plan to that followed by his own men. The shields were much smaller and lighter than he had seen before, and made of white steel of remarkable thinness. The loophole itself was very small, and must have been very difficult to detect from anything but a short distance. The shutter fitted closely and worked very smoothly. A metal stay held the plate in a slanting position, and rendered its fixing into the parapet a comparatively simple matter. The Sniper pounced greedily on as many of these shields as he could find, and stored them away for his own section's use.

The barrage had been heaviest in the space between the old German firing-line and supports, and little but raw earth and shell-holes remained of a once well-organised position. A few hundred yards away on the right the end of the embankment reared itself abruptly, giving to the place the appearance of a muddy tide race, gale-driven over a rocky shallow, with the rain-mists trembling overhead as the spray of ocean breakers. The Germans had tried to retreat over this area. But the barrage had caught them, and chewed them up, so that the Sniper felt a queer kind of satisfaction at the sight of a decently whole body. He did not waste any time in this locality, and having staked out a number of sniping posts, he hurried back to headquarters.

On the way down Hedge Row he met one of the trench-mortar officers engaged in the attack. The latter was little more than a boy, and painfully shaken by his recent experiences. The trench-mortar units always have a trying time. Their guns are close to the firing-line, their discharge note is characteristic, and the shell can be seen from the beginning of its flight, so that the shrapnel generally starts bursting around them soon after the first shot has been fired. This particular officer was shivering with cold and racked from want of sleep, yet he managed to grin cheerfully enough as he addressed the Sniper.

'Been over the line?' he queried. 'Pretty average hell, isn't it?'

The Sniper silently offered him his flask.

'No, thank you, my boy,' said the gunner. 'Cling to that as long as you can for yourself, and don't be playing the giddy prodigal son up here. You'll need every drop before you get quit of this show.'

After a further remark or two he went off to recover his guns. Much to his regret, the Sniper did not meet the boy again. Talk about 'ships that pass in the night'! The sorrow of sundered trench acquaintances is far more poignant. The little gunner got the Military Cross for his work in the attack, but he 'went West' shortly afterwards, and a wooden cross now marks his resting-place.

The evening merged into the darkness in a flurry of sleet and driving squalls, and the night threw its cloak over the misery of hundreds of human souls – those who went out chilled to the bone and haunted with the memories of the last three days; those who came in through the flooded communication trench and over the soaking open, depressed by the thoughts of the days to come. The relief was successfully effected. The survivors of the attack tumbled out through the storm to the rest billets. The new-comers settled down in the wallow their predecessors had left, to hang on and exist as best they might.

The ordinary winter conditions of Flanders had existed up to the last day of the attack, but from the time the Sniper's battalion took over the sector the weather broke down entirely. Rain and snow fell in turn, and during the infrequent spells of fair weather the ground froze. Veterans of the first winter of the war declared that it was their worst experience of the campaign; the wonder was that any men survived.

The trenches became a series of ponds filled with liquid mud over a bottom of plastic clay of such stickiness that men often had the boots dragged off their feet when attempting to pass along the line. The drainage system had disappeared in the bombardment; the dug-outs had been blown in. The men crouched down among the floods away from the icy wind which froze their clothing and whitened their hands and faces with its bite.

All the first day the Germans kept up a wicked shell-fire, and the number of casualties steadily increased. It was impossible to bring stretcher cases down from the firing-line during the day because of the blocked communication trenches. One dug-out fortunately was left capable of being repaired, and into this the wounded were carried to await the coming of darkness. The doctor and his assistants did what they could to make them comfortable, but their sufferings were heart-rending. It affected the rest of the men so much that the traverses on either side of the dug-out were cleared and their occupants moved out of sight and hearing.

During the afternoon the Sniper met Sergeant Ferguson coming out of the dug-out. The sergeant's face was white under its mud and his mouth was twitching.

'Billy's been hit, sir,' he said. 'Got it bad in the thigh. Don't go in just now,' he added, as the Sniper made for the dug-out. 'The doctor's busy with him. I could not stand it.'

Through the doorway the Sniper could hear a low agonised voice gasping out the name of the Almighty. It was Billy. The sergeant quivered at the sound.

'This sort of thing makes one bitter at times, sir,' he said. 'Billy belonged to a trade which would have kept him out of the Army. But he joined up and his place was filled. And now, according to the papers, the man who took his job is out on strike with all his mates for higher pay, while Billy is sticking this on a bob a day. There's something wrong about it, sir. Why should some have to suffer so much, while others not only do not suffer, but actually benefit out of the other man's suffering?'

John Brown came out of the dug-out and wiped his bloody hands in a pocket of snow. He had been helping the doctor with Billy. As soon as the sergeant had finished he began whistling 'We don't want to lose you'.

'That's the song that got me into the Army,' he said. 'Dorothy Ward sang it, and I was at the recruiting office before I knew what I was doing.'

'Bet you don't hear it sung now,' growled the sergeant. 'It would empty the house. Shut up, for Heaven's sake!' he exclaimed, as Brown began whistling again.

Old Dan came puffing round a traverse and made towards the group. 'What are the twa o' ye bletherin' aboot noo?' he asked.

'Sergeant has got the hump about the people sticking in soft jobs at home while we've got this,' said Brown, with an expressive sweep of his hand.

'It does gie ye the hump at times,' admitted Old Dan. 'But Ah'd raither bide oot here ten year than be at hame scrimpin' ma ootpit an' wastin' the country's time. Ah wouldna like ma bairns tae come an' ask me tae tell them the kind o' stories that you, for example, will be able tae tell your bairns when ye gang back, an' ken that Ah'd been lettin' ye doon at hame while ye were oot here.'

'But what will you do, Haggarty, if you find rival contractors have stolen all your customers?' asked the Sniper slily.

'What will Ah dae, sir?' said Old Dan with such emphasis as to make his hearers smile. 'Lang Jock o' the Vennel and Soapy Davie hae tried it already. But wait till Ah get a haud o' them. They'll no daur show face in Glesgie when Ah gae back.'

'That you, Jackson?' called the doctor from the dug-out entrance. 'There's one of your fellows in here would like to see you.'

'Dod! that's what Ah cam' along aboot. Hoo is the laddie, doctor?' said Old Dan anxiously.

'Badly wounded, but not dangerously. He'll do all right,' replied the doctor.

'Ah'm glad tae hear that,' said Old Dan thankfully. 'Dae ye mind if Ah come ben wi' ye, sir?' he asked of the Sniper.

Together they entered the dug-out and made their way among the wounded to where Billy was lying. There were two greatcoats wrapped snugly round the boy, and he was lapsing into a painless unconsciousness under the influence of a morphine tablet which the doctor had given him. He smiled wanly at his officer.

'Ah'm gled tae see ye, sir,' he said. 'Ah was wantin' ye tae write tae ma lassie. She'll think Ah'm hidin' somethin' frae her if Ah write. The sergeant's gotten her address. It'll no worry ye ower muckle, sir, will it?'

'I'll be only too pleased, Billy,' said the Sniper.

'Ah'm sorry tae be leavin' ye, sir,' murmured the boy, his sleepy eyelids closing. He drew the deep, satisfied breath of a tired child about to fall asleep.

'Billy, laddie! Dae ye hear me?' said Old Dan hastily.

'Ay, Dan'l. What is it?'

'Mind ye let me ken whaur ye are when ye get hame. Ah'll git the auld wife tae send ye somethin'. Mebbe ye'll be in hospital nearby her.'

'Ah'll let ye ken, Dan'l. Thenk ye kindly, an' mind ye keep yer heid doon.' A second later he was asleep.

Snow had begun to fall heavily, whirling in the wind into great solid pillars and masses, blotting everything from view beyond a few yards. Going down the trench, the Sniper met his sergeant standing by a loophole. The man was coatless and blue with cold.

'Where's your coat, sergeant?' asked the Sniper sharply.

'Left it behind me, sir. Going down for it presently,' replied the sergeant.

The Sniper went round the next traverse out of sight of the sergeant, and climbed out on to the rising ground behind the trench. The snow hid him from the enemy. He picked his way carefully over the treacherous surface to where some dead men were lying. Opening the pack of one of them, he pulled out the coat and returned to the sergeant.

'Put this on, sergeant,' he said. 'And when you have warmed it up properly, go and exchange it for the one you wrapped round Billy.'

Without a word the sergeant shook himself clear of the snowflakes and put on the coat. For once the man looked sheepish.

'You take some knowing, Ferguson,' said the Sniper. The sergeant had turned from him abruptly and was fumbling with the panel of his loophole.

The storm steadily increased and maintained its violence and the sufferings of the men became terrible. Trench-feet and frost-bite spread rapidly, and it looked as if the whole battalion would succumb to exposure. The garrison hid themselves away in nooks and crevices and the snow covered them over. At times the trenches looked deserted. But a word of command and out of the mush of the trench bottom mushy figures would rise to carry out the order.

To such an extent was the vitality of everyone lowered that wounds proved fatal from which men should easily have recovered. The Sniper saw one man struck in the leg by shrapnel. The leg was broken, quite a simple break – but he died within an hour. An hour afterwards another man was struck in the shoulder. The splinter hardly penetrated the flesh, and the Sniper felt tempted to dig it out with his knife. He wished he had done so; for shortly after the first field-dressing had been applied the man died in frightful agony, calling out on his comrades to shoot him.

It was impossible to provide any hot food, and soon there was a shortage even of cold rations. The Germans shelled the roads behind, interfering greatly with the movement of the transport, and the two-mile stretch over which the supplies had to be carried to the firing-line was a sodden morass where men were engulfed to the waist in places. Ration parties took hours to reach some sectors of the front-line trenches, and at times the men lost their way. But for the large number of dead lying around, whose packs provided tins of bully beef and other extras, many men would have starved. Yet they had to fight the rats for those supplies – big vicious brutes who came out from their swamped hiding-places and nuzzled about the bodies of the slain, even gathering threateningly round some live human who dared to dispute their possession of the spoils.

The Germans seemed to suffer even more severely both from the weather and the lack of food. The poor wretches were too miserable to move about, and the section got very few targets. Germans and British lay in their holes while the storm raged around them, each equally incapable of offensive action. A group of schoolboys could almost have overcome the defenders of either position.

One by one the men went down from exposure. There was a constant stream of sick men to the rear. The Sniper at last grew tired of the inactivity and all the drabness and filthiness around him. He determined on a sniping expedition into No Man's Land, for the sake of the excitement, and to try and bring up his section's successes to something like average weekly total.

CHAPTER XXIII

Two in a Tree

A T ONE POINT No Man's Land was unusually broad, owing to a withdrawal by the Germans from a part of the line rendered untenable through the capture of the sector on its flank. A group of huge pollarded trees stood more than half-way across, most of them badly battered and bare, but with one untouched giant in their midst heavily covered with ivy. The Sniper had picked out this tree for his hiding-place, and he set about making preparation to occupy it with a fair degree of safety to himself.

Aided by the sergeant and Old Dan, he covered a number of squares of black cloth with ivy strands, collected by his section from an old farm behind the lines, and furnished them with lengths of pliable wire at each corner, so that they could be easily fastened up in any position. Having carefully blackened his face and hands, he started out from the firing-line as soon as darkness fell.

It was no easy task crossing No Man's Land because of the mud and the water-filled shell-holes. But at last he found the tree, and, having scaled it with some difficulty, he carefully made his way inside the ivy screen and began making himself both comfortable and secure.

He could have chosen half a dozen resting-places in that tree. The bole was broad, and the space between the stumpy branches where they left the trunk had become filled up with twigs matted together by decayed foliage, while the ivy runners had descended from the boughs above, forming a regular canopy over his head and around him, through which he would be able to see, but with little chance of being seen himself. To make matters sure he fastened the squares of camouflaged cloth in a little screen round about him, and then he settled himself down to await the sunlight.

Towards dawn he dozed a little, but suddenly he awoke with the knowledge that he was not alone. He heard the deep-drawn breath of a man exhausted by some strenuous exertion. Evidently the intruder had just climbed the tree and was resting from his labours. He heard him begin to move about as over some preparations. Then there was stillness, and presently the sound of snoring. Whoever the new-comer was, he did not suspect the Sniper's presence. The Sniper got his rifle into position and waited for the dawn to disclose the man's identity.

Slowly the light crept into the sky. It filtered through the ivy tendrils, and gradually lit up the canopy's interior. At first the Sniper could see nothing which suggested the presence of a companion. But as the light grew stronger, he saw little more than a yard away from him a camouflage arrangement similar to his own, and inside it the grey-blue form of a German officer. The latter was still asleep; his rifle lay close beside him. The Sniper reached out cautiously and drew the rifle away.

The German woke at the noise and started up suddenly. His face paled a little as he saw the Sniper's ready gun pointing at him. He put up his hands above his head. 'I surrender,' he said, in perfect English.

The Sniper continued to stare at him, wondering what to do. He thought it a decidedly novel situation for two enemy snipers to choose the same tree.

'Let me see your ammunition,' he said curtly.

The German unloosed his cartridge belt and handed it over to him. The bullets were regulation service pattern. Had they been tampered with, the Sniper would have been inclined to shoot the man at once.

'My presence is rather awkward for you, I can see,' said the German calmly. 'If I were in your place, I think I would shoot.'

The Sniper relieved him of his revolver, and hung it behind himself out of the man's reach.

'I have another revolver here,' said the German, tapping a breast pocket.

The Sniper took the second revolver from him. It was a little black Walther pistol, .635 calibre, too small a weapon to be of any use at a distance, but a deadly little toy at close range. The frank way in which the German had disclosed its possession appealed to the Sniper. The man was a handsome, clear-eyed fellow, with nothing sullen or unlikeable about him.

'Will you give your parole?' he asked.

'Certainly,' said the German. 'I quite realise that by sniping law I should have been dead some time ago.'

He settled himself down in his resting-place and the Sniper began peering through the ivy at the German line in search of a target. It struck him that he was now in a very safe position. Even if the Germans saw him in the tree they would think it was their own man.

The dawn was now well in the sky, and he could see his surroundings fairly plainly. The German position was badly battered, and he realised that many sniping chances would come his way as soon as the full daylight chased the shadows away from the broken-down trenches. He turned to look at his battalion's position. It was in a similar plight, and the thought of the havoc that the German might have wrought there made him turn grimly towards the enemy line again. He determined to warn the artillery to root out this dangerous lurking-place as soon as his battalion left the trenches.

A German officer suddenly appeared in a battered communication trench about five hundred yards away. He walked along boldly, evidently well screened from the British lines; but at the junction of the trench with a support position, he paused and looked directly at the old tree. After a little he waved his hand.

The Sniper raised his rifle and prepared to shoot. A sudden sound beside him made him look at his companion. The German sniper was gazing wildly at him, the perspiration pouring from his forehead. When he glanced again at the German line, his target had disappeared.

'That was my brother,' said the German quietly. 'I thank you.'

The Sniper laid his rifle down beside him, and settled back in his post. All day the two sat there in silence, and the rifle remained unused. As soon as darkness fell he led the German into his lines and sent him down to headquarters under escort. With the escort went a written report of the whole occurrence. The Sniper did not go himself.

Later Old Dan came for him. 'That German wants tae speak tae ye, sir,' he said. 'He's just gaun doon the line.'

The Sniper followed Old Dan to where the prisoner was standing with his guard.

'I wish to thank you for your courtesy, sir,' said the German. 'When I am examined by your intelligence officers I shall tell them nothing. But I spoilt your sport to-day. I will tell to you what you like to ask.'

'I wish to ask nothing,' said the Sniper.

He shook hands warmly with the German, and watched the party disappear into the darkness. He saw the German turn round and wave his hand to him before the darkness swallowed him up. The day had not yielded the results he had hoped for. But he returned to the ruined dug-out which was his habitation feeling well satisfied.

Next day's weather proved more severe than ever. It rained and snowed incessantly, and the condition of the trenches became terrible. Whole lengths had to be abandoned, and No Man's Land in places came pouring over the position like a moving Irish bog. In the afternoon the colonel sent for the Sniper.

'The brigade want a patrol carried out,' he said when the Sniper appeared. 'They want to know if the old German firing-line by the canal bank is still being occupied.'

'That won't be easy, sir,' said the Sniper. 'No Man's Land is almost impassable there.'

'I know,' said the colonel. 'I have told the brigade that they are asking too much, but the information seems rather important. They leave it entirely at your discretion whether to go or not. My own instructions to you are not to go if the thing is too risky. By the way, you are going on leave next week. I have put your name first on the list. So be careful.'

The Sniper saluted and returned to his quarters. He meant to go, but he did not like the job. None knew better than he the difficulties it entailed. He would have laughed at the dangers of an ordinary patrol; but only that morning he had watched a German trying to make his way across the open over a gap in the enemy support lines. He had seen the speed of the man's first bold rush gradually changed into a slow, painful stagger, as the effects of the clinging mud began to be felt. Then a bullet had stretched him lifeless, a burden on the soil which had tricked him. But because of the manner in which the brigade headquarters had made the request, the Sniper decided that the patrol must be done.

When the section heard of the matter every single sniper asked to go with him. The Sniper chose the sergeant and John Brown. He had to speak rather sharply to Old Dan, who grumbled bitterly at being left out. As soon as darkness fell the three made their way over the embankment to the firing-line. Several times they stumbled over the dead lying there.

It was a night of the blackness of the pit. Here and there a patch of unmelted snow gave a fitful radiance which confused the eyes and made the darkness more impenetrable. Down on the right, a breeze unfelt and unheard by the men in the trenches ruffled the surface of the brimming canal, and at intervals the lap! lap! lap! of the troubled waters travelled across the lightless void like the cry of a soul lost in the Stygian waste.

Not a sound came from the enemy trenches: not a star-shell illuminated the shadows. Either the Germans were overcome by the wretchedness which the storm god had let loose over the land, or they were keeping a watch all the more potent and unpierceable because of its silence. In between, the silent hidden mud waited for its victims. As the men in the firing-line watched the party disappear into the blackness, they congratulated themselves on the safety of their own water-logged hollows, and wondered if any of the patrollers would ever return.

The Sniper at once led the way to the canal bank. There they would find the hard ground of the old towing path, and though he knew that German listening patrols would be likely to choose the same ground, he meant at all costs to cover at least half the journey as quickly and easily as possible. No German patrollers were watching by the canal bank. But at length he judged it unwise to use the path any longer, and, lowering himself face downward, he slid off into the shell-churned slime.

The mud seemed to reach up clammy fingers and feel all over his body. At every forward move a thousand icy handgrips closed over him and tried to drag him back. Foot by foot he struggled onward, sometimes on hands and knees, sometimes with a seal-like motion, his chin stemming the billowing surface slime. Never before had he been so glad of the experience and the hardening of muscles which innumerable nights spent in No Man's Land had given him.

The sergeant and John Brown laboured one on either side of him; but silently, so that no man could have marked the passing of the patrol. With every limb moving with the tirelessness of a machine, and every faculty alert and undimmed by weariness, the Sniper saw the German line loom up before him. Without any check in his progress, he passed through the shattered wire and looked over the parapet into the trench.

No sign of life was visible. Leaving Brown on the parapet top with several bombs in readiness, he slid down into the trench, followed by the sergeant. It was deeper than he expected, half-filled with water, and smelling of blood and filth.

With a bomb in one hand and a service revolver in the other, the Sniper moved along the trench in one direction; the sergeant patrolled in the other. It was eerie work. Everywhere the effect of British shell-fire was evident, piles of débris, broken-down traverses, and dead Germans. Sometimes he jostled a floating corpse as he passed along.

He climbed out on the parados and crept back along it. The dead were very thick there; men who had been caught by the barrage when retreating from the trench. But not a live German was to be seen. He returned to his starting-point to find the sergeant waiting with a similar report. Without doubt the position had been evacuated. Quickly climbing over the parapet, he led the way on the return journey.

At first the passage was easy, and with a sure instinct the Sniper skirted shell-hole and slime puddles. But in the middle of No Man's Land where the two barrages had met, not a firm foothold could be found. Now one would be engulfed and held, and after a fierce tug-of-war the other two would get him free, only to require assistance in clearing themselves. But the fear of the coming daylight lent them strength. With senses swimming, and chests heaving painfully, they staggered like drunken men into the meshes of their own wire.

Dawn was breaking as they were helped into the trench and down to headquarters. The Sniper mumbled his report to a sleepy adjutant, who wakened up quickly when he saw their exhaustion, and superintended the arrangements for their succour. He led them into the dressing station, stoked up the brazier, and helped them to a dixieful of hot soup. Then they lay down by the brazier and slept till their weariness left them.

An invitation came up from brigade headquarters for the party to go down and refresh themselves there. But the colonel did not disturb them. He knew they would prefer to remain with their own people.

They woke up next day at noon, feeling strange in their mud-stiffened garments, but gloriously hungry and fit. It was still sopping wet outside, but this was the last day of the battalion in the trenches, and the three ate their breakfast in the best of spirits.

With cruel irony the weather showed signs of clearing in the afternoon. The sun even began to shine through the clouds. The Germans immediately started shelling the ground behind the lines, and the advance relief party had a narrow escape when coming up to take over.

When the showing-round process had been completed, the Sniper thankfully turned his back on the firing-line and made his way towards headquarters. In order to save time he got out of the communication trench on a short cut through the wood. Here he came on a wounded man hobbling towards the dressing station. The man was only slightly wounded, and hardly needed the help which the Sniper gave him. But when the edge of the wood was reached the man decided to rest for a while before making a dash across the open to the shelter of the embankment. The Sniper had to get a report off to brigade headquarters, so he left him and hurried on.

The ground which he had to cover was under observation by the Germans, and he was only half-way across when they switched on a light barrage. The shells burst behind him and on his left, but, hurrying quickly forward, he thought he was clear, when he heard the note of a high-explosive shell travelling quickly towards him. He *knew* the shell was coming for him. The conviction leaped into his mind that his time had come. It was a curious feeling, utterly devoid of all fear. The dominant impulse within him was to throw himself into a position of defence like that of a boxer meeting the rush of an adversary. As he stared steadily in the direction of the approaching danger, a cloud of earth and black smoke rose from the top of the embankment at the very spot he was eyeing. The shell had struck there and exploded. Had its course been a foot or two higher it would have killed him.

About an hour afterwards he was passing along the base of the bank, when, glancing casually to the left, he saw the wounded man still sitting where he had left him. Thinking that his wounds might have weakened him, he hurried off to his aid. The man was sitting in a perfectly natural position, and had all the appearance of being asleep. The Sniper was bending down to rouse him before he realised that the man was dead. A shell splinter, possibly from the barrage that had nearly killed the Sniper, had scooped out the crown of his head, and the piece lay a few feet away in a bloody smudge of brains.

Just after darkness the relieving party came in, and the worn-out men roused themselves from their hiding-places and stumbled down the line. The Sniper stood by the path at the end of the embankment and watched the battalion march out. He reckoned that there were barely two hundred of them, and nearly eight hundred had gone in. Weather and shells had accounted for the rest, and yet the battalion had only been *holding* a sector of the line.

A soft rain had commenced to fall, unlike the fierce downpours which had been raging all through the week, but wetting and full of wretchedness. The wan light of the star-shells flickering through the misty drizzle showed up the decimated platoons as the column filed past. Many familiar forms were absent. The men were tired, as their slow, dragging footsteps showed. They staggered along, hunched up and miserable, haunted by the memory of comrades who had gone up with them so gallantly, but who had not come down. The further away files were straggly, with the men almost out of touch with one another. Single forms would come stumbling out of the shadow blocks of ruined wall or shattered copse, bob about in the steely radiance of a water-filled shell-hole, and then merge themselves again with the broader shadows which leaped across their path when the star-shells died out. The whole picture was symbolical of the agony, the human sacrifice and endeavour, by which the sacred ground of Ypres has been held through four winters of war. And all the time the Sniper was saying to himself, 'Thank God! To-morrow I go on leave. London after this! Oh, God!'

The battalion halted on the broad Lille road. Some of the men dropped out from weariness. Then the opening drone of the pipes was heard; the ranks were at once reformed; tired shoulders straightened suddenly; disordered equipment was drawn tight. The pipes swelled into the opening bars of 'Blue Bonnets'. With a click the men did the balance step, as though on the depot parade ground, and down towards Ypres Lille Gate marched the broken men, no longer broken, the spirit of the pipes firing their blood, as it has fired the warlike Scot throughout the ages.

The Sniper forgot about his leave. He was thinking what a glorious thing it was to be a Scottish officer marching with his men.

CHAPTER XXIV

Leave and Maimie

GOOD NIGHT, OLD MAN. Hope to see you again soon,' said the man whom the Sniper thought was the husband, shaking him by the hand. 'The others won't be long in going,' said the girl whom he thought was the wife, giving his sleeve a little tug, and hurrying the man to the door. And the Sniper suddenly awoke to the sordidness of the situation.

He had come on leave the day after his battalion had been relieved from the canal bank, sick of the discomfort and dirtiness of the trench area, filled with a great longing for the light and laughter of civilisation, for the sight of well-dressed girls, and people speaking his own tongue. And London had gone to his head like wine to the head of a hungry man.

The music and sparkle and warmth of the restaurants, the rustle of women's dresses, the sheen of silk stockings and bright eyes in the darkened streets, the whole gay diablerie of the city despite the war shadow over it, held out an appeal to men accustomed to live with nature ungarbed and raw, only to be resisted by those who had steady solid friends to greet them and substantial homes to go to. Those like the Sniper with no friends in town had London: and London welcomed such as he.

His first intention when he arrived at Victoria had been to go straight to bed, and to call on the Rankines the next day, though Cissie had informed him that in all probability he would find only the general at home. But a brother sniper officer of the same division had taken him in charge, and after a drink here and a drink there, a dinner at a restaurant whose orchestra made the wine bubble in his veins until every movement of a woman's head seemed an invitation, after a revue, and then a night-club, he was ready for anything.

At the club two girl friends of his cicerone were met with, and an invitation to accompany them to meet their husbands and some other people at their flat soon followed. There was not the slightest suggestion of open wickedness. Every phase of the evening had gradually merged into the next. The moral descent had been imperceptible, and his conscience had slept undisturbed through it all. But now the rose-coloured atmosphere which had made everything seem pleasant and inviting to his eyes, was rudely dispelled by the sight of this sleek foreign-looking bully clearing out of his way; and the Sniper, sober and sane, realised that it was time for a decent man to go.

He was filled with a sudden disgust at the people around him. However had he come to associate with such a crew? There was a girl of the street with tousled hair and a dishevelled blouse which she had recently unfastened to show the company the bruises on her shoulder made by a man's rude clutch; another girl busy teaching a weedy youth the words of a filthy song; a Jewish bookmaker, presiding at a card-table surrounded by several cloth-capped yahoos and girls, who had invited the Sniper to back the card he fancied, addressing him familiarly as 'Old Sporty'. Damn the fellow's impertinence! Myles, the other sniper officer, was sitting apart from the assembly, talking to his girl acquaintance. Now that the Sniper had recovered his sanity, the contrast between this clear-skinned, clear-eyed trenchman, and the pallid-featured, neurotic company struck him with a sense of shame. Myles himself must have felt disenamoured, for when the Sniper suggested returning to their hotel, he at once agreed, and rose to put on his British warm.

'You're not going, Scottie?' said one of the girls.

'Yes. I want to get to bed. Very tired, you know,' he said.

'Can't you stay here?'

'No, I think not,' he said firmly.

'Oh! If that's the sort of boob you are, the sooner you clear out the better. Bertie!' she called out to the Jew fellow who was preparing to go. 'There's no need for you to go now. I want you to stay.'

'Wasn't it awful?' said Myles a little later, when the two were plodding hotel-wards through the silent, taxiless streets. 'I used to know those girls – at the beginning of their career. They were quite nice then. Awfully sorry, old man, to land you such a dud.'

But his contrition had vanished overnight, and next afternoon he had got the Sniper into a similar predicament. The two had been seated in the lounge of their hotel, when, with a 'Oh, here's two girls I know! Awfully nice! Stand by me, old man, and take one off.' Myles had dashed off in the direction of two exceedingly pretty girls who were just entering. He was back in a moment introducing the Sniper, and before the latter could protest, he had spirited off his particular fancy, leaving his friend to entertain the other.

It was an awkward position for the Sniper. He intended to call on the Rankines, and his last night's experience had cured him of all vagrant ideas. Yet how best to extricate himself he did not know. The girl was a lady, with only that slight trace of the street about her which makes her type the more attractive. She was just the sort of girl whom the ' khaki fever' has gradually transformed into a *grande cocotte*, and for the life of him he did not know what to say to her. It was the girl who broke the silence.

'Why are you so silent, Scottie?' she asked.

'Well, to tell the truth, chérie,' he said, 'I was wondering how best to tell you that there is nothing doing with me. I've got to pay a call shortly. I do hope you will have tea with me, though.'

He was stammering and blushing before he had finished, and the girl laughed merrily at his confusion.

'Don't you worry, Scottie,' she said. 'It's a change to see a man bother himself out of consideration for me. I shall stay and have tea though. It doesn't do one any good with the waiters here, if they see you turned down.'

And so it was settled, and, with all cause of restraint removed, they started talking like any two ordinary individuals, about the war, life in town, the latest show, and all the current gossip. But for that indescribable something, the common brand of her class, however cleverly some may try to hide it, the girl might have passed as an eminently respectable lady friend enjoying her talk with a handsome young officer. At times the Sniper was struck with the tragedy of it all, and wondered whether this girl would develop into the type of harridans whom he had encountered the night before. But her merry wit kept him laughing in spite of himself, and he was just chuckling hugely at one of her sallies when he felt that someone at a neighbouring table had looked at him rather intently. Switching round in his chair, he saw Maimie Rankine.

The girl was sitting with an elderly general whom he inferred to be her father. She now seemed absorbed in what General Rankine was saying, but the Sniper knew that she had recognised him, and from her apparent indifference to his presence he had little doubt that she had also diagnosed the character of his companion. He guessed what she would be thinking of him, and he could hardly conceal his vexation at the wretched turn of luck which had changed a perfectly harmless situation into a very compromising one. He hurried through the remainder of the meal, and conducted his companion out of the lounge, seeing her safely into a taxi, and returning as quickly as he could in the hope of getting an opportunity to explain the circumstances to Maimie.

He saw her standing by the cloak-room waiting for her father, but as he approached she looked at him as though he were a stranger, and turned to help her father on with his coat. The Sniper went straight past her to the lift and up to his room. He lay down on the bed and stared up at the ceiling. Of his surroundings he was hardly conscious. All he knew was that he could not go to call on the Rankines, that Maimie had cut him, and that he must just give up thinking about her.

After a while thoughts of self-pity began to fill his mind. Why should he worry? He was not to blame. If Maimie Rankine could jump to a conclusion so hurriedly, well, let her. She was not worth troubling about to the extent of wasting his leave. There were plenty of other places in London to go to besides the Rankines'. He got up and went out into the street to find something to amuse him.

He entered a bar off Shaftesbury Avenue, and drank almost more than he could carry. The spirit fired his blood, making him think of going wild again if he fell in with a suitable companion. But dinner sobered him up considerably, and he walked back to his hotel. He had hoped to find Myles there, but that officer had not yet returned, and he wandered aimlessly about again, finally drifting into a revue. The show bored him. The sight of other men there with their friends filled him with envy. He did not know a soul. He wondered why Maimie Rankine had come back from France, and thought how fortunate her presence in town would have been, but for that ill-fated meeting. She might have come to this very theatre with him. Hang it all! What right had she to condemn him unheard? He had felt sure that she liked him, too. She had been just as pleased about the meetings on the Calais road as he had been. He had got to the stage of being annoyed with her again when the curtain fell and the audience began to leave their seats.

Going down the exit passage he suddenly saw Maimie standing there alone. The blood rushed to his face at the surprise of the meeting. He could hardly see what was to the right and left of him. His heart felt curiously painful as he noticed one or two men further up the passage casting admiring glances back at her. In her evening dress, with opera cloak hanging loose over her shoulders, showing her finely moulded neck and clear skin, she looked wondrously beautiful and desirable. He saw her flush as she recognised him coming. He somehow felt that she would acknowledge him. But he passed her without a glance, as though he had not noticed her from amongst the retiring crowd.

At the entrance he was jammed in the crush for a little, and he caught sight of her there again, beside the tall form of her father. She seemed to point him out to the latter, for General Rankine looked in his direction, and seemed to try to make his way through the pack towards him. But the pressure of the people around suddenly lightened, and, slipping away in the crowd, he hurried across the square. 'I'm hanged if she is going to get it all her own way!' he murmured. But he felt very miserable, and wished that somehow or other he had been forced to stay and speak to her.

A girl called to him from a deserted corner. He stopped unthinkingly. When he realised what her purpose was, he walked on abruptly. He arrived at the entrance to his hotel, but he was too restless to think of turning in, and he walked on. Though he had no friends in London, he knew the city well. Presently he found himself in the square where the Rankines lived. He looked up at their house: it was unusually well lighted. He wondered what was going on inside. An officer came out as he watched, got into a waiting car, and drove away. The Sniper looked at him jealously. Perhaps Maimie was a very close friend of his. In any case he was a lucky fellow to be able to call at her home.

He turned back in the direction of his hotel, thoroughly sick with himself and his surroundings. This was the leave which he had been expecting so eagerly! He had been far happier, and much less lonely, among the dead men and the mud up by the canal bank. Before he had covered half of the way back, his mind was made up – he would go back to France to-morrow. Big Bill might laugh at him; the whole regiment might be curious. But they would be glad to see him again. He would be among friends ready to talk to him for his own sake, and not because of the drinks he might stand them, or the money he carried in his pocket.

Early next morning he was in the middle of his packing when Cissie Rankine walked into the room. 'What the deuce are you doing here, Cissie, old man?' he exclaimed delightedly. And then he remembered the state of affairs with Cissie's sister and went back to his packing to cover his embarrassment.

'I came on leave last night, Ronny,' Cissie said. 'And I have heard from Maimie a little of what happened yesterday,' he added, looking squarely at the Sniper.

'I was not to blame for that. I merely took a girl off to oblige Myles. You remember him, and can understand what he is. I was coming to call on your people as soon I could get decently clear of her.'

'I know, Ronny. Damned unfortunate! Girls are mighty touchy over these things, and Maimie thinks such a lot of you. Where are you going?'

'I'm going back to the battalion.'

'You are not,' said Cissie decisively. 'You are coming back to lunch with me. Now don't be an ass, Ronny. I know how things are with you and Maimie, and I'm not going to stand by and see them spoilt. How would you have acted if you had been in Maimie's place? Come down and have some breakfast, and get some sense into you.'

He kicked the Sniper's pack into a corner and dragged him down to the dining-room. The Sniper was simply overwhelmed by the boy's unwonted strength of purpose. On his way to the Rankines, he began to feel dubious about his reception, and half-heartedly mentioned his doubts. 'Shucks!' said Cissie derisively. 'You're a lucky dog, so stop your sulking and moping.'

Maimie greeted him in the hall without a trace of constraint in her manner. It was as if neither of them had left France, and another meeting on the Calais road were taking place. She was genuinely glad to see him, and the Sniper soon felt at his ease. Cissie suggested a lunch in town and an afternoon show, and went out of the room to look up theatre advertisements. As soon as he was gone Maimie started explaining her presence in town – rather nervously, the Sniper noticed, as though she were afraid of a silence.

She had left the ambulance for good, she told him. Elsie, her sister, had just had a serious breakdown at school, and Mrs. Rankine had been obliged to go north to nurse her. She herself had been released from the ambulance 'on compassionate grounds' to come home and keep house for her father.

'I am a very good housekeeper, you know,' she said naïvely.

The Sniper then started blunderingly to explain the hotel lounge incident, but she stopped him immediately.

'Please say no more,' she said. 'I was perfectly horrid. I saw you alone in the theatre afterwards. I can't tell you how sorry I am for treating you as I did.'

Cissie came into the room a little while later, but he hurriedly bobbed out again. The sight of Maimie flushing and faltering over her apology had been too much for the Sniper. Somehow or other he had found his arms round her, and her hands stealing shyly up to his shoulders. And he was telling her all about his sorrows of the evening before, and she was listening to him, sympathising now and then with little hand pressures, but thrilled to think that a man should suffer out of regard for what she thought.

'I'm afraid we must leave you out of this lunch and theatre, little man,' the Sniper said when Cissie returned again.

'I was ever meant for a sacrifice,' murmured Cissie resignedly.

The rest of his leave passed all too quickly for the Sniper. Maimie and he spent it by going the round of all the shows. The general and Cissie manfully looked after the house themselves – no easy matter on account of the servant problem – and Maimie was free to spend the whole time with him, much to his satisfaction.

He even felt tempted towards the close of his leave to go to the War Office and ask for a few days' extension. But when he reported again at his battalion headquarters he was glad that he had not done so.

'Thank Heaven you have come back to time, Jackson,' was the adjutant's greeting. 'We are suddenly ordered down to the French front, after only a week of long rest, and half the officers are on leave. We have only ten to move the battalion with. I am sorry, Jackson, but I shall need to send you on at once as advance officer.'

'When do I start?' said the Sniper with an alacrity which made the adjutant think very kindly of him.

'Five o'clock to-morrow morning. Entrain at Watten. Here are your instructions. Now off to bed, my lad, or you will miss your start.'

CHAPTER XXV

Men of France

THE SNIPER WENT SOUTH with a dozen other advance officers. After a long day's journey they came to a little French town behind the sector which their division was to occupy. Next day they were to go up to their separate trench portions to learn the billeting arrangements, the trench positions, and all the other details to which taking-over officers have to attend, so that when their battalions arrive they may be able to direct each company and unit to its proper place, and point out to the commanders where they may draw all necessary stores. A considerate R.T.O. sent them on to the inn Lion Rouge, where the most comfortable quarters in the town could be found.

Jules Labré kept the inn Lion Rouge in the square by the Hôtel de Ville, and thither came many officers travelling up and down behind the front, to stay over the night until train time, to eat Jules's excellent dinners and drink his more excellent wines, and if truth be told, to indulge in many a gay bout of repartee with Madame Labré in the little back room where Jules dined his privileged guests.

This little back dining-room was the holy of holies of the Lion Rouge. Into the big dining-hall and coffee-room anyone who pleased might enter. But beyond these outer courts only the intimates of the Julian circle might go. There were the same old Frenchmen, staid and jolly, who had come to eat their dinners there even in the time of Jules's father; and one or two travellers whose credentials had been duly approved by long acquaintanceship. Always any officers of the allied armies, whom chance sent to the inn, were ushered in as honoured guests. And Jules himself sat down at the head of his table, and partook of what he provided for the guests, just as though he were a guest himself.

Jules was a wit renowned through many departments, and at dinner that evening the Sniper listened delightedly to his merry talk. Jules had gone very early to the war, had been wounded after the Aisne, and when he returned from hospital he walked with one foot supported from the ground by a little steel framework four inches high – of which distinction Jules was even more proud than of his Croix de Guerre, 'avec palmes'.

'Ah, my friends,' he said jestingly when the Sniper mentioned his wound, 'Messieurs right and left foot will no longer prove two so good servants as in the past. One has been exalted over the other.'

'The jokes of Jules are even better than his dinners,' said stately old Monsieur St. Felix, when the laughter had subsided. 'And as his dinners are the best in the world, see what a fine fellow I think him.'

As the night wore on, however, Jules became more thoughtful, and his sallies were heard less frequently. Even the officers noticed it, strangers though they were.

'You must not mind that our worthy Jules should seem melancholy, my friends,' said Monsieur St. Felix, in an effort to relieve the situation. 'To-morrow he goes before Major Médecin, and he fears lest he may be sent to the trenches again.'

'Oh, Monsieur! Monsieur!' burst out Jules reproachfully.

'Pardon me, old comrade. You understand,' exclaimed St. Felix quickly, and the Sniper wondered at the haste of his apology.

When the dinner was over Jules invited the officers to his private room to drink their coffee and liqueurs at his expense, and to talk. The Sniper learned afterwards that this was a common practice of the good-hearted landlord. He had lived in England, and loved the English. He liked to hear the news of the various fronts told him in the English tongue, and to do honour to the men who had come to the help of his country. But to-night little was said at first of the line and its happenings.

'You must pardon me, my friends,' Jules began almost immediately, 'that I should have been such a poor host this evening. But it is even as good Monsieur St. Felix has said. I am being called up to-morrow for medical re-examination. Not that I fear further service, Messieurs,' he added quickly. 'My life is my country's and it is my sorrow that never again can I strike a blow for her. No! It is the thought of what I shall see to-morrow – the sight of the other réformés, men like myself, and many worse, that makes me so sad.'

There are some subjects which one may discuss unreservedly with Frenchmen. There are others about which one dare not speak. And when Frenchmen talk of these things of their own accord, it is the great burning soul of France which speaks from their quivering lips, and they are as men possessed. As Jules went on with his theme the tears streamed unrestrainedly down his cheeks, and his voice often broke with emotion.

'In France all men belong to the state, and the state does with them as it pleases. Even those who have been wounded must go before the Officiers Médecins, who shall say if they are fit to do still more for their country. And, Messieurs, I have seen the old Major Médecin himself weep at what he saw coming before him. For some come without arms, and some who cannot walk, and some who cannot see. Men, Messieurs, with whom I played when we were boys together. There is Henri, Léon, and Gaston. And Julie, Henri's wife, who leads him. Julie! whom I remember as a merry, laughing girl; whom I loved ere yet my José had come to the village. Now so quiet and sad, but oh so proud! My friends! Your country has done much for France – how much, we Frenchmen who have fought for France know. But of your sufferings much has still to come. I pray the good God that you may not be called to suffer even as my poor country.'

Here the depth of his feeling overcame their host, and he broke down entirely. The officers sipped their wine in silence, making no attempt to console him. Each man was thinking of the little bundles of red and blue rags, all that remained of gallant Frenchmen, and the rusty shattered rifles and mouldy equipment, on which they had stumbled in out-of-the-way places behind and in front of the lines. Their appreciation of what the landlord was saying was too great for them to put their sympathy into words. It was Jules himself who broke the silence, and restored the early cheerfulness of the evening.

'Pardon me, Messieurs. Pardon me,' he said. 'I have made you sad. Then friend Jules will make you merry again. For to-morrow it is for you à la garde, à la guerre.'

He soon had them laughing, though the morning gave them some idea of what it must have cost the honest fellow. For as they crossed the square fronting the Hôtel de Ville on their way to the station, they saw the gathering of the réformés. And some there were without arms, and some who could not walk, and some who could not see. Though most of these officers were veterans of the war, the sight of these broken men of France brought home to them as never before what France had done, and suffered, in the common cause of humanity.

There were several French officers waiting to greet the Sniper when he arrived at the headquarters in the little village which formed the reserve position of the sector which his battalion was to occupy. The colonel, his second-in-command, and one or two juniors were present. But the man who made the greatest impression on him was Paul Durand Delongres, his guide and friend during the days which elapsed before the arrival of his battalion in the sector. Delongres was a student of Paris, and a poet, who had laid down a facile pen to win even greater distinction with his sword, a man whose nimble fancy painted the empty spaces with laughing sprites, and who laughed with them.

To hear him tell the merry jest that in winter-time the French sought the comfort of the village, and only sent a man up occasionally to see if the trenches were still there, made the listener forget for the nonce the grimmer side of trench warfare. But an hour later when he was conducting the Sniper through a ruined village, which French military genius had converted into a fortress, he stopped and addressed him.

'You asked me a little while ago, Monsieur Jackson, what I thought of peace. Look around you, my friend. This is my native village. Over by the church there, many of my people lie buried. In yonder house I lived with my father and my mother. Where are they now, eh? I do not know. In this quiet spot, I learned to love everybody and everything – the birds, the beasts, the sweet scents of the tender plants. And oft of an evening, I lay and wondered at the beauty of the nightingale's song as she sang to the play of the moon sprites among the untrodden clover of my father's fields. When I see what is around us now, I find it very difficult to think kindly of our mutual friend over the hill there. No, Monsieur Jackson, there shall be no peace until atonement has been made. A fool may set a fire agoing. But a wise man is required to put it out with least damage. And as for poor clumsy Monsieur le Boche! – I have it in my heart to pity him.'

He was still smiling, almost gaily. One observing him from a distance might have fancied that he was recounting some merry anecdote. But there were unknown depths of fury and pathos in his voice, unmistakable despite the grace of speech and manner which cloaked them, rendered all the more terrible thereby. And the Sniper, noting this under-current, also felt inclined to pity the men who had called it into being.

Paul Delongres fell a few weeks later in the first day of the great attack, last of a family trampled out by the war. But the French armies have hundreds of thousands of his like – men who have been bereaved of parents, sisters, brothers; who have seen the desolation of their country, the broad track of the battle-line where scarce one stone stands upon another, where the very fields stink with the foulness wrought thereon; who yet smile and joke, and swagger, and fight on. And while such men live France never can be vanquished.

At length the Sniper's battalion arrived in the little village, and after the exchange of many warm greetings the Frenchmen marched away. The change was effected suddenly, as all such changes are, and the villagers went to bed one evening with the blue coats in their midst, and woke up to find the blue replaced by khaki. The rush of business which followed the opening of shops and cafés made the change exceedingly popular, and the thrifty French folks quickly adapted themselves to the needs and manners of the new-comers. The language question offered some difficulty at first, but to people accustomed to convey so much by gesticulation the various signs which the Tommies used to indicate their wants were easy of interpretation, and the desire to please animating both parties ensured the harmony of the trafficking.

The veterans of the battalion who had picked up a smattering of French in the early campaigns before the transfer to the Ypres sector, were eagerly called upon by the younger men for assistance, and many a free drink they earned in return for their services. But in spite of their good offices amusing incidents occurred by the dozen, and throughout the morning of the first day the village echoed with the shrill laughter of the women and the deeper-toned merriment of the men.

The Sniper happened to be in the back room of a little farmhouse café about half a mile from the village, bargaining with the owner for a quantity of straw, when two of his section entered the front room – Mackie and young Geordie Smith.

'That's fine breid up there, Geordie. See if ye can buy half a loaf,' he heard Mackie say.

'Ah dinna ken the French for breid but Ah'll have a shot at it. Hey, lassie!' said Geordie, addressing the girl in attendance, and pointing up at the bread. 'Gie's hauf a loaf.'

The girl's eyes followed the pointing finger, and immediately reached down the bread, giving Geordie back a franc and a half out of the two-franc piece he had tendered.

'Dod! the lassie understands braid Scotch,' exclaimed Mackie. 'See if ye can buy some matches.'

But Geordie was not nearly so successful in this second attempt. No matches were on view, so he could not point to them; and though he spoke the words more slowly and more slowly, the girl only shrugged her shoulders and laughed.

'Ah doot Ah'm bate, Mac,' he said disgustedly.

'Try her wi' yer pipe, Geordie,' Mac encouraged.

Geordie pulled out his pipe, his pouch, his pipe-cleaners, everything connected with a smoker's outfit, to no avail; and though he went through the weirdest contortions and scratchings, the girl only laughed the louder. Old Dan's amused chuckle interrupted the pantomime.

'Whatever are ye young deevils tryin' tae dae? Want tae musmurise the lassie?' he asked.

'Naw, Dan'l. We're tryin' tae get some matches.'

'Then why no ask for them? Hey, Mawm'sel! Vohyay alumet.'

The girl immediately raked out five boxes of matches in return for Dan's half-franc.

'Dod, Dan! Ye can fairly dae it,' said Geordie admiringly. 'What's the word for breid?'

'Doo pan.'

'Dew pan? Holy Moses! We were richt, Mac. It's just braid Scotch only the meanin's different. All-you-met an' dew pan.'

'Ay, Geordie! Dew pan is just a fancy name for pan loaf what Baldy Johnstone sells in the Tron. But, Dan'l? What does 'vohyay' mean?'

'Ah dinna ken, laddie. The officer telt me it was a polite way o' askin' efter anythin', an' it's aye workit wi' me. Vohyay shokolat. Vohyay caffay.'

'Vohyay glass o' beer, Dan'l?'

'Wee, wee! Mersee, Moshoo!' said Daniel, with such a comical air of profound learning that the Sniper went laughing out of earshot.

CHAPTER XXVI

The Hunters' Chance

A WIDE EXPANSE OF OPEN country lay between the new British position and the German lines, with lots of places where a sniper could lie hid without having to depend on specially made sniping posts, but the section quickly adapted themselves to the new conditions. At first the Germans proved venturesome fellows, not afraid to crawl out into the open to get a better shooting position, and before the Eastshires cleared No Man's Land of them, they had secured several successes. During the third tour of the battalion in the sector the struggle came to a head, resulting in the decisive defeat of the Germans, and after that the section held complete mastery. Matthew Oldheim started the row by getting one of the most persistent of the enemy snipers not long after the fellow had severely wounded the divisional commander's aide-de-camp as the latter was following the general along the firing-line.

The American had fast been making good his claim to be considered on equal terms with the Five as one of the super-snipers of the section; and as he had been chief designer to an important engineering firm before the war, his mechanical genius was now proving a veritable godsend to the Sniper in adapting to the use of the section the new camouflage practices which were being developed by the Army generally. Indeed he contrived for his own use several devices which, in slightly more finished form, afterwards became regular ordnance issues.

In this case he simply fixed an empty biscuit-tin to the parapet and waved his cap behind it. The German obligingly put a bullet through the tin, and a light stick shoved through the holes roughly gave the direction from which he had fired. But though Oldheim kept careful watch for a long time he could find no other sign of the German's presence.

'He's in dat hole, sir,' he said disgustedly to the Sniper, indicating a shell-hole a little in front of the firing-line. 'But de darn fellah is lyin' as close as a prairie hen.'

He raised his hand just a little too high above the parapet, and the German promptly fired at it, fortunately only succeeding in skinning Matthew's knuckles.

'Drat de tantalisin' fellah!' exclaimed Oldheim angrily. 'Dere I been lookin' for him more dan one hour, an' de only time I not lookin' he shoots his gun off.'

He danced about in the sloppy trench almost frantic with rage and disappointment.

'I get you yet, you German nigger,' he yelled, shaking his fist at his enemy.

Crack went another bullet, this time clean through the cuff of Oldheim's coat-sleeve.

'He's a good shot,' said Sergeant Ferguson, critically examining where the German's bullets had hit. 'You'll get it in the head next, Oldheim. Stop your nonsense, man.'

The Sniper bound up the injured knuckles, and the American immediately snuggled down at his loophole again.

'I get dis fellah next time sure,' he said.

The Sniper walked away thoughtfully and hunted out the bombing officer of the battalion.

'Bring along your grenade rifle and a couple of grenades,' he said. 'I want you to shift a rat for me.'

'Glad to fire at a louse for something to do,' grunted the bomber, starting to collect his appliances.

'Do you see that shell-hole over there?' said the Sniper a moment or two later. 'Put a grenade into it for me. A sniper is hiding in it.'

'Right,' said the bomber, carefully clamping the rifle into position.

The first grenade burst ten yards from the hole; the second right on the edge. The German took fright and bolted for his lines.

Before he had gone a yard, Oldheim flung his rifle over the parapet and bowled him over.

During the night a sniper patrol went out and brought the dead German in. He was found to be dressed in a camouflage suit, on which the colours were so blended, that a man wearing it and lying on the ground was completely invisible fifty yards away.

'Why, the chap must have been watchin' ye a' the time, Matthy,' Old Dan commented. 'Nae wonder ye couldna see him. Ye micht have got one clean through the heid wi'oot ever kennin' it.'

The sergeant earnestly urged the Sniper to do his best to retain the dress for the section's use, instead of sending it back for examination by the British camouflage experts. The Sniper managed to induce the colonel to back his request, and after some doubt the dress was finally left at the Eastshires' disposal. The sergeant immediately made an application to try it in No Man's Land.

'Where do you mean to go, sergeant?' the Sniper enquired when the request came before him.

'That old French dug-out, sir, up the old communication trench.'

'But that won't give you any better field of fire, sergeant?'

'I am sure it will, sir.'

'How do you know?'

'I am quite sure, sir.'

'Your knowledge is a bit uncanny at times, sergeant,' said the Sniper, giving the man permission.

The old dug-out had once been behind the French firing-line. But some time ago the Germans had slightly advanced their position, and now it lay in No Man's Land, two-thirds of the way from the British lines. As far as the Sniper could see the place did not overlook the German trenches in the slightest degree, but he had too often been astounded by the sureness of the sergeant's instinct for seeking out a kill to refuse the man's request, no matter how unpromising the venture seemed. He decided to go with the sergeant, in the hope of finding out something to add to the Divisional Summary of Intelligence.

During the night the two left the firing-line and made their way to the old dug-out. It was so close to the enemy trenches that they could hear the Germans talking to each other quite clearly. When dawn broke the sergeant was hunched up among the tumbled-down sandbags of the dug-out wall, his camouflage dress making him look part of the structure; while the Sniper, through his periscope carefully placed in a little crevice among the rotten material, was ready to observe the results of any shooting. But his position was not high enough, the German parapet blocking his view completely, and he dared not raise the periscope any higher for fear of attracting attention. Where the sergeant was lying, however, was a full two feet above the level of his view-point, and he waited hopefully for the result of his companion's investigations.

'I can just see over the German parapet at that point where it has sunk a little, sir,' the sergeant whispered softly. 'There's a dump there outside a row of what looks like dug-outs.'

'Do you see anyone?' asked the Sniper eagerly.

'Yes! There's a German bending over a brazier cooking breakfast. I'll wait till he is nearly finished. He is just going back to the dug-outs.'

The Sniper instantly divined the sergeant's idea. The cook would be dealt with as soon as he showed signs of lifting off the meal, and hungry men would come out to enquire what delayed their comrade only to expose themselves to the waiting sniper. The Sniper sat down in the dug-out to await developments.

'That's the cook,' he thought, as the sergeant's first shot went.

A minute or two later the sergeant fired again, then three times in quick succession.

'I've got five, sir,' he whispered.

'Better come in now,' the Sniper whispered in reply.

They were scarcely forty yards from the enemy firing-line, and he knew that the sergeant's position was much too exposed to defy detection from the German observers if he lay there all day, more especially with such a casualty roll to make the search all the more thorough. He had no fear of the sergeant not being able to get under cover without attracting attention, but, realising that it would be a lengthy process, he turned his attention to searching No Man's Land for enemy snipers lying between the lines. After half an hour he turned to see how the sergeant was getting on. The latter had only moved a foot and he had still two more to go before he could duck under cover.

Shooting was going on from several points in No Man's Land, which meant that German snipers were to be found there, and he quickly went back to his observation. A small mine crater lay between him and the British trenches with quite half of its further side visible to him. He had examined it before, but as it was an ideal position for an enemy sniper he began to investigate it bit by bit again. As he looked, a portion of the earth seemed to rise out of its side and move along out of his field of vision. It was a German who had been lying there all the time, camouflaged to look exactly like his surroundings. The Sniper immediately snatched up his rifle and fired. The German pitched in a heap on the crater wall, and went rolling out of sight.

The dug-out structure behind him screened the Sniper completely from the enemy firing-line, but in his eagerness to get the German he had forgotten the presence of other hostile snipers in No Man's Land, and had taken little precaution to hide himself. Fortunately he got under cover immediately, for a German had seen him, and a bullet grazed the top of a sandbag and buried itself in line with his head on the other side of the gap through which he had fired. The size of the hole it made showed that the bullet had been a doctored one. The Sniper began at once to search for this fellow, determined to bring him to book.

The two marks made by the bullet roughly gave him the direction of his enemy, and he carefully examined the ground through his powerful prismatic periscope. Knowing the kind of place a sniper would choose, he soon decided on a hummock of earth thrown up by the explosion of a large shell. But the German was skilfully camouflaged, and though the Sniper examined the position till his eyes ached with the strain he could find no trace of him. He determined to draw the German's fire, knowing that his periscope lens was powerful enough to show up the puff of fumes from the muzzle of the rifle.

Still keeping the point under observation, he poked his cap on the top of his rifle over the edge of the shelter as far away from himself as he could reach. The ruse proved successful, the German fired, enabling the Sniper to see the exact spot where his enemy was lying. But the German made a bad shot, and nearly hit him instead of the cap; the bullet – not a tampered one this time – sliced through the rotten material of the dug-out wall a few inches from his head, making him duck involuntarily.

He had just got his eye back to the periscope again when a shot rang out above him. A white chalky mass rose a foot or two from the hummock and collapsed into the shell-hole. It was the camouflaged German; and the sergeant had fired. The man had silently 'grown' up out of the dug-out while his officer had been immersed in his search, and, spotting the German as the latter fired, he had killed him.

'Good shot, sergeant,' said the Sniper. 'You gave me a start though. I'd forgotten about you.'

'I've been watching you for over an hour, sir.'

'Good gracious! It's nearly two o'clock,' said the Sniper, glancing at his watch in surprise. 'Shows how time flies when one gets busy. Let's get out the bully.'

No more firing took place in their vicinity during the day, and with the first shades of night they made their way quickly to the home firing-line. When about a third of the way across the sergeant suddenly pulled the Sniper down and pointed towards the enemy trenches. Dimly outlined against the sky was a group of men climbing over the parapet.

'A patrol coming out to examine the dug-out, sir,' whispered the sergeant.

'Much good may it do them now,' the Sniper grunted.

Old Dan met them when they climbed into the trench, eager to hear their news.

'It's dawmn guid work, sir,' he said. 'But it's a peety ye couldna get the deil in that wee bit plantain on oor left. He's been firin' intae bays seevin, eight, an' nine, a' day. Ah doot he's done for Maister Lawrie.'

'What's that, Haggarty?' asked the Sniper quickly.

'Ay, sir. Ah got the men cleared oot as soon as he started. But Maister Lawrie would gae alang the trench, an' the Alleyman slappit one richt in his stummick.'

'Lawrie! Oh, what a pity! We must get that fellow, corporal. Are you sure he is in those trees?'

'Yes, sir. Ah'll get him a' richt, if ye'll leave the job tae me.'

'Right, corporal!' agreed the Sniper.

Old Dan was missing from the trenches next morning and all through the day. He had gone out to the plantation before dawn, and, having found the German's sniping post, an elaborate nest of green canvas in the tallest tree, he had settled himself down to wait for the coming of its occupant. He confessed afterwards that he went to sleep – 'Ah'm an auld man, ye ken, sir,' he said in explanation – and was only wakened when the German's head appeared through the entrance in the morning. A quick bayonet thrust disposed of him quietly, and the corporal settled himself down in the post to await the coming of the day.

There was shooting from the trees all through the day-time, and the rumour went round the firing-line that Old Dan had been killed by the German – as trench rumours will go round. Cissie Rankine burst excitedly into the Sniper's dug-out with the news, as the Sniper was in the midst of a particularly trying report to brigade headquarters.

'The German is still firing away from those trees, Ronny,' he exclaimed. 'Old Dan must have been killed.'

'See where any of the bullets were striking, Cis?' asked the Sniper patiently. Had it been anyone but his intended brother-in-law he would have bundled the interrupter out of the dug-out.

'No,' said Cissie.

'Well, run away, little man, and ask the Germans where the bullets are going. Old Dan is having a bean-feast.'

Late that night, as the Sniper was just dropping off to sleep, he heard Old Dan's shuffling footsteps passing by the dug-out.

'How many did you get, corporal?' he called drowsily.

'Just a baker's dozen, sir. Ah'll no worry ye wi' the report the nicht.'

'All right, Haggarty. Good night,' muttered the Sniper, falling asleep with the sound of Old Dan's response still in his ears.

CHAPTER XXVII

The Mine that Failed

I T SOON BECAME APPARENT that something more was intended than a mere extension of the British line. The country consisted of rolling ground not unlike the Surrey Downs, and the opposing firing-lines ran along the edges of a well-defined valley. The Eastshires' position consisted at first of little more than this firing-line, but an advance trench was soon added half-way down the slope, and when a third trench was begun almost at the bottom of the valley, even the rawest recruit knew that trouble was coming. The intensive training which the battalion was put to do during the rest periods, the arrival of drafts to complete the establishment, the gradual recall of men from out-jobs down the line, all pointed the same way.

There were indications also of the immensity of the effort intended, and the thoroughness of the preparations being made. Navvy battalions worked unceasingly in laying new roads and broadening and strengthening tracks already in existence. Rumbling transport deposited steadily increasing piles of road metal at points where almost instantaneous repair work would require to be done in the event of any damage occurring. Huge ammunition dumps, carefully camouflaged against enemy airmen, began to grow out of the rearward country as though a coal-field were suddenly being developed with scores of pits spewing up refuse heaps; and men whispered of guns encountered every night-time moving up towards the firing-line, guns which miraculously disappeared as soon as the trench area was reached.

One night the Sniper was short-cutting across to a village where a chum battalion was billeted. On the way he passed a group of men lowering a huge black snout on wheels into a yawning pit. He had occasion to pass the same way during the day-time, but only green swarding met his eye.

Somewhere beneath, however, a great siege howitzer was lurking until the appointed time for it to push aside its covering and spit forth its venom.

The Germans were fully conscious of the approaching blow, and the volume of their artillery fire considerably increased. They harassed the men working on the new trenches and on the roads behind with shrapnel and high explosives; whenever the wind was favourable each side gassed the other, so that men went about with gas helmets at the ready as never before; and the refreshing green verdure clothing the country became covered with ghastly patches where the poisonous vapours had rolled thickest; and the birds ceased to sing in the coppices where wild life had been rampant with the northern journey of the sun.

A rare struggle took place between the rival tunnelling parties, the Germans seeking to destroy the new positions which were growing up against them, the British striving to ward them off and strike forward on their own account; and mines were blown and camouflets, until sometimes the valley was filled with billowing white fumes as though geysers or hot springs had suddenly found vent, and the meadowland between the lines became white and disfigured with craters and fissures and heaps of erupted subsoil.

The Germans at last succeeded in evading the cordon of the British listening galleries, and it so happened that their sap head was directed against the junction point of the Eastshires and the left adjoining battalion, on which flank Big Bill Davidson was commanding his company. Fortunately the distance had been miscalculated, and the explosion failed to damage the firing-line.

The night on which it took place was the quietest in the experience of the battalion for many a long day. Not a shot was being fired, and the line was wrapped in one of those mysterious trench silences which herald the coming of big events. The Sniper and Cissie were seated together on the fire-step near the right extreme of the sector, discussing home affairs. But somehow or other the conversation refused to flow easily, and each found himself breaking off in the midst of a sentence to listen for something without the other appearing to notice the break. The brooding deviltry of the trench area filled their souls with a vague apprehension, and fidgetings and murmurings floating round the traverses on either side of them showed that the men were also uneasy.

Suddenly away to the left a pillar of flame rushed heavenward. Solid and clear gold at the base, leaping up to pure flaming whiteness, merging at the summit into a misty radiance flecked with crimson splotches and rent by incandescent scintillations, the monstrous beacon lit up the countryside as far as eye could reach. A roar like the concentrated thunder of ages annihilated the silence. The earth quivered; its mud-covered surface heaved like a swell-ridden ocean. Then the stillness of the heart of a cyclone, as the disturbance passed on, and the roar reverberated in the distance. The ear was only beginning to detect the first faint sound of the falling débris, when the illumination was swallowed up by the swirling shadows, dying away as quickly as the radiance of a candle snuffed out.

The Sniper and Cissie were flung violently against the parados, and blinded by the awful glare. Before their eyes could become re-accustomed to the darkness, the hostile artilleries awoke to life, and the night was made light again by the flashing of the guns.

'Oh Lord! They've got Bill,' sobbed Cissie, making off towards the danger area.

'Hold on, Cissie!' exclaimed the Sniper, grabbing the excited boy by his equipment and dragging him back. 'You can't leave your position. Listen! Bill's got them on the hop.'

From a point on the left nearly half-way across No Man's Land, came the sharp staccato bursts of Mills' grenades and the hoarse voices of men in conflict, audible because of their variant keys in spite of the turmoil of the artillery battle. Presently the sounds ceased, and reassuring news soon came travelling down the line. Big Bill had gallantly rushed his company into the crater, easily repelling the advancing Germans, and making the ground his own. The Germans had only succeeded in advancing the British line still nearer the ultimate objective, and their effort gave Big Bill an opportunity of gaining a well-merited Military Cross.

The blowing of that mine confirmed an idea which had been forming in the Sniper's mind for some time, that the Germans were making serious efforts to mine the whole of his battalion's position. He had become very friendly with the tunnelling officers in charge of the British mining operations in the sector, and had proved himself very useful by bringing to their notice all the various indications of enemy mining activity in the district.

Thus the unnatural growth of sandbags at any part of the German line, especially when these sandbags under the action of the weather sweated into a colour unlike those filled with ordinary surface soil, and the streams of water from pump pipes hanging over the parapet when the water's clearness showed that it came from a much deeper depth than the muddy drainings of a trench bottom, were manifest signs of enemy burrowings into the bowels of the earth.

The tunnellers were always glad of such information, and often asked for particular details. But of their operations they told him nothing, for the work of the British miners is one of the closest kept secrets of the line. The Sniper's own duties were specialised enough for him also to have resented any misplaced curiosity on the part of an outsider, and he was content to pass on to his friends all the information he collected without asking any questions. That was one reason why they liked him and welcomed his visits to their dug-out.

Recently he had noticed that their requests for information were becoming more frequent and eager. He sensed an undercurrent of anxiety in all they said. And he was not one bit surprised when he heard at headquarters that a German mine was suspected under a part of the line almost ready to be blown. He knew that the tunnellers were working night and day to cut the gallery leading to the explosion chamber. One night he got a distinct impression from their general attitude that they were more than doubtful about arriving in time.

From a careful study of the aeroplane photographs, along with direct observation of the German line, he felt sure that he had located the exact position of the German shaft. He placed it right in the firing-line behind one of the thickest entanglement belts of the sector. The impulse came to him to take a hand in the game, and with the impulse came the premonition that he must strike at once.

He knew that it would be no use applying for permission to brigade headquarters. They would want a detailed plan of operations, and that would take up valuable hours. He felt it was one of those undertakings best carried out first, and then submitted for approval if successful, carefully covered up if a failure. On the night in which he inferred that the tunnellers were playing a losing game, he went out into No Man's Land along with the sergeant and Old Dan.

After an hour's crawling they had worked their way inside the German wire belt to the base of the parapet at the point behind which he thought was the mine shaft. A clanking windlass confirmed his deductions. Taking advantage of the noise it made, he prized out a sandbag and carefully fitted into the cavity several slabs of gun-cotton, the top slab containing a primer filled with detonator and fuse.

The gun-cotton had been annexed from the tunneller's dug-out. There also he had secured a long length of instantaneous fuse of the variety calculated to burn an unbelievable number of yards per second. He would have preferred a detonating battery and electric leads, but the sergeant had failed to find one in the engineer's dump at headquarters, which he had surreptitiously visited, and the Sniper had counted himself fortunate to have secured the fuse.

After tamping the charge well home the three crawled away into No Man's Land, trailing the fuse behind them. It was as fine a piece of patrol work as any one of the trio had ever done, and not a sign of their presence had they given the Germans. But none of them saw anything remarkable about it. It was only a means to an end, on the attainment of which the whole of their consciousness was centred.

They found a shell-hole at a convenient distance, and from this hiding-place the Sniper lit the fuse. A tiny pin-point of light streaked towards the German line. He had hardly ducked down his head when a blinding flash fanfared up from the point where the mine shaft had been, and the ground shook with the force of a mighty explosion. A shower of débris rained around them. He heard Old Dan's guttural swear as a lump of earth struck the back of his neck. Immediately after, the line woke to life, and No Man's Land was full of cracking bullets and whistling shell fragments which each startled side fired at the other. Sometimes in a lull of the tumult he would hear Old Dan complaining about the dirt which had worked down his neck, and he giggled hysterically at the thought of the old fellow being conscious of such minor evils in the midst of the awful hubbub around them.

When silence settled down again the three crawled in to the home firing-line. They found an awakened garrison eagerly discussing the cause of the explosion in the enemy lines. But, carefully avoiding each group of debaters, the three made their way to their quarters and tumbled in for a belated rest.

The Sniper was awakened next morning by the senior tunnelling officer. 'Here, get up,' said the tunneller. 'I want some information from you.'

'What is it, nuisance?' said the Sniper sleepily.

'Last night nearly half a hundred weight of gun-cotton disappeared from our dug-out along with one detonator, and all our instantaneous fuse.' The tunneller paused to eye the Sniper questioningly. 'A mysterious explosion took place in the German lines. Now, what about it, you blighter?' he demanded.

The Sniper cursed him into a state of believing his innocence, and the tunneller departed feeling that he had unwarrantably disturbed a very weary and overworked man.

But late that evening he came back again and shook hands with the Sniper warmly.

'You will soon hear from the colonel what it is about,' he said, when the Sniper enquired the reason for his demonstrativeness. 'This morning we struck the German gallery. We found the explosive all ready to be fired, with detonators and everything fixed up. But following the wires to the shaft, we found them broken and the gallery blocked by a pretty stiff fall, just below where the explosion took place last night. Oh, don't look so innocent, my lad. One of my men noticed you pinching the gun-cotton, and saw you and your two villainous N.C.O.s climbing out of the trench. We are mighty grateful to you, mighty grateful. If you had not carried out that stunt the whole of the firing-line would have been blown sky-high by now.'

He stayed a long time with the Sniper; and the colonel also actually paid a congratulatory visit just after dinner. From their conversation the Sniper gathered that his exploit had meant far more than the saving from destruction of a mere length of trench with its garrison. The German mine would have destroyed many British galleries destined to play an important part in the coming attack. He also learned that the attack was only a matter of a few days.

Before the tunneller left he took a long, earnest look at the photograph of Maimie Rankine which the Sniper had hanging on the dug-out wall. Then without another word he went out into the night. When great events are imminent in the trench area, the trenchman's womenfolk and home are very near to him.

When the tunneller had disappeared Sergeant Ferguson came in for a few minutes. The nightly visit had grown into a habit with the sergeant. Generally he came to talk about the work of the following day. But sometimes he would sit in silence, smoking one of the Sniper's cigarettes and sipping a very weak whisky and soda, while the Sniper worked away at his daily report for the brigade. To-night was one of his silent visits.

'I suppose the attack comes off very soon, sir,' he said, after a long pause.

The Sniper nodded abstractedly and went on with his writing. Then another long silence.

'Old Dan would make a good sergeant, sir,' murmured the sergeant.

'What has set you thinking like that?' asked the Sniper, coming completely out of the absorption of his writing as he realised the trend of the sergeant's thoughts.

'Nothing, sir. Only I've been out here a long time now, without getting a scratch, and I know I must go some day. Don't think I'm moping, sir,' he said hastily. 'I thought it my duty to the section to say who the most suitable man was, in case I don't get a chance later.'

'I have as great opinion of Old Dan as you have, sergeant.'

'I thought as much, sir. Only some people think him too old to be out here. I saw the brigadier looking at him rather curiously the other day, and it worried me. It would break the old chap's heart if he were sent home.'

'Old Dan is not going home, sergeant. And I hope also that you will be the last to go,' said the Sniper warmly.

He resumed his writing again and finished off his report, but with an effort. The sergeant's words had set him thinking. As time goes on in the trenches without anything happening, the trenchman sometimes lapses into a state of mind in which he imagines that nothing ever will happen to him. Then suddenly the grim reality forces itself on his consciousness that sooner or later he must go down the line – on a stretcher or otherwise – or remain there for ever. The law of chance works very hardly with the infantryman.

The Sniper noticed that the sergeant took a long wistful look at Maimie's photograph when he was leaving, just as the tunneller had done. When the man had gone, the Sniper sat silent far into the night with the photograph in his hand.

CHAPTER XXVIII

The Break-up of the Section

THE DAY CAME AT last whose morrow would see the battalion in the trenches preparing for the attack, and on that day the men of the battalion took communion. It was no official parade. The padre simply let it be known that services would be held at certain hours, and left men and officers to decide for themselves as to putting in an appearance. But all the earlier services were crammed, and when it came to the officers' turn, every one of them attended, though two or three of them subscribed to other tenets than those contained in the Presbyterian faith, and more than one of them on account of their youth had not yet got beyond the adherents' gallery of the Scottish kirk. But this was a day of days, the last time that all would meet together, and so one by one they walked slowly down to the tent and very self-consciously took their seats inside.

The simple service began. The old familiar hymns were sung. At first there was a difficulty about the singing. These men had lived with each other and fought together. But as Scotsmen they were wont to read into the heart of a comrade more by his silence than by his spoken words. Therefore they were shy of giving too open an expression to the deepest sentiments of their being, and during the first verse the padre had to carry on alone. Then the colonel took up the harmony. One by one the others followed his lead, until the tent was athrob with the stately measures, and the whole camp filled with the melody of the old psalm tunes.

The sacred cup was passed round. The short service drew to a close. During the singing of the last psalm – 'All people that on earth do dwell' – the Sniper noticed that the colonel was not joining in. He was standing a little apart from the others looking over the edge of his Bible. On his face was the expression of one who heard in the singing the voices of comrades long gone under, the same tones, the same tricks of inflection, who yet recognised that the spirits of those comrades were still quickening in the breasts of the men filling their places around him; who knew that the honour of the corps which he had cherished so long would remain untarnished in their keeping.

After the service was over, when the younger officers hung modestly behind to allow the senior men to get on ahead, the colonel paused until the juniors were forced to join his party. As fellow communicants, as comrades linked by the same beliefs and joined together by the same holy cause, the officers of the regiment walked in a group back to their quarters.

Over by Albert that evening the shrapnel was bursting thickly. The guns were roaring out their threat of the coming strife, lighting the heavens with their flashes, and tinging the distant horizon with the blood-red reflections of exploding shells. But in the rest camp there was a brooding content, and in the hearts of its dwellers the strength of men who have renewed the covenant which had kept their fathers steadfast throughout the ages.

In the early grey of the morning the Eastshires fell in while the guns were roaring out their final hate before the commencement of the attack. The Eastshires were brigade reserve. Before the attack had been an hour in progress they were called on to reinforce the forward waves. A long stretch of almost unbroken wire had been encountered, and one battalion had lost fairly heavily in trying to force its way through. The survivors were bunched together in a sunken road, out of which the Germans were bombing them from the shelter of their trenches. The enemy artillery had locked No Man's Land with a perfect hell of a barrage. Yet through it the Eastshires must go if the day was to be won.

Towards a break in the wire Big Bill rushed his company. He fell shot through the head as he entered the gap. Jimmy MacLauchlan went down on the parapet. But the rest of the company swept through under Cissie, and the advance waves were able to make progress.

A strong German counter-attack rolled up from the left, directly opposite to where the Sniper was waiting to go over with his section. It crumpled in the flank of attack, seriously threatening the centre, and the Sniper, seeing danger, gathered what men he could together and broke in on the German bombers as they worked triumphantly down the trench.

He could remember racing his sergeant for the German trench, and shooting down a German officer even as the latter was raising his pistol arm. But after that came a confused buffeting blank, with a definite picture evolving only here and there. Once he found himself looking round at a crouching German about to bayonet him in the back, and Oldheim rushing round the traverse to kick the German's face off in the nick of time.

Often he heard Old Dan bellowing out some weird cry of war, and more than once he saw the sergeant step coolly inside the guard of an opponent, sending his bayonet home into the man's throat. But all these scenes gradually merged themselves into a nightmare of blue and brown rushing shapes, transfused with a flaring red which seemed to scream. Then the nightmare itself vanished, and he felt himself sinking into a soft dream river, down which he was carried in someone's arms – someone whom he dimly recognised as Old Dan – down into a darkness where oblivion rushed over him.

He awakened to find himself lying under a pile of blankets on a bed made of wire netting stretched over a wooden frame, set by the wall of a timbered structure which the light of an acetylene jet told him was some sort of dug-out. Round a bucket of glowing coke in the centre of the floor were seated Old Dan, Oldheim, and Brown, Mackie and young Geordie Smith, all five writing steadily, and he wondered at their unusual intentness of expression. He raised himself into a sitting position. At once a hundred aches and pains ran through his body and a glance at his torn clothing brought back the memory of the attack.

'Ah notice ye're stirring, sir. Hoo dae ye feel?' asked Old Dan's voice from the fire.

'All right, corporal. How is the attack going? Where are we?' he enquired eagerly.

'We're in a dug-out below the trench we captured yesterday. The attack was nigh on a mile in front o' us afore we cam' in here. It's further on the day, they say.'

'Have I been asleep for a day?'

'Ay, sir. The doctor examined ye an' said it would be the best thing for ye. The colonel cam' in, tae, just afore the relief. He's awful pleased wi' ye, sir. The battalion mairched oot last nicht.'

'I suppose the rest of the section went at the same time. Did we have many casualties?'

He noticed that the men looked strangely at each other, and seemed to hesitate long over the reply.

'We were hit vera sair, sir,' Old Dan said slowly. 'There's fowerteen wounded and seevin deid, baith the Saunderses amang them. This is a' that's left o' us.'

The Sniper sat on the edge of the bed and stared at the speaker in silence. Old Dan's words kept going through his mind, sentence after sentence, like the figures of an arithmetical problem to which a dullard is trying to find a solution. It seemed too incredible, too colossal a wipe-out to be possible.

'What happened to Ferguson?' he asked.

'He's hame by noo. He got an awfu' sair one in the leg. Ah doot he'll lose hauf o' it. Ah thinks Andra would have been better pleased if he had gotten it through the heid. He gret sair when they were takin' him awa' at the thocht o' leavin' the section when he was maist needed. He said ye'd unnerstan'. He couldna help himself leavin' ye. He was awfu' gled that ye had come through a' richt.'

'Yes, I understand,' murmured the Sniper.

'We stayed ahint tae get the laddies in. Sall Ah show ye whaur we laid them, sir?'

The two climbed out of the dug-out together, and out of the trench to where seven white crosses at the edge of a riven clump of trees showed up dimly in the darkness; and there the wise old man left the officer to mourn his dead alone.

He called him half an hour later to a scanty meal of bully beef, biscuits, and tea. Then the six of them packed their kits and staggered away down the shell-hummocked road to their battalion billets.

CHAPTER XXIX

The Auld Section

A QUIET WAS OVER THE village, and a stillness, and the turmoil of war was far removed. Up on the western high ground, where the roofs and gables of Estaminet Moulin edged themselves above the tree-tops, the big arms of the mill stood up blackly against the reddening sky, like the arms of a mitred priest raised in blessing on the peaceful community clustering beneath. Down in the village a bell was chiming, each note an entity of sound, clear and distinctive, unmistakably compelling, with never a jarring chord to mar the melodious cadences of the Benediction call.

Sometimes, so still was the atmosphere, the ear could detect the subtle intermingling of many footfalls, as down every roadway centring on the church streamed the inhabitants of the district. For though these people dwelt amidst peace and plenty, far removed even from the fringe of war, they were part of the great emotional heart of France, stirred to the uttermost by patriotic fervour; and at this Benediction service they were crowding towards the little place of worship to intercede for their beloved land.

Inside the church the lamps were burning feebly, but the altar was ablaze with tapers, and the white draperies of the apse cast a reflection down the nave on the kneeling congregation. The old organ sounded at intervals from its loft beneath the belfry; the aged priest by the altar broke into the service chants with that tender quavering voice which tells of a great age. His accent bespoke him a refugee from the Flemish border. And so he was – a man of four score years, driven from his retirement by the invaders, back in harness again that a younger man might be free to fight his country's battle.

The firing-line now ran through the little village which was once his charge. His church and home were in ruins. His flock was scattered, he had suffered the loss of everything he held dear; and just because he had suffered, yet carried his sorrows triumphantly, men and women flocked to hear him, filling the little church as never before, to take comfort from his strength for the anxieties and griefs which war has spread throughout the length and breadth of France.

On a chair behind one of the pillars supporting the organ loft, where a little recess hid him from the eyes of such as might be curious, knelt the Sniper. It was his last night with the battalion, and though of a different tongue and faith to its congregation, he had come to the little church, drawn by the same religious appeal which holy places make to all hearts in times of doubt and care. The Eastshires had left the fighting area; they were back in their long-rest billets fifty miles further up the line. But only a remnant was left of them, seven officers and scarce a hundred men. Big Bill Davidson and Jimmy MacLauchlan were dead. Cissie Rankine was home in a London hospital, out of the war for good. And of his section . . .

Trench acquaintanceship is a much more real and enduring thing than the usual relationship of man and man in normal times. Men live very closely together there. They do their job knowing that the lives of comrades depend on their efforts. They look to comrades to do the same by them. A friend is not an individual with whom to while away a few hours or days. He is a man on whose quick bayonet stroke, or ready support with platoon or company, one's life may depend. The connection gradually comes to be taken for granted. It is only when a comrade drops out and the support is lacking, and still more when a stranger comes to take his place, that his personality obtrudes and the sense of his loss strikes the heart with a pang far greater than the ordinary sorrow of bereavement.

What trenchman can ever forget the horrible sick sensation at the sight of a new-comer sitting down at the mess table in the place once occupied by a chum gone under? Then the trench area becomes a horrid place, haunted by the souls of the dead, who come to talk with him in the night-time, continuing some previous conversation so naturally that he wakes in the morning thinking them still alive, and learns again of their death with all the shock of a fresh bereavement.

The Sniper had eagerly grasped at the chance of getting away from it all by going down the line as a sniping instructor. The colonel had made him the offer of the appointment two days after reaching rest billets. An hour ago word had come that the transfer had gone through. 'The regiment can ill spare you, Jackson,' the colonel had said to him. 'You did splendidly in the attack. You will hear more about that shortly. And personally it means a lot to me. The adjutant and yourself are the only ones of the older officers left now. Captain Allan is going on the staff next month, and you of course would have taken his place. But you need a rest badly. I know you will do the regiment credit down at the base.'

He was not insensible to the appeal which the colonel had made to him, nor to the feeling of regret at breaking with his battalion. But the thought of the free and careless life awaiting him down the line made him look forward to the change as though to a long-expected holiday. Had his section been spared to him he would never have dreamt of leaving. But he could not face the task of building it up again, of training raw recruits whose every mistake reminded him of the super-men whom he had lost. Far better let a new man take on the job, with a new man's freshness of spirit, and no recollections to haunt him of what had been before. Old Dan would provide the necessary experience. Old Dan was sniping sergeant now. How keen the old fellow had been over the selection of the new-comers! How proud he was of his stripes!

'I'd better let the old chap know that I'm going,' the Sniper murmured, as the Benediction ended, and, leaving the church, he moved off in the direction of the section's billet.

The village was waking to life with the return of the churchgoers; lights were beginning to play out on the streets as housewives turned up the wicks of lamps thriftily lowered till their return. The gentle evening breezes carried to his ear the chatter of the young folk, a silvery laugh, the catch of a trench song or two, all mellowed by the softness of the evening air. The estaminets sent out a clatter of cups and a clink of glasses, and a murmuring hubbub of conversation. He could see the revellers as he passed by the open doorways. Their fine new uniforms and clear full-blown features, their merry laughter and careless gestures, spoke of new drafts from the depots still to be 'blooded'. In marked contrast were the sombre groups of the older men sitting apart and talking quietly among themselves.

'Talking of the chums they have lost,' he thought, and passed by as quickly as he could.

The last house of the village was the farm where the snipers were billeted. Knocking gently, the Sniper raised the latch and entered the big stone-floored farm kitchen. The farmer and his wife, the farmer's father, a disabled franc-tireur of '70, and the solitary labourer, were grouped round the stove, and at a table a little removed from the hearth were seated Corporal Oldheim and Corporal John Brown watching Old Dan making up some indents.

'Ah was comin' round tae see ye, sir,' said Old Dan, springing up immediately from his seat. 'There's some indents here for signing.'

The Sniper listlessly affixed his signature. He wanted to tell Old Dan the news of his departure, and have done with it. But the old fellow would not give him an opportunity. He was bubbling over with enthusiasm as to the progress the new men were making, and the Sniper began to experience a curious disinclination to interrupt him. The sergeant was so keen.

'See thae score sheets, sir,' he was saying, unfolding a number of papers, which bore the results of the day's ranging. 'Ah tell ye, sir, we've gotten a haud o' a pickle o' rale guid shots that only want a wee bit feenish put tae them tae bate onythin' in the line.'

Certainly the totals indicated excellent shooting, and in the old days, when the question of a suitable man for one of the few vacancies in his section always received long and careful consideration, such marksmanship would have made him quite as enthusiastic as his sergeant.

'Yes, Haggarty,' he said. 'I'm glad you have been able to pick out such good material for my successor to work on. You know I am leaving the battalion. I'm going on Tuesday to begin work as a sniping instructor down the line.'

He spoke the words lightly enough, but he was keenly conscious of the effect they were producing on his hearers. Oldheim and Brown were leaning over the table, gazing at him open-mouthed in dismay. Old Dan was sitting bolt upright in his seat, staring fixedly at the wall in front of him. The Sniper was startled to see that the lines had come back to his face, the droop to his jaw, and the flaccidness to his lips, all the signs which he had noticed before in his quondam corporal's appearance when the latter was under stress of great emotion. Old Dan actually looked older than his sixty odd years.

The Sniper turned away to the group by the fireplace. He was afraid at the moment that Old Dan would look at him. To cover his intrusion into the family circle he reached down an old-fashioned chassepot from its perch on the wall and pretended to examine it closely. A remark he made on its well-kept condition sent a flush to the veteran Frenchman's ashen cheeks, and a sparkle to his dimming eyes.

'Ah to be young again!' murmured the old French sniper, and the Sniper hastily replaced the gun and retreated.

'I'm sorry my news has upset you, sergeant,' he said.

The remark seemed to bring Old Dan out of his abstraction.

'Dinna say sergeant tae me, sir. Say it tae Oldheim or Broon. If ye're gaun, Ah'm gaun, tae. Ah don't want tae hinder ye gaun, sir. It's the like o' ye that's wanted sae badly at the schools. Ye've done mair than your bit, an' ye've a young lady tae conseeder. But it's suddenly come ower me that an auld man like me would be better at ame savin' his prayers, than oot in this bluidy business. Ah'll awa' an' see the colonel the noo,' and he rose from his chair abruptly and disappeared through the doorway.

With a curt 'Good night,' the Sniper left the farmhouse. He heard Old Dan's footsteps echoing down the road, but he did not follow him. From the barn across the courtyard, where the main body of the snipers were billeted, rose a gay trench melody. Silently he stole up to the half-open door and looked inside. The light of half a dozen candles, carefully socketed in empty biscuit tins to guard their flames from the straw, revealed the blanketed forms of over a score of men reclining comfortably on the fodder with which the floor of their billet was thickly strewn. Some were lazily cleaning rifles, some altering telescopic sights, others writing letters home; but all were crooning softly in harmony together:

'Down the communication trench near the middle of Whizz-Bang
    Lane,
I've got a nice little sandbag villa where the Crumps and the Johnsons
    rain;
Not very far from the sniper's post,
Where the aerial torpedoes trouble me most,
I've got the German machine-guns on toast,
Down in Whizz-Bang Lane.'

He liked the look of the men. There was good stuff among them, and good spirit – material which Old Dan's cunning hand could have moulded almost to any degree of excellence he chose. Hang it all! Why had the old fellow taken his defection so badly? 'Defection!' The word hurt the Sniper, although he had used it unconsciously. But what Old Dan had said really justified his going, whatever the old fellow's manner of speech might have indicated. He had done his bit. He could do useful work at the school. He had his girl to consider. But was he considering her? He knew what Maimie would have said; what she had said already. She had written to him rejoicing in his escape, sympathising with him in the loss of his section, and wishing him luck with his new recruits. Yet in spite of it all he had decided to go. For a man will give life itself to win a girl, but having won her his greatest care is to preserve his life so that he may continue to keep her.

He walked away from the barn out along the roadway. The night air was cool and fresh, but it seemed to suffocate him. His brain was on fire with the tumult of his thoughts. Why the dickens was he worrying about a matter already settled? He was *going*. But though he repeated the affirmation many times, the words brought him no satisfaction.

He passed his billet and took the turn up towards the Moulin Estaminet. He could not think of turning in as yet. Upwards he climbed until he stood on the crest of the ridge and the whole plain of Flanders lay spread out before him shimmering in the moonlight. Away on the left the faint glimmer of the distant channel lightened the horizon. Behind him was the black background of the forest-clad bluffs of Normandy. He flung himself down in the shadow of the mill and let his thoughts run riot.

Down in the village someone was singing 'O Lovely Night'. It was a corporal of A Company, a man who had been a professional singer before the war. His glorious voice rose and fell in all the melodious soul-haunting cadences of the song, and the Sniper listened spell-bound, almost fancying that he could hear some spiritual lover hailing the advent of his mate. The song seemed to open the flood-gates of his unrest, and the moist earth drank into its depth the influences disturbing his soul.

The soft evening breeze stirred the grasses around him, filling the air with low whisperings and hummings. He seemed to hear the voices of dead comrades calling his name and trying to cheer him. The mystery of the night bewitched him. A gentle gust eddying round the mill played on his forehead, and he thought for a moment that it was the touch of a healing hand on his brow. He stood up to his full height, stretching his shoulders back with arms bent at the elbow, thrilling to feel the strength of them.

'God! It's good to be alive,' he said. And after a little he added, 'And it's good to be here. Great Scot! How did I ever come to think of leaving them?' He was thinking of his section as he spoke the words.

A man came walking over the ridge, his figure silhouetted against the moon-bathed sky. He came directly towards the Sniper as the latter stood in the deep shadow of the mill, and brushed against him as he passed.

'That you, Haggarty?'

'Yes, sir. Is that you?'

'Glorious night, isn't it?'

'Ay, sir. One o' the nichts it does ye guid tae be alive in.'

'Seen the colonel?'

'No, sir. Ah cam up here tae think things oot, an' dod! Ah'm no gaun tae see him. Ah'm gaun tae stay an' carry on. Somehow Ah feel it's no fair tae Andra an' the laddies that are left, mair especially as ye're gaun, sir.'

'I'm not going, sergeant.'

'Ye're no gaun! Did Ah hear aricht, sir? Ye're no gaun!'

'No! I'm not going.'

'Oh, the Lord be praised! The Lord be praised! We'll have the auld section again.'

Old Dan was wringing the Sniper's hand till the knuckles went cracking and crunching. The tears were streaming down his wrinkled cheeks, the drops glistening like precious stones in the moonlight.

'We'll build up the auld section again. The auld section. The auld section,' he kept murmuring.

'Ay, the auld section,' murmured the Sniper.

Then those two walked slowly down into the village and its slumbrous shadows, the content of a thousand years of peace filling their souls.

THE END